DEATH DIVE

Depth Force Thrillers
Book Two

Irving A Greenfield

DEATH DIVE

Published by Sapere Books.

24 Trafalgar Road, Ilkley, LS29 8HH,
United Kingdom

saperebooks.com

ISBN: 978-1-80055-793-2

CHAPTER 1

Captain Jack Boxer's gray eyes were riveted to the Digital Depth Readout. There were dark circles under his eyes, and he leaned wearily over his Command Computer Console.

"Going to night lighting," Boxer said, pushing the switch to change the *Shark*'s interior light from white to red.

Boxer glanced over to the Combat Information Center, where the red light gave the men a ghostly, if not demonic, appearance. He pursed his lips. If it were not for the inherent strength of the *Shark*'s hull all of them would have been ghosts... He looked back at the DDROT. "Six zero feet," he said over the MC. "Prepare to raise sail ... raise sail!"

"Sail raised... Holy Christ, we've got a goddam malfunction!" Harris, the executive officer, exclaimed.

Boxer switched on the damage control computer at the same time he keyed the damage control officer. "Check the sail's hydraulic system," he said. His own DCC showed no malfunction.

"Sail jammed," Harris reported.

Boxer cursed under his breath.

"Skipper," the DCO called, "the DCC shows no malfunction."

"But there is a malfunction," Boxer exploded. "The sail is jammed!"

"Skipper, about four zero percent of the sail is up," Harris said.

Boxer shook his head. That wasn't even enough to allow the bridge party to crawl into the sail and make their way topside. He looked at the DDROT. "Three zero feet," he announced.

"Stand by to surface!... Bridge detail on deck through number one hatch... Stand by... Diving planes neutral position."

"Diving planes in neutral position," the diving officer responded.

A null came up on the diving plane indicator.

"Secure diving planes," Boxer said.

"Diving planes secured," the DO answered.

The DDROT showed one zero feet; then the red numbers were replaced by green flashing lights. "Surface ... surface," Boxer said over the MC. "Bridge detail on deck!"

Cowly undogged the hatch and, pushing it open, lifted himself through it. The other five men of the detail went after him.

Boxer took several deep breaths and the sharp tang of the sea air filled his lungs... "Mister Harris," he said, "pass the word to open all hatches."

"Aye, aye, Skipper," Harris answered.

Boxer activated the deck MC. "Mister Cowly," he said, "can you reach the bridge?"

"Negative," Cowly answered, over his handset.

"Post lookouts forward and aft," Boxer said.

"Aye, aye, Skipper," Cowly responded.

Boxer keyed the DCO. "What's the problem?" he asked.

"Everything shows normal," the DCO answered.

"Mister Harris," Boxer said, "lower sail."

"Negative on that," Harris responded. "It's frozen where it is."

"DCO," Boxer said, keying the man again, "I want a repair detail on that sail. I want that sail either up or down!"

"Aye, aye, Skipper," the DCO answered.

"And I want a repair detail on the diving planes," Boxer said. "I want to know the extent of hull damage."

"Aye, aye, Skipper," the man responded.

"I'm going up on deck," Boxer told Harris. "Tell engineering to reduce speed to one zero knots."

Harris nodded.

"Notify Tom I want a team of scubas to have a look at the hull under water."

"No other boat could take the punishment this one took," Harris said.

"Except the one the Russians put on our tail," Boxer replied. "I sure wasn't ready for it," he added ruefully.

"You'd think the Company would have known about it," Harris commented.

Boxer shrugged. "Their boys don't know about the *Shark*, or at least they didn't until we engaged their sub. But now they know just as much as we know about them. You can be sure they monitored and made tapes of everything from the sound of our engines to the sound of our voices."

"But they couldn't find us," Harris answered. "They had to depend on their sonar."

"Yeah, they were blind all right … this time. But maybe next time, or the time after that, they won't be."

Harris shook his head. "That's something I don't want to think about."

"Neither do I," Boxer said. "But if we have an Under Water Imaging System, you can bet that they'll have one soon."

"There's no arguing that," Harris replied.

"Skipper," Cowly radioed from the deck, "I think I know why the sail froze."

"Tell me," Boxer answered.

"The deck flange around the sail's well has been damaged," Cowly reported.

"I'm coming topside," Boxer answered; then to Harris he commented, "The depth-charging!"

Harris nodded.

Boxer went topside through the number-one hatch. The night was warm. The sky was full of stars and the Southern Cross was clearly visible. A light breeze blew from the southwest.

Boxer went to where Cowly was standing and looked down at the well flange. The surface that, with the flange, formed part of the seal around the sail's well was cracked and dented in several different places.

"All it would take," Cowly commented, "is some sand and a few small stones to jam it. And with the pounding we took there must have been sand all over the hull."

Boxer nodded. The *Shark* had been caught in an undersea canyon and tons of debris had fallen on her from the depth-charging. Every bit of power the *Shark* could produce was used to free her from the grave into which the Russians had put her.

"The pressure seal is gone. We probably have some water in the well."

Cowly agreed.

Lt. Cmdr. Larry Parker, the DCO, and his work detail came up on deck.

Boxer showed him the damaged flange. "It's going to have to come off and a new one must be put down." Then looking up toward the top of the sail, he said, "My guess is that a new one will have to be put on there too."

"We might be able to patch the one down here," the DCO said. "But even if we could, it probably wouldn't be watertight."

"The way it is now," Boxer answered, "we'll ship water every time we dive, or if we run into a heavy sea."

"There's no contradicting that," the DCO answered.

Boxer ran his hand over his beard. "The way it is now," he said, "we can't even use our ATI…" He pursed his lips. "If we should encounter any aircraft — How much higher would she have to be raised so that we could use our ATI system and SRS? We have to be able to use both systems. Without our Surface Radar System we'd really be in trouble."

"Another ten percent," the DCO answered.

"Shit!"

"It might—" The DCO stopped abruptly.

"Go ahead and finish what you started to say," Boxer told him.

"It's a crazy idea."

"We could use a crazy idea, if it might work. Right now I don't have any idea, crazy or sane."

"Suppose we flood the well with sea water and really build a head of pressure … maybe we'd get some movement out of it. Then we could pump the well dry and secure the sail in its place. I don't think we'd get much movement but some is better than none."

"How much water do you think that well would hold?" Boxer asked, already wondering how deep the *Shark*'s hull would ride during the time the water was in the well.

"The deck would probably be awash," the DCO said, answering the question.

Boxer looked at the sea. It was calm. The *Shark*'s deck was a good five feet above it. But in any sort of a big blow, the deck was always awash, especially if they were under way at anything over six knots. "Got a guesstimate of how long it might take?" he asked.

"With the welding—"

"What welding?"

9

"If the sail came up," the DCO said, "I'd weld it into place. That way we'd be able to dive to … maybe three or four hundred feet, without any problems. If we went deeper I wouldn't vouch for the integrity of the weld."

"That would mean burning open the weld when we're inside the *Tecumseh*."

"Or going into dry dock," the DCO answered. "I don't think the *Tecumseh* could handle the kind of repair that would be needed."

Boxer keyed Harris. "What's the weather look like? Hold it for a minute." He put his hand over the radio's mike and said to the DCO. "You didn't tell me how much time you'll need."

"Outside guess would be about fifteen to twenty hours."

Speaking to Harris again, Boxer said, "I need good weather for twenty-four hours."

"You just might get it," Harris answered.

"Roger that," Boxer answered and nodding he said to the DCO, "Get those repairs under way."

"Aye, aye, Skipper," the DCO answered.

Boxer keyed engineering. "All engines stopped," he ordered. Within a matter of minutes the *Shark* was dead in the water.

Boxer sent for First Class Petty Officer Norman Yellan, nicknamed Yellin' Yellan, and said, "I want you to take a team of scubas over the side and investigate the hull and diving planes. The starboard plane is damaged. I want to know how badly."

"I'll need lights," Yellan said. "And those lights will bring sharks."

"How many men do you think you'll need?" Boxer asked.

"Four — myself to do the inspection and four more to keep the sharks from inspecting the inspector."

"Okay," Boxer said.

"I'll get right on it, Skipper," Yellan answered.

Boxer remained on deck until the Scuba team was in the water; then he went below. It would be an hour or so before Yellan would be able to make his report and Boxer needed a respite. With the exception of a catnap here and there he had been on continuous duty for almost four days, and it was catching up to him.

Coming up to the bridge, Boxer said to Harris, "All repairs and inspections are under way."

"I've made a roster of officers and men to serve lookout duty ... two hours on, four off."

Boxer nodded. "Pass the word to them and tell them I don't want any arguing about it. It has to be done and that's it."

"Are you going to get some sack time?" Harris asked.

"If I don't," Boxer answered, "I'll fall asleep on my feet. You could use some yourself."

Harris smiled. "Rank has its privileges ... you first, Skipper."

"I won't argue," Boxer said. "You take the CONN. We won't be going anywhere for the next ten to fifteen hours. Yellan will be coming up with a damage report. I don't think there's anything major with the hull, or we'd have known it by now. But there's something wrong with the starboard diving plane."

"If it can be fixed," Harris answered, "I'll have it done."

Boxer nodded. "I'm going to take a look-see at James and tell him what's happening. I'm sure he knows we've stopped."

"Good idea," Harris said. "He'd appreciate being filled in."

Boxer yawned and walked slowly off the bridge. A few minutes later he was standing over James's bed in the sick bay. "I came down to tell you that we've stopped to make repairs. The sail is jammed. With some luck we'll be able to get it up a bit more so we'll be able to use our radar gear."

"Thanks for telling me," Hicks said with a wan smile.

"How are you doing?" Boxer asked.

Hicks nodded. "Okay, I guess, for a man who has a hole in his chest."

"Is there anything you want?"

"Anything I'd want I couldn't have now," Hicks answered with a grin.

"As long as you're thinking about women," Boxer said, "you'll be fine."

"Thanks again for risking your neck to bring me back to the *Shark*."

With a quick motion of his hand, Boxer waved Hick's thanks aside. "You would have done the same for me."

"I've been lying here, trying to decide whether or not I would have. I'd like to think I would, but I'm not sure I would have ... at least not then. Now I would. But not then. I hated you too much."

"Forget it!" Boxer exclaimed. "It's past and done with."

"There's something else... There's Tracy."

Boxer shook his head. "I haven't any claim on her and she doesn't have any claim on me. But now is not the time to talk about her. Sometime, when you're well and you still want to talk about her, we'll talk. But not now."

"Okay," Hicks said with a sigh. He closed his eyes.

"I'll stop by again," Boxer said.

"Thanks for stopping by now," Hicks answered, without opening his eyes.

"Hang in there," Boxer said and he left the sick bay. A short time later he was stretched out on his bunk. He had dimmed the overhead light in the cabin, and now, with his eyes closed, he was slowly drifting into the darker world of sleep...

Captain First Class Igor Borodine stood on the bridge of the *Q-21* and looked at the stars veiled by a curtain of dust that only five days before had been the island of Torpay, a secret Russian missile base. Now, there was nothing but empty ocean covered with a light brown dust, which, he was sure, had radiated out from the center of the explosion in all directions for hundreds, if not a thousand, miles or more. That the island had been destroyed by an American strike force off a submarine was almost impossible for him or any of his superiors to believe. Yet it had happened.

The Americans had managed to plant and detonate a small atomic bomb inside the island's active volcano. The resulting explosion had changed the local geography and caused a six-foot tidal wave to move in all directions for some two thousand miles. Even now there were numerous weak undersea earthquakes...

Borodine shook his head... It was an incredible feat that had cost the lives of the men who'd accomplished it. The submarine, its crew, and the strike force lay buried in an undersea canyon twenty-five hundred feet deep. If the sub's hull had not been crushed by the boulders that had fallen on her from the depth-charging by Soviet destroyers, then there was the strong possibility that many, if not all, of the crew and the strike force were still alive...

That thought caused Borodine to shiver... The men in the submarine would eventually die of starvation and, before that, possibly turn cannibalistic. Despite the fact they had been his enemies, Borodine hoped they would die long before they'd resort to eating one another.

"Comrade Captain, I understand that the salvage ships should be here in a matter of days," Vassily Markov said. He was the political officer aboard the *Q-21*.

Borodine was so involved with his own thoughts that he had completely forgotten Markov was on the bridge with him, as were the helmsman and two other junior officers, who were occupied with their own tasks.

"The estimated time of arrival is ten hundred tomorrow morning," Borodine answered.

Markov leaned against the inside of the bridge. "How long do you intend to cruise this area?"

"Not too much longer," Borodine answered.

For several moments neither Markov nor Borodine spoke; then Markov asked, "Do you think there's any chance that our salvage people will find any evidence of the American submarine?"

"None."

Again there was a protracted silence between them; and again it was Markov who spoke first. "All of our armed forces are on a Step Two Alert," he said.

Borodine shrugged. "There are only two possibilities: the submarine is entombed under thousands of tons of rock; or a miracle occurred and it escaped. Either way the salvage people will come up empty."

"So your considered opinion," Markov said, with just a hint of sarcasm in his voice, "having the salvage people come out here is a waste of time?"

"It will give them excellent deep water-diving experience," Borodine replied.

"Costing additional millions of rubles."

"It was not my decision to send them here," Borodine said.

"If we are to make a pre-emptive strike, then we must be prepared to justify it to the rest of the world."

"What would be left of it?" Borodine answered.

"Think what you will of my decision to—"

"I would prefer not to have to fight World War Three, Comrade. We wouldn't win and neither would they."

"But they attacked and destroyed one of our bases. How can you justify that?"

"I can't. But one base isn't worth the world."

"I doubt if your thinking would be the same had you been sunk or badly damaged by the American submarine," Markov said hotly. "Just think of the men who were killed on the island and the equipment that was destroyed."

Borodine almost shook his head. There wasn't any point in discussing the situation with a man like Markov. He would never understand the Americans took the only course of action open to them. They could not allow the base to become operational.

"Don't tell me you wouldn't destroy that submarine this very moment, if you had the opportunity," Markov sneered.

"I wouldn't hesitate an instant," Borodine answered. "But that is an individual action between two professionals. It would not involve the deaths of millions of people."

"Those millions of people," Markov countered, "are just as much our enemy as the men aboard the submarine that destroyed our base."

"Our secret base," Borodine corrected.

"It was our base!" Markov exclaimed.

Borodine pursed his lips. "We have a difference of opinion, Comrade. It is not unusual for such differences to arise between men in situations like this one. The two of us are looking at the same thing, but we see it from different perspectives."

"It is more than a difference of perspectives, Comrade Captain," Markov said. "I want nothing less than the total destruction of our enemy, while you appear to be content to play a game with your professional counterpart. You are not a knight, if I may use the analogy, going out to joust for the honor of your lady. But you are a highly trained technocrat, who commands a highly sophisticated killing machine, and whose sole reason for being is to destroy the enemies of your country."

Realizing now that the helmsman and the two other officers on the bridge were listening to the conversation, Borodine said, "And that, Comrade, was exactly what I did. I destroyed, with the aid of several other professionals, the enemy of our country. Now if you'll excuse me, I have work to do below." Then turning to one of the junior officers, he said, "Captain-Lieutenant Popov take the CONN."

"Aye, aye, Comrade Captain," Popov answered.

Borodine lowered himself into the open hatch and hurried down the steps that led from the bridge to another hatch and finally to the main deck inside the hull of the _Q-21_.

"Anything wrong?" Viktor, his executive officer asked, as Borodine came into the CIC area.

"Markov," Borodine answered in a whisper.

"Still?"

Borodine nodded. "I just don't like the son of a bitch."

"I know," Viktor answered. "But for your own safety don't make it so obvious. He's a dangerous man."

Borodine shrugged and walked up the three steps to the interior bridge. He sat down and was about to monitor the boat's systems when COMMO signaled him. "Yes?" he answered.

"We have a Mayday, Captain," the officer on duty said. "An airliner is on fire and is going down."

"Latitude and longitude?"

"One zero degrees south latitude; one seven five east longitude."

Borodine punched the aircraft's position into the *Q-21*'s NAVSYS. Instantly a grid map of the Pacific Ocean appeared, showing the position of the *Q-21* and the position of the aircraft. It was located three hundred and fifty miles southwest of the *Q-21*.

"Captain, the plane is going down," the duty officer said.

Borodine called Viktor to the bridge. "A commercial aircraft went down three five zero miles from here," he explained. "We can be in the vicinity of the crash within ten hours."

"And you want to go after it?"

Borodine nodded.

"Radio Moscow for permission," Viktor said.

"Before I'd get a *yes* or *no*, it would be too late to do anything."

"You make the decisions," Viktor told him.

Borodine smiled. "Yes I do." He hit the klaxon button twice; then over the MC, he said, "Prepare to dive. All hands prepare to dive..."

"Stand by to dive," Borodine said, setting sixty feet into the DIVSYS. "Setting forward planes at five degrees... Forward ballast tanks flooded."

The *Q-21* tilted slightly and began to sink beneath the waves.

"Two zero feet," Borodine announced over the MC system. He activated another switch. "Main ballast tank flooded. Four zero feet ... five zero feet..." He moved the diving planes into their null position. "Six zero feet ... trimming ballast to hold at six zero feet."

The boat's bow rose slightly; then it settled down.

Borodine watched the dive indicator; the bubble came to the center of the instrument. "Dive complete," he announced.

"Holding steady as six zero feet." He switched from night lighting to daylight, he dialed thirty-five knots into the SPED-CONT and put a new course destination into the NAVSYS. Then, over the MC, he said in a calm voice, "We're answering a Mayday from a commercial airliner that has gone down three five zero miles from here. Lieutenant Popov will be in charge of the rescue detail. Every man not on duty when we arrive at the crash site will be part of the rescue detail. Lieutenant Popov report to me for further instructions."

"Comrade Captain," Markov said, as he came up to the bridge, "I must protest —"

"I would not expect you to do anything else," Borodine said, winking at Viktor.

"I will radio Moscow and —"

"As soon as the rescue operation is over, Comrade Captain, you have my permission to radio Moscow. But until then, no one but myself is authorized to send radio messages from the *Q-21*."

"But I have the authority to —"

Borodine held up his hand. "Comrade Captain, if you'll excuse me, I have a great many things to do before we reach the scene of the crash."

Markov turned on his heel and walked stiffly away.

"He's not going to forget this," Viktor cautioned.

"I am doing what any captain would do," Borodine answered. "I am following the law of the sea, nothing more and nothing less. I am truly sorry for him, if he is unable to understand that."

"If he weren't your enemy before," Viktor said, "he is now."

Borodine shrugged but didn't answer.

Boxer slept, dreaming of his last visit with Gwen. Her naked body was soft against his. No longer in her bed, they lay stretched out on a white sand beach, beyond which the water was silvered by moonlight.

Someone was calling him...

Gwen vanished...

"Stand by ... stand by for depth charges!" The explosions ripped the beach apart. The sand and the sea came up over him. He was buried alive!

"Skipper ... Jack, get up!"

Boxer opened his eyes and found himself looking at Harris. "I was dreaming," he said, shaking his head as if the movement would erase whatever memory was left of the dream.

"COMMO picked this up," Harris said, extending a message to him.

"What is it?" Boxer asked, rubbing the sleep out of his eyes.

"A Mayday from an airliner," Harris answered.

Boxer took the message paper and read it. "How far are we from them?"

"According to NAVCOMP and COMMCOMP one five zero miles."

Boxer pulled himself to a sitting position and swinging around planted his feet on the deck. "Do we go or don't we?" he asked, looking up at Harris.

"Could be a trick."

Boxer shook his heads. "The Russians think we've bought it. According to William's last message they have their whole damn military machine on condition two, hoping to find evidence that will allow them to go to condition one."

His voice dropping to a whisper, Harris said, "I didn't realize that we were that close to war."

"We're not. The Russians won't find anything. They won't find us and they sure as hell aren't going to find anything left of the island. But what do we do about this?" Boxer asked, waving the message in front of him.

"If we go, we blow whatever cover we have left," Harris said.

Boxer nodded. "And if we don't go, how do we — how do I — manage to live with that for the rest of my life?" He ran his hand over his beard. "Has COMMO picked up any transmissions about the crash?"

"It only lasted about forty-five seconds," Harris said. "The position is way off the major shipping lanes."

Boxer took a deep breath and slowly exhaled. "How are the repairs going?"

"The diving plane should be repaired within the hour. The sail has a long way to go before we see any results."

Boxer stood up and put on his jumpsuit. He went to his COMMCOMP and switching on the MC, he said, "Now hear this ... now hear this... All hands, this is your captain... We will soon change course to answer a Mayday... A commercial aircraft is down some one hundred and fifty miles from our present position... Mister Cowly and Mister Redfern will be responsible for the rescue operation... All personnel not on watch at the time of the rescue report to either Mister Cowly or Mister Redfern... That is all." He put the mike down, looked at Harris and said. "In my shoes, you'd have done the same."

Harris nodded. "There'll be flak," he said.

"I'm hoping not too much," Boxer answered. "But I'll have to take what comes. If I ignored this, I couldn't ever again think of myself as a seaman, much less a man."

CHAPTER 2

The *Shark* was moving half as fast on the surface as she could submerged. Spinning a phosphorescent wake, her huge cigar-shaped hull sliced through the waters of the South Pacific.

Boxer was on the bridge of the sail, scanning the horizon with infrared binoculars for any signs of the wrecked aircraft. At the same time two lookouts fore and aft searched the sea for ships and the sky for planes. Though they were off the main shipping lanes and aircraft routes, a submarine traveling on the surface was an inviting target, especially now that Russia was more bellicose than usual.

Having to make a long run on the surface would have bothered Boxer even if the *Shark*'s radar gear was operational. But doing it blind, and with his boat damaged, made him very uneasy. If he had to order a dive, he wasn't at all sure the *Shark* would be able to surface again — especially if he were forced to dive deep. Boxer pushed that possibility from his mind and concentrated on the search.

Light coming into the eastern sky was already erasing some of the dimmer stars; Because they were so close to the equator, daylight would erupt suddenly without the gradual change from darkness to dawn that took place in the northern and southern latitudes.

The sun was just below the horizon. The clouds in the east were purple, became dark pink; then took on the color of a faded rose. The arc of the sun was above the horizon. The clouds turned white and it was daylight.

Boxer switched off the infrared optics and continued to scan the water.

Cowly keyed him and reported, "James has taken a turn for the worse."

"I'm coming down," Boxer answered.

"Want a cup of coffee?"

"After I see James," Boxer said. He climbed over the side of the sail and made his way down the ladder to the deck. He was just about to lower himself through the number-one hatch, when one of the bow lookouts called out, "Target two five degrees off port bow!"

Boxer trained his glasses on the area. There was wreckage in the water — and survivors. "Good work ... you spotted it!" he told the man. He keyed the bridge. "Mister Cowly bring the *Shark* to course one two degrees; reduce speed to six knots; then pass the CONN to Mister Harris and ready the rescue detail. The wreckage has been sighted."

"Aye, aye, Skipper," Cowly answered.

Boxer summoned the fore and aft lookouts. "Go below; get yourselves some coffee and then report to Mister Cowly."

"Aye, aye, Skipper," the senior man answered.

"Good work, Jackson," Boxer said again. "Damn good work!"

The seaman grinned and disappeared into the open hatchway.

The *Shark* was put on its new course and it began to slow.

Boxer made his way to the bow and scanned the sea. He could see a portion of a wing; two people were on it and at least four were clinging to it. The tail section of the aircraft was still afloat. There were many people in the water, and at least three inflatable rafts were visible.

Cowly and Redfern came up on deck.

"There are some survivors," Boxer said, handing his glasses to Redfern.

"Sharks!" Redfern exclaimed and handed the binoculars to Cowly.

"I count four circling," Cowly said, giving the glasses back to Boxer.

Boxer keyed COMMO. "Patch me into the deck MC," he said.

A few seconds later, the COMMO said, "Go ahead skipper."

Boxer cleared his throat. "Ahoy… This is the captain of the submarine… We'll come to a dead stop close to you… Some of the crew will go into the water to assist you… Try not to struggle… Those of you who can swim to the side of the submarine will be taken aboard by men on deck… Please remain calm." He didn't need his glasses to see that several of the survivors were waving at him. He keyed Harris. "Have the rescue detail come on deck," Boxer said.

Moments later the men clambered up through several of the hatches.

Boxer keyed the EO. "Stop all engines."

"All engines stopped."

The *Shark* began to lose headway.

"It's all yours," Boxer told Cowly and Redfern. "Get those people aboard. We're a sitting duck out here like this."

Within moments, the *Shark* was within fifty feet of one of the rafts. There were two men, a child, and a woman on it.

"Can you make it to us?" Cowly asked, using a bullhorn.

"No paddle," one of the men answered.

"Yellan," Redfern said, "better start earning your pay."

"Sure," Yellan answered with a grin. He signaled to his team and ten of them leaped into the water. He and another man swam directly to the raft, while the others headed toward the people in the water.

"Sharks!" one of Yellan's men called out.

"Shark detail go!" Redfern shouted.

A half dozen men with bang sticks went into the water.

Yellan eased the raft alongside the *Shark*.

"Take 'em aboard," Cowly ordered.

Three men clambered down the sloping side of the *Shark*. Two pulled the raft up onto the bulge of the hull. The third man reached down into the raft, took the child out, and handed it to Cowly, who was standing by.

"Take the boy below," Cowly said, handing him to another man, "and see he has milk and cookies."

"Aye, aye, sir," the man answered.

The woman came out of the raft next. She was middle-aged and disheveled.

Cowly reached down and pulled her onto the deck.

Sobbing, she fell into his arms. "I thought we were going to die," she wept. "I thought I'd never see my children again."

Cowly patted her on the back. "You're safe," he said reassuringly. "You're safe now." And he passed her to another member of the rescue detail.

The man came out of the raft and made his way up to the deck. He was younger than the woman. "I must send a radio message," he said. "There are people waiting for me in L.A."

"You'll have to talk to the skipper about that," Cowly said.

"Where is he?"

Cowly looked toward the sail, where Boxer and Redfern were standing. "He's busy now, sir, but I'm sure he'll speak to you after we complete the rescue operation."

"I must speak to him now!" the man insisted.

Cowly signaled to one of the crewmen. "Take this man below," he said, "and give him some coffee."

"Aye, aye, sir," the man answered.

"You can't just brush me off like that. I'm Byron Hayes. I demand —"

Cowly not only recognized the name, he also recognized the face. Byron Hayes was the film and TV star who was aboard the *Mary-Ann* when she collided with the *Sting Ray*. He was one of the people who testified against Boxer at the Board of Inquiry.

"Sorry, Mister Hayes, you must go below now," Cowly said quietly. "I wouldn't want to have you taken forcibly." And he turned his back on him.

Yellan's men were herding more people toward the *Shark*.

Suddenly there was a muffled explosion and a geyser of water broke the surface off the port side.

"Got too close for comfort," one of the men shouted.

"Several dead here," a second man called out. He was swimming close to a half dozen people in inflated life jackets. "Sharks —"

"Look out!" Yellan shouted.

The man screamed.

"Get that man aboard," Boxer shouted.

Two more men went into the water.

Blood swirled red around him.

A second dorsal fin came toward the man.

Suddenly several more sharks were in the area.

"Taylor, White," Redfern yelled. "Get two M-22s up here and take those sharks out."

Boxer came over to Cowly. "How many would you say were still out there?"

"A couple of dozen, at least."

Boxer looked off to the southwest. The sky was leaden. "A squall line is coming toward us. This sea is going to start changing soon."

Cowly nodded.

"Get one of the docs on deck," Yellan shouted from the water. He was bringing the injured man alongside. "Shark got a good chunk of his right side."

Ross lifted himself out of the hatchway and moved down to the water's edge. Two men carrying a gurney followed him.

Within moments the injured man was lifted out of the water and put into the gurney. Half his side was gone and what remained was badly shredded and bleeding profusely.

As the medical team passed, Boxer raised his eyebrows.

Ross shook his head.

Ross and White began to shoot at the sharks.

Another bang stick went off.

Boxer and Cowly went out on the bulge and helped four more survivors come aboard the *Shark*. Two were middle-aged men. One was a young man in his teens, and the fourth was a young woman.

"Never thought I'd make it," she said, reaching up for Boxer's hand.

"You're okay now," Boxer answered, looking at her long enough to see the handcuffs on her left hand.

"Skipper," Harris said, coming on the radio. "The barometer is dropping fast."

Boxer suddenly realized the breeze had freshened considerably and the water was roiled. "Roger," he answered. If the radar was operational he would have been able to get an exact reading of the squall's speed and direction, and how far away it was from the *Shark*. But now as he turned to look at it, the best he could do was estimate it was still five to ten miles away — and moving in on them very fast.

"What's going on?" the woman asked.

Boxer looked at her. She was wearing a simple blue pants suit. Her shoulder-length auburn hair was disheveled. He guessed she was somewhere in her late twenties, or early thirties. He took hold of her wrist. "Who was on the other end of the cuffs?" he asked.

"A man," she answered without flinching. "A New York City detective. He separated us when we were going down. He couldn't swim."

Boxer let go of her wrist. "Boomer," he called to one of the men, "take this lady below and have one of the machinist mates take off her jewelry."

"Aye, aye, Skipper," the man said.

Boxer turned his attention back to the scene in front of him.

Yellan and two of his men had reached the tail section of the aircraft and were trying to coax several people to swim for the *Shark*.

Redfern was giving the order to launch an inflatable boat from the deck, while several of his men were pulling survivors out of the water.

"Cowly," Boxer said, "we don't have much time before that squall hits us."

"Are we going to take the dead aboard?" Cowly asked.

"Negative," Boxer answered.

Suddenly the wind began to make a moaning sound and the water became choppy. The *Shark* started to roll slightly.

Boxer keyed the EO. "Give me one zero zero rpms," he said.

"One zero zero rpms," the EO answered.

As soon as the engines started up, the *Shark*'s roll lessened and she began to push gently through the water.

Boxer keyed Harris. "Bill tell Mahony to put us into a tight circle."

"How are things up there?"

"Hectic," Boxer answered. "Weather is closing in."

"How much longer do you think we have here?" Harris answered.

"Not much I hope," Boxer answered. "Here comes the rain!"

Harris signed off.

A cold, hard rain slashed down, cutting visibility to a few yards.

Boxer forced his voice above the sound of the wind. "Tom, how many men have we got out there?"

"Eight in the water and four in the boat," Redfern answered.

The sea was running now. The waves were three to four feet, and breaking over the *Shark*'s deck.

"Cowly," Boxer called, "how many people have we taken aboard?"

"Harris told me sixty. He had them counted as they went below."

"Five minutes more —"

"Target bearing three zero degrees," the SO reported. "Range twenty-five-thousand yards... Speed two zero knots... Depth two zero zero feet."

Boxer keyed Harris. "ID that target," he said.

"CONCOMP IDs the *Q-21*," Harris answered.

"Christ!" Boxer swore. Suddenly he realized Cowly was looking at him. "We don't have five minutes," he said. "We don't have one minute. We might as well be dead already."

"But we've got men out there," Cowly protested.

"And I've got a boat, a crew, and sixty survivors here under my feet," Boxer answered. He keyed the COMMO. "Am I still patched into the deck MC?"

"Sure are, Skipper."

"Patch me into the MC below as well."

"Done."

"All hands," Boxer said, hoping Yellan, the rest of the men, and the other survivors would hear him above the sound of the rain and the wind. "We are abandoning the rescue operation… We are abandoning operation… Prepare to get underway immediately… Prepare to get underway immediately… Prepare to get underway immediately… Battle stations… All hands, battle stations!"

Tom came running down the deck. "What the hell is going on?"

"Battle stations, Mister," Boxer answered. "Get below!"

The men on deck scrambled through the hatches.

Boxer was the last one through number one hatch and dogged it shut. He ran to the bridge. "I have the CONN, Mister Harris," he said. "Helmsman bring her to course one eight zero degrees," he said.

"Coming to course one eight zero degrees," Mahony answered.

Boxer sat down at the COMMCOMP and set the *Shark*'s speed at twenty knots. "Section officers report," he said.

One by one all of the section officers reported their men on station.

Boxer keyed the sonar officer. "Give me a target indication every two minutes."

"Aye, aye, Skipper."

"Harris," Boxer said, "I want all the survivors in the mess area."

"That's where they are, Skipper," Harris said.

Boxer switched on the MC. He was sweating profusely and took the time to run a handkerchief over his face before he said, "Now hear this ... now hear this ... shortly we will be under attack from the *Q-21*...

Suddenly a man came running up to the bridge. "I demand to see the Captain. I must speak to the captain!"

Boxer cut the MC transmission. "Mister Cowly get this individual back to the mess area!"

"You?... Jack Boxer?" Hayes questioned.

Cowly came alongside of Hayes. "I don't want to have you taken back," he said.

"But you're out of the navy!" Hayes exclaimed, still looking at Boxer.

"Mister Cowly," Boxer said, "I gave you an order."

"Aye, aye, Skipper," Cowly answered, grabbing hold of Haye's right arm and twisting it in back of him.

"Let go of me!" Hayes cried, struggling to be free.

"Move!" Cowly ordered.

"I'll make you pay —"

"Move!" Cowly exclaimed again, shoving Hayes in front of him.

"Target bearing three zero degrees ... range twenty-three thousand five hundred yards ... speed two zero knots ... depth two five zero feet."

"You haven't heard the last of this," Hayes shouted before he was forced back into the mess area.

Boxer took a deep breath, exhaled, and switched the MC on again. "This is the captain... We're going to have to fight on the surface... If I have to dive ... well, the *Shark* is damaged ... and even if we did manage to sink or damage the *Q-21*, we might not be able to surface again." He replaced the MC mike in its cradle and leaned back.

Cowly returned. "We've got some very jittery people in the mess area, Skipper."

"There's some jittery people all over this damn boat, including the one you're speaking to now," Boxer answered.

"Skipper," the SO said, "target has increased speed to thirty knots."

Boxer keyed the CIC. "Activate the ECM."

"ECM activated," the officer in charge reported.

"Cowly, Harris, each of you choose another man to go with you and prepare to launch the minisubs. Let's see what Borodine will do with you guys around him. Try to get in a shot at him. You won't be able to sink the _Q-21_ but you sure as hell could damage him."

"When do you want to launch?" Harris asked.

"It'll take ten minutes to arm them. Say twenty minutes from now." He switched on the outside TV cameras. Instantly, the sea, as seen from the bow of the _Shark_, filled the screen. The water surged up over the bow and drowned the water-shielded lens. "When we slow to launch you guys, we'll roll more than we're doing now, but you shouldn't have any trouble getting out from under us."

"One or both of us could ram —"

"Only if there's no other way," Boxer said, "and only on my command. Is that understood?"

"Aye, aye, Skipper," Harris responded.

"Only on your command, Skipper," Cowly said.

"Better get things under way," Boxer told them. He shook their hands. "Good luck."

The two men wished him luck.

"We're sure as hell going to need it to get out of this alive," Boxer replied; then picking up the MC, he said, "Launch crew, stand by to launch minisubs numbers one and two... Arming crew arm minisubs for maximum fire power." He glanced at the clock on the control panel. It was 0730 hours. "Launch will take place at zero seven five zero."

Boxer checked the barometer. It was still falling. The squall might well be turning into a regular tropical storm. If it did, Borodine would have an even greater advantage than he had now. A rough sea would slow the *Shark* down considerably, probably to ten knots or less, making her an easier target than she otherwise would have been.

Boxer switched on the minisub bay cameras and watched the two undersea craft being armed. That he might have to sacrifice one or both of them to save the *Shark* was a real and horrifying possibility.

Borodine studied his COMMCOMP. There was no doubt about it: the target identified by the *Sea Savage*'s computer was the *Shark*. He looked up at Viktor. "How is it possible?" he asked. "We searched for her and found nothing. I'd have sworn she was trapped in that undersea canyon."

Viktor shook his head. "I don't know how. But she's here and we have a second chance to destroy her."

The SO keyed Borodine. "Target bearing three three zero degrees ... range ten thousand yards ... speed twenty knots ... still on surface."

Borodine rubbed his clean-shaven chin. "Why hasn't Boxer dived? He knows we're here. He must —" Borodine stopped. "If his sonar gear was damaged, he wouldn't know we're here."

Viktor agreed and added. "That might explain why he's on the surface. He could be trying to make repairs."

Borodine keyed the engine room. "Speed control going to automatic ... setting speed at four zero knots... Inform me immediately of any equipment changes."

"Aye, aye, Comrade Captain," the engineering officer answered.

The SO came on again. "Comrade Captain the target has initiated its ECM system."

"So much for Boxer not knowing we're here," Borodine commented.

"If he knows we're here, why hasn't he dived?" Viktor asked.

Again Borodine rubbed his chin. "There are only two possibilities: one, he's damaged in a way that we can't determine; two, he's trying to lure us closer to get a better shot at us. But the second appears to be less probable than the first because he's moving too slowly. No, I think he's damaged."

"Damaged, but still very dangerous," Viktor said.

Borodine nodded. "My guess is that Boxer answered the Mayday. I wouldn't be surprised if he had started to take survivors aboard before the weather turned and we showed up."

"What kind of captain would use his damaged boat to pick up survivors?" Markov asked, coming up behind Borodine and Viktor. "I couldn't help overhearing what you said, Comrade Captain. I'll tell you what kind of captain: a mad one or a —"

"A very good one," Viktor said.

Markov's eyes narrowed. He looked at Borodine.

"Boxer is obeying the law of the sea, as we were when I decided to respond to the Mayday," Borodine said.

"Ah, but you guessed the *Shark* was here. You really didn't believe it had been destroyed. You were gambling that you'd find it."

"You're wrong. I was absolutely certain the *Shark* was down, lost with all hands."

"This time, Comrade Captain, make sure she does go down with all hands," Markov said with a smile; then he turned and left the bridge.

"Comrade Captain," the SO said, "the target is slowing down."

"Heading the same?"

"Yes."

"Range?"

"Eight thousand yards and closing fast," the SO said.

"I don't like it," Borodine said. "He shouldn't be slowing down. He should be running away from us with every bit of power he has. We'll go to battle stations."

Viktor reached over and hit the klaxon button three times. The sound tore through the *Sea Savage* and sent the men running to their stations.

"I'm going up to periscope depth and have a look around," Borodine said, setting a depth of forty feet into the automatic dive control system. "This time Boxer won't get away. This time he's in check…"

CHAPTER 3

Boxer watched the arming of the minisubs on the TV monitor. When both craft were ready to be launched, he automatically reduced the speed of the *Shark* to four knots. "Open bay doors," he ordered.

"Bay doors opened," the launch officer said.

"Dive as soon as you're free of us," Boxer told Harris and Cowly. "Launch craft number one."

"Craft number one launched," the LO said.

Boxer watched it exit the bay. It moved quickly away from the *Shark*. "Launch craft number two," he ordered.

The second minisub moved out of the *Shark*.

Boxer switched on the Underwater Imaging System. The minisubs were already well below the *Shark* and were beginning to turn toward the *Q-21*.

"Target bearing three zero degrees … range seven thousand yards … speed four zero knots … closing fast," the SO reported.

Boxer increased the *Shark*'s speed to fifteen knots. "Mahony," he ordered, "stand by to take the helm… Helm going to manual control." He switched off the AUTONAV system. "Mahony, come to nine zero degrees," he said.

"Coming to nine zero degrees," Mahony answered.

"Target bearing one five degrees … range six thousand five zero zero yards … speed four zero knots … depth one five zero feet," the SO signaled.

"Stand by to fire ASROC one and two," Boxer said.

"ASROCS armed and directed," the FO reported.

"So, where are our minisubs?"

"Four thousand yards from target... New target ... bearing one eight degrees ... range six thousand yards... Closing fast... Torpedo ... torpedo!"

Boxer quickly checked the ECM indicator. The system was functioning. "Helmsman, come four five degrees," Boxer said, after clearing his throat.

"Torpedo changing course," the SO said.

"CIC compute course intercept for ASROCS and torpedo," Boxer said.

"Course intercept computed... Firing time for ASROCS one five seconds from now."

Boxer looked up at the digital clock. "One zero seconds to firing time ... eight seconds..."

"Primary target bearing one five degrees... Range —"

"Fire ASROCS!" Boxer ordered.

"ASROCS fired," the FO reported.

Boxer turned his attention to the UWIS screen.

"Primary target bearing one five degrees ... range five thousand five five zero yards ... speed forty knots ... depth forty feet."

Boxer saw the two ASROCS enter the water. Seconds later the explosion distorted the UWIS image. The dull sound pushed its way through the water to the *Shark*.

"Torpedo destroyed," the SO said.

"Helmsman come to two two zero degrees," Boxer said.

"Coming to course two two zero degrees," Mahony answered.

Boxer had six more ASROCS he could use before he'd have to resort to other weapons, or send an arming crew topside to load ASROCS firing tubes again. With the *Shark* rolling the way she was it would be almost impossible to do it.

Harris keyed him. "Will attack from Noreen," he said.

"Roger that," Boxer answered.

Cowly signaled. "Going in from Sierra."

"Coordinate," Boxer said.

"Target bearing one three degrees ... range four thousand five zero zero yards ... speed four zero knots ... 32 depth four zero feet... Target closing fast."

Borodine watched the approach of the two small targets on the CIC board.

"The one coming in on our starboard side will be close enough to use it," Viktor said.

Borodine nodded. "Open starboard ports."

The operations officer changed the position of a toggle switch. "Starboard ports opened."

Borodine went to his COMMCOMP and adjusted a set of controls; then he typed ACTIVATE LAZR PWR.

Moments later, the COMMCOMP responded:

LAZR PWR FULLY ACTIVATED
REQUEST FIRE COMMD

Borodine typed:

FIRE RANGE 1000 YDS
RANGE 1200 YDS
RANGE 1150 YDS
RANGE 1100 YDS
RANGE 1050 YDS

Boxer gave his attention to the UWIS screen. The *Q-21* was a long dark shape below the surface of the water. He watched Cowly and Harris move in for the attack. With any luck —

Suddenly Harris's craft disintegrated.

RANGE 1000 YARDS
TARGET DESTROYED

Borodine deactivated the laser weapon system, keyed the operations officer and ordered the starboard optical port closed.

"If it only had a longer range," Viktor said, "we could destroy the *Shark*."

Borodine nodded. "Move the equipment to the port side; there's still another target out there."

"Aye, aye, Captain," Viktor responded with a smile.

"Oh my God!" Boxer exclaimed.

The sound of the explosion reached the *Shark* seconds after it occurred.

Boxer keyed Cowly. "Abandon attack … abandon attack!" Boxer sucked in his breath and waited for Cowly's response.

"Roger that," Cowly answered.

"Target bearing one three degrees … range four thousand yards … speed eight zero knots … depth four zero feet… Torpedo … torpedo … target… Skipper, two — three — torpedoes closing fast."

"Course four three degrees," Boxer ordered. "Hard on the helm."

"Coming to course four three degrees," Mahony answered.

"CIC direct ASROCS three, four, and five at incoming torpedoes… Fire when ready," Boxer said.

"ASROCS armed… Ten seconds to firing," the FO said.

Boxer's eyes went to the digital clock. The seconds were leaping by.

"Targets turning to bearing four seven degrees ... range one thousand yards —"

"ASROCS fired!" the FO announced.

Boxer made up his mind to risk diving. He hit the klaxon button twice. "On manual control ... make three zero zero feet ... one zero degrees on bow planes ... flood forward ballast..."

The *Shark* pitched slightly forward.

"Making three zero zero feet," the DO said.

"DC keep those pumps working in the well," Boxer said.

"Aye, aye, Skipper," the DCO answered.

"Flood all ballast," Boxer ordered. He watched the depth gage. The *Shark* was going down very fast.

"Two zero zero feet," the DO said.

"Stand by to fire stern torpedoes five and six," Boxer ordered.

The sound of three dull explosions passed below the *Shark*.

"Arm torpedoes... Set bearing... Set target soundtrack... Load torpedoes."

"Torpedoes loaded and ready to fire," the TO said.

"Open torpedo tube doors," Boxer said.

"Torpedo tube doors open."

"Fire in one zero seconds," Boxer ordered.

"Targets bearing two seven five degrees ... range twelve thousand yards ... speed fifteen knots."

Boxer pressed the red abort button. "Torpedo firing holding at three seconds... SO, ID new targets." He was afraid this might be part of a Russian squadron on its way to or from the Indian Ocean. He took a moment to look at the UWIS screen. Cowly was closer to the *Shark* than he was to the *Q-21*.

"New target ID ... aircraft carrier *George Washington* ... escort destroyers: *Stanley*, *Harris*, *Seward*, and *Barly* ... guided missile frigates: *Paul* and *Victor*."

"Abort torpedo firing mission," Boxer ordered. "Close torpedo tube doors."

"Torpedo firing mission aborted ... torpedo tube doors closed," the TO said.

"Primary target bearing fifteen degrees ... speed forty knots ... diving."

"Cowly return to base," Boxer said.

"Roger that," Cowly answered.

"Helmsman bring her to two seven degrees," Boxer said. "COMMO signal carrier group we're approaching them."

"Aye, aye, Skipper."

Boxer switched on the MC. "Secure from general quarters ... secure from general quarters."

"Stand by to retrieve minisub," Boxer said, slowing the *Shark*'s speed to ten knots. "As soon as minisub is aboard, stand by to surface... Mister Berness, stand in for Mister Harris until Mister Cowly is aboard."

"Aye, aye, Skipper," Berness answered.

Exhausted, Boxer leaned back. This time he was lucky and he knew it.

"Diving to one thousand feet," Borodine said calmly, though he fully understood the danger. "New course one zero degrees."

"Secondary target moving toward the primary target," the SO reported.

"I had no idea there were two minisubs aboard the *Shark*," Borodine admitted.

"Carrier group holding steady on bearing four five degrees," the SO said.

"Stand down from battle stations," Borodine announced over the MC system.

Markov came to the bridge. "How will you explain this to your superiors?" he asked.

"Explain what?" Borodine asked.

"That you failed to destroy the *Shark*."

"I think I managed to keep the Americans from destroying the *Sea Savage*," Borodine said. "By now I'm sure you know about the American carrier group."

"You still had the time to sink the *Shark*," Markov insisted.

Borodine nodded. "I would have, or could have sunk the *Shark*. But an instant after the *Shark* had been hit, the Americans would have begun to hunt me. I wasn't going to gamble on them not being able to find me. You agree, I hope, it's better to be alive than dead, or as Shakespeare put it: "Tis better to run away and fight another day.'"

Markov glared at him.

Borodine watched the DDROT. They were approaching one thousand feet. Slowly he moved the diving plane control and watched the bubble indicator. When it indicated the boat was level, he placed the electronic plane control into its null position and switched the automatic stabilization system. The *Sea Savage* would remain at a depth of one thousand feet as long as the ASS was activated.

"Are we returning to Nikor Islands?" Viktor asked.

"No, we're returning to Vladivostok," Borodine said. "Our mission is over."

"It wasn't very successful, was it Comrade Captain?" Markov said.

Borodine shrugged. "If by that you mean we didn't sink the *Shark*, I'd have to agree that we weren't successful. But then the *Shark* didn't sink us. By that measure," he said with a smile, "I'd have to say we weren't completely unsuccessful."

CHAPTER 4

The carrier group heaved to and to the astonishment of the men who could see her, the *Shark* surfaced and lay off the port side of the *George Washington*. The rain had stopped and though the waves were two to three feet high, the sea was calmer than it had been before the *Shark* had dived.

Within minutes Boxer was aboard the Washington and facing Admiral D'Arcy, commander of the group.

D'Arcy had been Boxer's base commander in Staten Island, New York, and the ranking officer of the board of inquiry that recommended he be reduced in rank and be tried by a court-martial for dereliction of duty during the crash between the *Sting Ray* and the *Mary-Ann*.

Boxer was prepared to let bygones be bygones and thank him for showing up at just the right time. But D'Arcy glared up at him from behind a desk, and when he didn't have the courtesy to offer him a chair, Boxer said. "I have survivors aboard —"

"Speak when you're spoken to," D'Arcy snapped.

"Just a minute," Boxer said, "I'm not under your command and I don't like your tone."

D'Arcy's face turned red. "Just tell me what you're doing here."

"That is none of your business, Admiral," Boxer answered. "I started to tell you I have survivors on the *Shark* and several of my men, hopefully, are alive and with additional survivors not too far from here. Now if you'll order a rescue team for them, I'd be much obliged."

D'Arcy leaned forward, picked up a phone and said, "Send rescue teams one and two to assigned coordinates." Then he put the phone down and said to Boxer, "I heard rumors about you and your crew —"

"Admiral, I have survivors aboard the *Shark* and not enough room for them and I have an injured man who needs medical attention."

"First, I want some answers," D'Arcy said. "Just how much were you and that sub out there involved in this fracas over Torpay?"

Boxer shook his head. "You're going way over your head, Admiral. I'm not on your team and I don't have to answer you."

D'Arcy stood up and pursed his narrow lips. "You had something to do with this situation between our country and Russia didn't you?"

Boxer was becoming annoyed. He didn't have to put up with the crap D'Arcy was giving him and he wasn't going to. "Listen, Admiral, you take my survivors and we'll part company."

"I don't think so," D'Arcy said. "I'm holding you aboard this ship until we make port."

"You're an ass, Admiral," Boxer said.

"And furthermore —"

"Before you do anything so stupid," Boxer said, "you'd better check with Admiral Stark or Admiral Kaiser. I hope you remember who they are?"

"Then you are still navy, aren't you!" D'Arcy exclaimed triumphantly.

"You're an even bigger ass than I thought you were," Boxer commented. "I am not navy; I resigned from the navy."

"What about that sub out there?"

"What about it?"

"Who do you report to?"

"D'Arcy, contact Stark," Boxer said sharply. Then he turned and started for the door.

"Just where do you think you're going?" D'Arcy roared.

"Back to the *Shark*."

"Guards!"

Two marines entered the admiral's quarters.

"Don't do something that'll cost you, Admiral," Boxer said.

D'Arcy hesitated; he said, "Guards escort this man to the flight deck and see that he is safely aboard the submarine."

"What about the survivors?" Boxer asked.

"In good time," D'Arcy answered. "I'll take them aboard in good time"

Boxer looked at the two marines. "Let's go guys," he said. "The admiral has some heavy thinking to do." He strode toward the door but stopped before he opened it. "I have a man with a bullet wound in his chest," he said, looking at D'Arcy.

"I'll make arrangements to have him transferred to sick bay," D'Arcy said.

"Thanks," Boxer said. He opened the door and stepped into the passageway. Flanked by a marine on each side, Boxer headed for the elevator that would take him to the flight deck.

As soon as Boxer was back aboard the *Shark*, he went straight to the sick bay.

"Everything all right?" Hicks asked.

Boxer nodded. "Now it is," he said. "But it was touch and go there for a while."

Hicks managed a weak smile. "If anyone could come out of a tight spot, you can."

"If it weren't for the arrival of the carrier group … well, the spot would have been too tight for me to get out of."

"Did we lose anyone?"

Boxer nodded. "Bill," he said in a tight, low voice. It was the first time he had consciously thought about or mentioned Harris to anyone. "Never had a chance."

"Sorry," Hicks said. "I know he was more than just your EXO to you."

"He was a very good friend," Boxer answered.

Suddenly Boxer was keyed by the damage control officer. "I put a detail on deck to finish the weld," he said. "Should have it done in a couple of hours."

"Roger that," Boxer said.

"Will the survivors be transferred to the carrier?" Hicks asked.

"I'm not sure. Admiral D'Arcy is being pig-headed about it … but you're going aboard. You need better medical attention than you're getting here."

"I'm okay," Hicks said.

Boxer shook his head. "You're going."

"Now who's being pig-headed?"

Boxer ignored the jibe and said, "D'Arcy'll try to pump you about the operation, about me and about the *Shark*."

"He won't get anything."

Cowly keyed Boxer. "Skipper, medics are aboard."

"Send them to sick bay," Boxer said; then shaking Hick's hand, he said, "I'll see you in the States … we'll go out and do some drinking together."

"Sure we will," Hicks answered; then he said, "Jack, we have to talk about Tracy before I go."

"I haven't any claim on her," Boxer said.

"Neither have I. But I'd like to have, if she'd let me."

"Are you asking me not to sleep with her again?"

"I don't have any right to do that and even if I did, I wouldn't. I just wanted you to know how it is between us."

"The last time I saw Tracy," Boxer said, "we argued. I'm not sure she'll want to see me ... or even if I want to see her."

The medics came into the sick bay.

"There's your man," Boxer said, gesturing toward Hicks. "Tell your chief surgeon I'll be aboard in a while to speak to him."

The medics started to salute; then stopped.

Boxer smiled. "Yes, I'm the skipper," he told them.

They looked questioningly at Hicks.

"He sure is the skipper," Hicks answered.

Boxer winked at him and said, "See you soon." Then he left the sick bay, went to the Communications Center and sent a long coded message to Williams, explaining everything that had happened to the *Shark* after he had made his decision to pick up survivors from the downed airliner.

He knew that Williams and the others at the Company wouldn't like any of it. But he hoped that Stark would understand why he had had to do what he did.

"If there's any answer," Boxer told the COMMMO, "bring it to me immediately."

"Aye, aye, Skipper," the man answered.

Finally, Boxer returned to the bridge. Cowly was seated at the COMMCOMP. He looked tired, almost haggard. "Did you see Bill get hit?" Cowly asked in a low voice.

"Yes, I had him and the *Q-21* on the UWIS screen. He was about a thousand yards from the *Q-21* before he got it."

Cowly shook his head. "What hit him?"

Boxer shrugged. "I didn't see any torpedo wake."

"Neither did I," Cowly said. "I was two thousand yards away from the starboard side and sixty feet above the *Q-21*... I didn't see any wake either."

From the tone of Cowly's voice, Boxer knew he was having difficulty coming to terms with Harris's death. He also knew that neither Cowly nor he could afford the luxury of having such a difficulty, at least not while they were aboard the *Shark*.

"We'll talk about it later," Boxer said. "Now we have more important things to do."

Cowly looked at him for a moment; then he stood up and said, "Yes, sir. I'm sorry if I bothered you with a minor detail."

"Whether you like it or not Bill is dead and we are responsible for getting the *Shark* and everyone aboard her safely back to the States. For now you're my EXO."

Cowly remained silent.

The COMMO keyed Boxer. "Admiral D'Arcy wants to see you in his quarters as soon as possible."

"Roger that," Boxer answered. "Tell the admiral I'll be there shortly."

"Aye, aye, Skipper," the COMMO answered.

"You have the CONN," Boxer said, leaving Cowly on the bridge.

Cowly accepted the responsibility with a nod.

An aide brought Boxer to D'Arcy's quarters.

"Sit down," D'Arcy said, pointing to a chair at the right side of his desk. "I've been ordered back to the IO," he said. "There's fighting between several of the Gulf nations. More of a religious war than anything else. But the President and his advisors think that two carrier groups will get our message across better than one."

Boxer nodded.

"I'll take your wounded man with me and have him flown back to the States from the Seychelles."

"Thanks."

"You were right," D'Arcy said. "I spoke with the CNO on the scrambler. He told me whatever you did was none of my business and to assist you in every way possible."

Boxer remained silent.

"You'll have to keep the survivors you have, and any others my men find aboard the *Shark*. I'll issue rations for them."

"We don't have the facil—"

"It's the best I can do," D'Arcy said, leaning forward and offering Boxer a cigarette from a beautiful ivory cigarette box. "Try one. They're Turkish."

Boxer lit up, tasted the aromatic smoke and nodded.

"I owe you an apology," D'Arcy said, blowing smoke off to one side.

"No apology is needed, or wanted," Boxer answered. D'Arcy was more man and more officer than he previously had given him credit for being.

"I don't apologize often," D'Arcy persisted. "But I do apologize to you." And he offered his hand across the desk.

Boxer shook it.

"My helicopters are on the way back," D'Arcy told him.

"How many more —"

"I'm afraid I have bad news for you."

Boxer leaned forward.

"Several of your men were drowned," D'Arcy said.

Boxers jaw tightened.

"Ten more civilians were rescued," D'Arcy said.

"Do you know the names of my men?" Boxer asked.

"Yellan, White, Forbes and Dexter."

"Four," Boxer commented, shaking his head.

"I'm sorry," D'Arcy responded.

"My EXO was killed earlier today … just before we made sonar contact with you."

"You mean you were fighting —"

"A Russian submarine, the *Q-21*," Boxer said. "My own boat is damaged. Her sail won't retract or go up, I can't use any radar. I had to run on the surface."

"But you were submerged when you signaled us."

"It was a risk I had to take. Had the *Shark* remained on the surface, it would have been destroyed. I answered the Mayday, so did the Russian captain. I didn't think he'd do it, and he was sure that the *Shark* had been sunk." Boxer pursed his lips. "Both of us were wrong," he said, stubbing out his cigarette.

"Admiral," a voice said, over the ship's intercom, "our birds are on radar… ETA five minutes."

"Roger that," D'Arcy answered. Then looking at Boxer, he asked. "Would you like to go down to the flight deck?"

"Very much," Boxer answered.

D'Arcy stood up and led the way to the door.

CHAPTER 5

Boxer watched the last ship of D'Arcy's carrier group disappear over the horizon. Except for the *Shark*, the ocean was finally empty.

The DCO keyed Boxer. "Skipper, we're ready to try to lift the sail."

"Roger that," Boxer answered, looking toward the sail.

"Pressure now one zero zero psi ... going to two zero zero," the DCO said.

A low scraping came from the sail. Slowly it began to move up.

"Another foot should do it," Boxer said.

"Roger that," the DCO answered.

The scraping became louder. Boxer knew that the sides of the well and the sail were being badly scored.

"That's it," the DCO said. "My men will weld it into place ... the water in the well will hold the sail up... Radar gear is operational."

"Good work," Boxer said. Moments later he climbed up to the bridge and switching on the MC, he said, "Now hear this ... now hear this... This is the captain... We will get under way in three zero minutes... We'll be running on the surface... Because of the unusual condition on deck, all hatches will be closed and secured as if we were running submerged... Memorial services for the men we lost will be held in one zero minutes after we're under way... That is all." He put the mike back in its cradle and pushed the MC switch into its OFF position. For several minutes, he looked out at the ocean and thought about Harris and the other men who had been killed… Harris had been a good friend and had given up a chance to have a command of his own to be with him aboard the *Shark*. He had a wife and two young sons. Despite the fact that he'd spent so much time at sea, he was a good husband and father. As for Yellan and the other men, Boxer didn't know them as well as Redfern did. But all of them were courageous, dependable men and —

COMMO keyed him. "Skipper, message from the *Tecumseh*."

"Read it," Boxer said.

"Will be on station two four hours from now."

"Have Mister Cowly figure out ETA at two zero knots and relay it to the *Tecumseh*. Also, say that we have six zero additional people aboard, including one five women and children. Use the Alpha code when you send it."

"Roger that," the COMMO answered.

Boxer swung himself over the side of the sail and climbed down to the deck.

"Welding is almost finished, Skipper," the chief in charge of the detail said.

"The sooner the better," Boxer answered and went below.

Cowly was on the bridge.

"I want a written report of what you saw when you were about to attack the *Q-21*," Boxer said. "Every detail you can remember. Have it on my desk by eight hundred hours tomorrow."

"Aye, aye, sir," Cowly replied with the same sarcastic tone in his voice that had been there before.

"Stow that 'sir' crap," Boxer said. "If you want off the *Shark*, hand me your resignation with the report I asked for."

Cowly paled.

"The one thing I don't need aboard the *Shark* is an EXO who doesn't understand that all of us are expendable, that even the *Shark* is expendable, and would be sacrificed should the situation require it. Notify Mister Redfern I want to see him in my quarters."

Cowly nodded.

Boxer left the bridge and went directly to his cabin. Cowly's attitude had pissed him off. He had just sat down when two sharp raps on the door broke into his thoughts. "Come in," he said.

Redfern entered the cabin.

Boxer got straight to the point. "Tom, do you want me to write to the next of kin, or do you want to do it?"

"Yellan didn't have any next of kin," Tom said. "As for the others, I'll do it."

Boxer nodded.

"The rescue mission cost us more men than the attack did," Redfern said.

Boxer shrugged. "It might have cost all of us."

"Would you do it again?"

Boxer nodded. "Yes, I'd do it again."

"Some of my men think you made the wrong decision," Redfern said.

"What do you think?"

"You made the wrong one, Jack," Redfern answered.

"Cowly thinks so, too," Boxer responded.

"Sorry I can't back you on this one."

"You've got to call it as you see it," Boxer answered, "just as I had to do what I had to do."

The DCO keyed Boxer. "The weld is completed, Skipper."

"Roger that," Boxer said. "Are all of your men below?"

"Yes."

"Keep a close watch over the pressure in the well... We wouldn't want that sail to begin slipping.

"Aye, aye, Skipper," the DCO answered.

Boxer switched on the MC. "All hands prepare to get underway... Engineering make fifteen knots... Navigation will be done automatically... Memorial service will be one zero minutes from now." Boxer switched off the MC. And bending over the mini COMMCOMP, he interfaced with NAVCLOCK and AUTONAVSYS; inserted the *Shark*'s speed, present position, and rendezvous point with the *Tecumseh*, then switched the entire system to AUTO.

"When is our ETA with the *Tecumseh*?" Redfern asked.

Boxer typed the question into the COMMCOMP.

ETA FIFTY-SIX HOURS
AT CURRENT SPEED WITH
NO CHANGE IN WIND
AND/OR CURRENTS

"Any chance *Q-21* might be waiting for us?" Redfern asked.

"There's a chance," Boxer answered. "But I don't think so. I think D'Arcy's carrier group made Borodine run to fight another day."

"I'm not in the least bit sorry about that."

"Neither am I," Boxer said. "Believe me, neither am I."

"It's almost time for the memorial service," Redfern said.

"Do you want to say anything about your men?" Boxer asked.

"I guess I should."

Boxer nodded, and with a sigh, he said, "Let's go, Tom; I suspect the men are already waiting for us."

Boxer and Redfern stood close together on the bridge. Boxer read the service straight out of the book. The men off duty and all of the survivors were a short distance from the bridge and didn't have to rely on hearing his words come over the MC.

When Boxer was finished with the final prayer, he closed the book, lowered it in front of him, and said, "I have a few words to say to everyone aboard the *Shark*. To the men, women, and children who are aboard, let me assure you that we will deliver you safe and sound to the States." He paused before continuing. "The men whose names I read off died to save you. If it is at all possible, let their deaths make your lives worthwhile. That would be a fair exchange."

A low murmur of approval came from the group of survivors.

"Now, to the men who serve aboard this boat... We have accomplished the impossible: we are alive and the *Shark* is still a formidable fighting machine. We came out of a living death and because we went to the aid of people less fortunate than ourselves, we were forced into yet another battle that cost the life of our EXO, my friend of many years and my comrade in missions. Yet, even knowing that he'd die, I'd undertake the same mission again."

Boxer paused and looked at the faces of the men below him. There were many furrowed brows.

"Sometimes a CO makes an unpopular decision, but the one I made to rescue the people we have on board had nothing to do with being popular or unpopular. I made it because I'm a seaman and was taught to believe that a distress call must be answered, if at all possible. For me there was no other decision than the one I made." He took a deep breath and exhaled slowly. "Those of you who believe that the decision was wrong are most certainly within their rights and should, if sufficiently troubled by it, request a discharge from your obligations to the *Shark*. But before you do, think about what your decision might have been had you been in my place. Now Mister Redfern has something to say to you."

Boxer took a step backward. He had had no idea his heart was pounding, but now he could actually hear it.

"To my team," Redfern said, "I can only say that for me to command you is a privilege, and for myself to be under the skipper's command is no less a privilege. We've done the impossible and are here as proof of that. I have to admit that I didn't agree with the skipper's decision, but like all of you who don't agree with it, I didn't agree with it after the fact — after the *Q-21* came after us. Until that time, I guess I felt we were doing the only thing decent human beings would do: help those in distress. Well, we did do that. The survivors aboard are proof of what we did. But doing it cost the lives of some of our men. That's the way things sometimes happen. Sometimes people have to die so that others might live."

Redfern stepped back, looked at Boxer, and nodded.

CHAPTER 6

Everything aboard the *Shark* was running smoothly. The resumption of the normal routine had an almost calmative effect, while the continual presence of the survivors provided the men with the tangible evidence of their sacrifice and their courage.

Boxer permitted himself the luxury of winding down. He even found Cowly less hostile and was pleased that his EXO did not submit his resignation when he turned in his report on the destruction of Harris's minisub.

Boxer had several of the junior officers gather information from the survivors to prepare a roster of their identities and of those of their next of kin. Then he had Redfern interview them to find out as much as possible about the accident. There had been an explosion, then a fire in the port engine. But all of the survivors agreed the explosion had come first.

The evening of the second day Boxer was topside and had climbed up to the bridge just to look around, when the officer of the watch keyed him and said, "Skipper, one of the survivors wants to speak with you."

"Roger that," Boxer said. "I'll be in my quarters in one zero minutes."

"Aye, aye, Skipper," the OW answered.

Boxer reluctantly left the bridge and returned by way of number-one hatch to the bright interior of the *Shark*. He went to his quarters without first stopping at the bridge as he usually did, and he was just about to ask the mini-COMMCOMP to give him the *Shark*'s position so he could check it with the fixed navigation satellite, when someone knocked twice at the door.

"Come in," Boxer said.

The door opened and a young sailor said, "Skipper, this is the woman who wants to speak to you."

Boxer recognized her. She was the one wearing cuffs on her wrist. Boxer stood up. He nodded to the sailor and to the woman, then he said, "Please come in and sit down."

She stepped across the bulkhead and entered the cabin.

Boxer closed the door, aware that she was examining the cabin. "It's not much, as the expression goes," he said, laughing, "but it's home."

"Was I that obvious?" she asked.

"Yes," he answered and gestured toward one of the empty chairs. She was wearing a regulation jumpsuit and it fitted her very well, revealing the curves of the body it covered.

She sat down.

Boxer took a few moments to fill and light his pipe before he said, "I'm sorry but I don't know your name."

"Dee Long," she said.

"Well, Miss Long, what can I do for you?" he asked, finally sitting opposite her.

"You can help me start a new life," she said.

Boxer's thoughts raced. He knew exactly what she meant.

"None of the other survivors know why I was on that plane," she said. "They don't even know that the man with me was a cop. You and the sailor who cut the cuffs off are the only ones who know about them."

"He might have told some of the other crewmen," Boxer said, stalling for time to get his thoughts arranged.

"You could tell them I was carrying something, the way those agents always do in films."

Boxer puffed on his pipe. "You want to tell me what —"

She leaned forward. "I embezzled a hundred thou from the company I worked for," she said calmly.

"Why? Didn't you think you'd be caught?"

She pursed her lips. "I was sleeping with my boss," she said, looking straight at Boxer. "I gave him what he wanted. As for the money … well, one day I saw the opportunity and I took it without giving too much thought to the consequences. I guess I thought I could frighten him into —"

"You mean blackmail him, don't you?"

She nodded. "Okay, blackmail him into forgetting about the money … but he wouldn't. He was angry."

"He had a right to be angry," Boxer said. "I'd be angry too, if someone had taken a hundred thousand dollars from me."

"The money didn't mean anything to him," she said. "He's worth about twenty million. He was angry because I told him he was a lousy lover … and he was. I had sex with him because it made my life easier, if you know what I mean?"

Boxer nodded.

"If the plane hadn't crashed, I'd be sitting in jail now waiting to stand trial. I'd be facing ten years, maybe more."

"What happened to the money?" Boxer asked.

She lowered her eyes. "Most of it is in a safe place," she said.

"Oh."

For several moments neither of them spoke; then Dee cleared her throat and said, "Half of what I have is yours."

Boxer was tempted to say, all. But instead he remained silent.

She raised her eyes and looked straight at him. "Do we have a deal, Captain?"

For the first time since she had come into the room, Boxer noticed her eyes were smoky gray and there was a small birthmark on the right side of her neck. He put his pipe into the ashtray. She was asking him to do something extraordinary. Part of him wanted to do it and part didn't. Although she was an embezzler, he admired her candor and knew it took uncommon courage for her to be that open with him.

"Do we have a deal?" she pressed.

"I can't give you an answer just like that," he said, snapping his fingers.

"Captain, you make more serious decisions every day you're on this submarine. You make life and death —"

"Yes, you're right. But they're different. I was trained to make them. What you're asking me to do — Well, for starters, you're the first embezzler I ever knew."

"I'm also a woman," she said.

Boxer nodded. He was becoming increasingly aware of that fact.

"I don't want to go to prison," she said in a choked voice. "You can have most of the money. I just need a few thousand to buy a new identity and tide me over until I get settled."

"I don't need or want your money."

"Captain, anyone can learn to need eighty thousand dollars," she said.

"I'm not interested in your money."

For several moments Dee said nothing; then she stood up. "Are you interested in this?" she asked, and began to unzip the top of her jumpsuit.

Boxer stood up and grabbed hold of her hand, stopping it from moving any farther down. "I'd be lying if I said I wasn't. But not as a trade-off for your freedom." He forced her hand up, closing the zipper.

"Can't you see I'm desperate?" she said, her eyes filling with tears.

Boxer ran his hand over his beard. "I can't pretend I didn't see the cuffs. I'm sorry ... I wish I could."

"Please tell me you'll think about it?" she pleaded.

"I'd only be lying to you," he answered gently.

"I had to try," she said with a weary sigh.

"If I were in your place, I would have tried too," Boxer said.

Dee shook her head. "You'd never be in my place to begin with." She turned and walked to the door.

"I'm sorry," Boxer said.

She shrugged. "Maybe I'll get lucky and something or someone will turn up to help me out of the mess I'm in."

"I hope so," Boxer answered. "I really hope so."

Dee turned, smiled at him, and said, "Thanks for listening and not lecturing me." She blew him a kiss, opened the door, and left the cabin.

Boxer dropped down on his bunk, put his hands behind his head, closed his eyes, and wondered what it would have been like to make love to Dee.

The *Shark* rendezvoused with the *Tecumseh* fifty-six hours after she parted company with D'Arcy's carrier group.

Speaking to Rugger, captain of the *Tecumseh*, on the walkie-talkie, Boxer said, "Come to course two four zero degrees... Stop all engines."

"Roger that," Rugger answered in his gravelly voice. "Will take fiver ... repeat fiver miles to come dead in the water."

"Fiver miles copied," Boxer said. He was on the sub's bridge. The *Shark* was five hundred yards off the *Tecumseh*'s starboard side.

By comparison to the converted supertanker that served as the *Shark*'s mother ship, the *Shark* was puny indeed. The *Tecumseh* was fourteen hundred feet long and weighed two hundred thousand tons. She carried the *Shark* inside of her and also held a cargo of a million gallons of crude oil. Driven by atomic power she could do thirty knots. The *Tecumseh* measured seventy-five feet from her water line to her bridge.

Boxer turned to Cowly, who was standing alongside of him, and said, "have Berness ready the survivors. I want them off the *Shark* first, then Tom's men."

Cowly nodded. "Once we're aboard the *Tecumseh* are you going to speak to Hayes? He's been kicking up a fuss since he found out you had a long conversation with Miss Long."

"Yeah, I'll speak to him," Boxer said, watching the *Tecumseh*: he could tell from her wake that her engines had already stopped.

"Jack," Cowly said, "I've been trying to find the right time to say something to you. But that time never seems to come. So, I'll say it now."

Boxer looked at him.

"I want to apologize —"

Boxer waved him silent. "Let it go," he said, offering his hand.

Cowly shook Boxer's hand.

"Now let's go below and tuck the *Shark* inside the *Tecumseh*," Boxer said with a grin.

A few minutes later, Boxer was at the COMMCOMP, looking at a target display of the *Tecumseh*'s position relative to the *Shark*'s. In radio communication with Rugger, he asked for a reading of the current direction and speed.

"Zero zero on that," Rugger answered.

"Starting dive," Boxer said, blasting the klaxon twice. "This will be a manual controlled dive … diving planes five degrees … DO make nine zero feet."

"Making nine zero feet," the DO responded.

Boxer watched the depth gauge. "Flood forward ballast tanks," he ordered.

The *Shark*'s bow dropped slowly down.

"Two five feet," the DO reported.

"Helmsman come to two four zero degrees," Boxer said.

"Coming to course two four zero degrees," the helmsman responded.

"Target bearing two four zero degrees," the SO reported. "Range four zero zero yards ... speed decreasing."

Boxer signaled the engine room. "Four zero zero RPMS."

"Four zero zero RPMS," the EO answered.

"Six zero feet," the DO announced.

Boxer switched on the UWIS. The bottom of the *Tecumseh*'s hull came into view. He keyed Rugger. "Have you in visual sight," he said.

"Opening bay doors," Rugger answered.

"Seven five feet," the DO answered.

"Target bearing two four zero degrees" the SO reported. "Range two hundred yards ... speed zero... We're closing fast."

Boxer keyed the engine room. "Stop all engines."

"All engines stopped," the EO answered.

"Nine zero feet," the DO reported.

"Hold her steady nine zero feet," Boxer said, watching the dive-level indicator bubble come into position. "Diving planes in neutral."

"Diving planes in neutral," the DO responded.

Boxer's eyes were riveted to the monitor. "Steady as she goes, helmsman."

"Steady as she goes," Mahony repeated.

"We're moving under her," Boxer said, switching to the forward and aft deck UWIS sensors. "EO two zero zero rpms in reverse."

"Two zero zero rpms reverse," the EO said.

The *Shark* hesitated.

"In position," Boxer said. The *Shark* was between the two huge doors. "Zero rpms."

"Zero rpms," the EO answered.

The *Shark* remained motionless beneath the *Tecumseh*. "Diving planes up three degrees."

"Diving planes up three degrees," the DO said.

"Blow forward and aft ballast," Boxer said.

The sound of hissing air filled the *Shark*. Immediately she began to rise into the hull of the *Tecumseh*.

"Diving planes in neutral," Boxer said, watching the progress of the berthing on the monitor. The bay, though filled with water was brilliantly illuminated. "We're in," Boxer announced. "Doors closing... Secure diving planes."

"Diving planes secured," the DO answered, with a loud sigh of relief.

"Secure from surfacing procedure," Boxer said.

Each duty station reported secure.

Boxer keyed Rugger. "What's our destination?"

"Seattle ... unless other orders come along... I just radioed you were secure."

"Thanks," Boxer said.

"Everything is ready for our additional passengers," Rugger said.

"Good," Boxer answered. "I'll see you in a while."

"Roger that," Rugger answered.

Boxer turned to Cowly. "Have Mister Hayes report to me," he said.

"Aye, aye, Skipper," Cowly answered.

Boxer checked the monitor. Already the level of water in the bay had begun to fall. He switched off the UWIS and announced over the MC, "This is the captain... Everyone aboard the *Shark* will soon be transferred to the *Tecumseh*... For security reasons, I cannot tell you the port we will make but I can tell you that we are heading for the States... Conditions aboard our mother ship will be less cramped than aboard the *Shark* and much, much safer... I want to take this opportunity to congratulate all of you on your behavior during the difficult times we shared... Think of your trip back to the States as an unexpected cruise and enjoy it." Boxer switched off the MC and was about to stand, when he saw Hayes. He was being escorted by one of Redfern's men. Boxer smiled, nodded to the escort, and said, "That will be all."

"Aye, aye, Skipper," the man answered.

"Well, Mister Hayes," Boxer said, "what is it that you want?" The man's face was darkened by a three-day beard and his hair was unkempt.

Glaring at Boxer, he said, "I want to send a radio message to —"

Boxer shook his head. "Your name will be radioed to the proper authorities. But there will be no personal radio messages from you or any of the other survivors. That is final."

"I promise you," Hayes snarled. "I'll make you pay for this."

Boxer nodded. "You'll try, I know that."

"I happened to have been on government business."

"I'm impressed," Boxer answered wearily.

"I demand —"

Boxer stood up. "Aboard the *Shark*, even if you were the President himself, you couldn't demand. The only person here who can demand anything is me ... and I don't demand,

Mister Byron Hayes, I order, just as I'm about to order you off the bridge. Now go, Mister Hayes. Go before I have you removed."

"Boxer, by the time I'm finished with you, you'll have wished to God you hadn't rescued me."

"I didn't rescue you," Boxer answered. "One of my men did. Now go!"

Hayes turned around and left the bridge.

Boxer gestured to Cowly, who had been standing only a few feet away. "That man and a few others like him bug the shit out of me."

"I gathered as much," Cowly said with a smile.

Boxer smiled too, looked at the monitor, and said, "Have Mister Berness get the deck detail ready to break open number-one and number-three hatches."

Cowly nodded and asked, "Do you think Hayes can hurt you?"

Boxer shrugged. "He knows a great many important people … but I'm not going to worry about that now."

Rugger keyed him. "Skipper, I have a good Scotch waiting for you."

"I'll be with you in a few minutes," Boxer answered. "I could use a few drinks, a hot shower, and several hours of sleep."

"They're all yours," Rugger told him. "Oh, a few minutes ago we received a port change. We've been ordered to Norfolk, the long way around."

"Through the Strait of Magellan?"

"That's the long way," Rugger said.

"Any reason given?"

"None."

"Deck detail standing by, Skipper," Cowly interrupted.

"Ten four," Boxer told Rugger; then nodding to Cowly, he checked the monitor again. The water was below the deck and some of the *Tecumseh*'s crew had already put out gangplanks. "Pass the word to open the hatches," Boxer said.

"Hatches open," Cowly responded.

"Well," Boxer said, "we can relax for a while."

CHAPTER 7

Boxer enjoyed the leisure aboard the *Tecumseh*. The days were warm and for the most part filled with sunshine. The nights were star studded, giving him the opportunity to learn the positions of several of the less familiar constellations of the southern sky.

He followed the developments in the Middle East and the Gulf with interest, and though there was sporadic fighting, the presence of two American carrier groups was enough to hold the killing to a minimum. Russia was still making war-like noises, for propaganda effect. Three days after the *Shark* and the *Tecumseh* had rendezvoused, the Russians had returned all their armed forces to normal status.

Boxer had the time to think about where he had been and what he had done. Often in the middle of the night, awakened by a nightmarish distortion of the dangers he had experienced since he had taken command of the *Shark*, he'd throw some clothes on and leave the cabin to stand by the railing and let the sea and the sky work their calmative magic on him.

Boxer was not given to brooding. But when he did brood, he did it privately. Though he spoke to no one about it, Harris's death affected him deeply. Like Mallon, his engineering officer aboard the *Sting Ray*, Harris also had gone to Annapolis with him. They had been friends for all of their adult lives. Boxer had been Harris's best man. He knew Peggy, knew their children. He even knew Harris's parents. Yet despite his feelings for Harris, he never mentioned his name to any of the men. The grief he felt was his own. If he'd share it with anyone, it would be with Peggy. She understood their friendship.

Boxer made it part of his daily routine to see all of the survivors at least once during the day, including Hayes, who always turned his back to him whenever he saw him. But most of the time, he sunned himself, and by the end of the fourth day, he had acquired a beautiful tan.

Though practically all of his time was free, Boxer spent a certain amount of it going over the details of the operation on Torpay with Tom Redfern, the Marine major in command of the hundred-man strike force aboard the *Shark*. Both men agreed it had been a "smooth operation."

On the afternoon of the fifth day, Boxer and Tom were enjoying the sun, ensconced on beach chairs, when Boxer said, "Did you know we have a felon aboard?"

"I wouldn't care if we had two, three, or a hundred felons on board. As long as they don't felon me, I'm at peace with them." He raised his glass and took another sip of gin and tonic.

"She's standing over by the railing on the port side," Boxer said.

"She?" Tom asked, looking at Boxer, who nodded, and then at the woman at the railing. "That lovely-looking creature?"

Again Boxer nodded.

"What did she felon about?"

"About a hundred thou from her boss," Boxer said, pouring more vodka over the ice in his glass.

"You're funnin' me," Tom said.

"She told me herself. She was being extradited when the plane went down."

"And the cop she was with?"

"Drowned."

"Then how do you know —"

"She was wearing bracelets when she was fished out of the drink."

"Bracelets?"

"Cuffs. The cop with her couldn't swim. He had the good sense to uncuff himself as soon as the captain announced they were going to ditch."

"Hey take a look at your felon now!" Tom exclaimed.

Dee was climbing over the rail.

"Boxer was on his feet. "Don't," he shouted. "Don't do it!" But his voice was carried away by the wind. He began to run. "Stop her," he yelled. "Someone stop her!"

She was on the other side of the railing now. Barely managing to keep her footing, she looked up toward the bridge; then down at the water.

Boxer pounded across the deck toward her. Some of the people he passed looked up at him. He was breathing too hard to shout.

She saw him.

Boxer forced himself to shout, "Dee, don't do it!"

"Must," she answered. She let go of the railing and threw herself forward.

Boxer reached the railing, vaulted over it, and cannon-balled into the water below. He crashed into the sea and then his body sprung open. With powerful strokes, he started for the surface. He had to get away from the undertow caused by the movement of the ship; then get clear of the suction from the huge propellers.

The ship was sliding by, dragging him toward it. He fought his way out of its wake.

Finally, the *Tecumseh* passed him ... but now he was being sucked back to its stern, where the propellers would cut him into pieces before Rugger could stop them.

Boxer struggled to pull himself away from the ship. Every part of his body ached. He felt as if a huge hand had closed around him. His strength was ebbing. He was no match for the propellers, but if he stopped swimming, even for a moment, he'd be sucked to his death.

Boxer forced himself to continue to stroke. Slowly, he began to feel the drawing ease. He was able to put more distance between himself and the ship. Now he could look for Dee.

Boxer hoped she could swim well enough to avoid the suction of the propellers, and he hoped her instinct to live was stronger than her will to die, now that she was close to dying.

Above him, Boxer could hear the wail of the siren on the *Tecumseh*. He stopped swimming and tread water. He looked for Dee. She was a few yards to his left. She, too, was treading water.

"Dee," he called, "Dee, over here!"

She looked at him. "I can't... I can't... I don't have the strength."

"Float," he called back. "Float!" He started to swim toward her.

The *Tecumseh* had already passed them.

Boxer still could feel the pull of its propellers. He guessed Rugger had already stopped the engines and the propellers, already slowing down, would stop completely soon, leaving the ship dead in the water — but about five miles from where they were.

"I don't want to die," Dee shouted. "I don't want to die!"

She was thrashing wildly, and despite her change of mind, she would fight him when he came near her. He was afraid that any sharks nearby would soon be attracted by her vigorous motions. He glanced up at the stern of the *Tecumseh*. Someone was throwing a life preserver into the water.

"I'm going down," Dee screamed. "I'm going down!"

He turned toward her.

She was already under.

Boxer dived. He saw her and the next instant had hold of her. Gasping for air, he brought her to the surface.

The sudden roar of the helicopter made him look up. He had forgotten there was one aboard the *Tecumseh*. Suddenly a small package was jettisoned from the aircraft. The instant it hit the water it inflated into a raft. Moments later four men in wetsuits dropped into the sea.

Dee was gasping and coughing.

Two of the men swam toward Boxer. "Get her on the raft," he said.

"Sure thing," one of them answered.

"Hey you down there," a voice said over a bullhorn, "we'll have you out of the drink in a couple of minutes."

Boxer looked up and saw Tom in the helicopter's open door.

Within minutes, Dee was lifted into the helicopter by a sling. Boxer followed; then the four men from Tom's strike force were taken aboard.

The helicopter's pilot started to turn toward the *Tecumseh*, when Boxer stopped him. "Go low over the raft," he said, and taking hold of one of the rifles aboard, he fired a half-dozen rounds into the raft. It was beginning to sink even as he replaced the weapon in its rack. "Better no one knows we've come this way," he said to Tom, who only nodded.

A short time later they landed on the *Tecumseh*.

"You do the damnedest things," Tom commented to Boxer later that night over coffee. "It's one thing to put your life on the line because of duty. But —"

Boxer held up his hand. "No lectures please, and I promise never to tell you how it felt to drop over the side of this ship."

"The other officers at the table laughed.

"Can't refuse an offer like that," Tom said. "But," he added, raising his glass toward Boxer, "I offer a toast to you, Jack Boxer, captain of the *Shark*, I'm proud to say that I serve with you."

One by one the men at the table raised their glasses to Boxer.

Flushed, Boxer accepted the toast with a nod and a simple, "Thank you."

After coffee, Boxer filled his pipe, lit it, and smoked contentedly. Later he watched an hour of TV, picked up from a satellite by the special electronic equipment aboard the *Tecumseh*. But the program was mindless and he was restless. He gave up trying to become interested in it and went on deck.

The ship was still in the tropics, though in another two days — three at the most — it would be in a more temperate zone. A three-quarter moon hid most of the stars but silvered the calm surface of the sea.

As he stood at the railing, Boxer couldn't help wondering why Dee had wanted to kill herself? He understood she would probably go to prison for several years and that prospect was frightening. But even in prison, she would still be alive. He pursed his lips and realized that no matter how frightened he had been — and there were times when he had been so terrified it had taken every bit of his willpower to keep himself from trembling — he had never been so frightened that he had wanted to die.

Boxer knocked the warm ashes from his pipe into his hand and dropped them over the side. He put the empty pipe into his shirt pocket and went inside. He intended to go to his cabin and read a while before going to sleep. But when he reached the door, he changed his mind and went instead to the sick bay, where Dee was.

She was the only one in the room.

Boxer stood at the foot of the bed and looked down at her. She was asleep. One arm was at her side and the other rested on her stomach. Her hair fanned out on the pillow.

Suddenly Boxer realized she was looking at him. "I thought you were asleep," he said.

"No. I was resting with my eyes closed."

"Are you all right?" he asked, knowing it was a foolish question.

She managed a small smile. "Yes." Then she added, "I guess."

"You'll feel much better in the morning," he told her. "I'll stop by and —"

"Thanks for coming in after me," she said.

Boxer nodded.

"The instant I jumped, I was sorry, and then when I started to go down —" Her voice was suddenly choked off by weeping. "It's true, you know, your whole life does flash by you."

"Yes, I know," he said.

"I can't say that I enjoyed looking at parts of mine."

Boxer remained silent.

"Would you hand me a tissue?" she asked, pointing to a box on the top of the medicine cabinet beside her. "For some reason, I hurt all over. Bruised. Know what I mean?"

Boxer stepped around to the side of the bed and, handing her a tissue, said, "I'll come by again tomorrow. Now the best thing you can do is sleep."

"I really am sorry," she told him. "It was a stupid thing to do. I've done a lot of stupid things."

"We all do," he answered, anxious to leave. He was becoming more and more ill at ease.

"Thanks," she said simply.

Compulsively, he bent over her and kissed her on the forehead. She smelled clean. Straightening up, Boxer said, "See you tomorrow."

"See you," she answered.

Boxer left the sick bay and returned to his own cabin. Sometime later, as he was lying in bed waiting to fall asleep, he found himself wondering if Dee was experiencing some sort of reawakening, or was she just pretending to feel contrite in the hope that he would not hand her over to the authorities when they reached port?

"I wouldn't have any way of knowing," he said, thinking aloud. "No way of knowing at all." Then with a deep sigh, he rolled over on his side and instantly fell into a deep sleep.

CHAPTER 8

Bruce Kinkade, director of the CIA, sat at the head of the highly polished table. Though he was very angry, nothing in his brown eyes or in the expression on his cleanly shaven face showed any emotion other than complete calm. He was a man of middling height, with a bald pate and stubby fingers. He wore a simple gold wedding ring on the third finger of his left hand and a star sapphire on the forefinger of his right hand, which was rumored to have been given to him by the King ibn-Saud as a token of the King's appreciation for service rendered to Saudi Arabia.

To his right was Mister Thomas Williams, responsible for coordinating all of the *Shark*'s missions for the Company and the navy. He looked very much like a college professor, which years before he had been at one of the most prestigious universities in the northeast. But now, as a cover for the Company's operations, he was the president of the Thomas W. Williams Company, owner of the supertanker *Tecumseh*.

The man seated on Kinkade's left was Admiral Stark, Chief of Naval Operations. Tall and lean, he looked as if he belonged on the bridge of a warship, rather than at a conference table in the Company's headquarters in Langley, Virginia.

Next to Stark was Admiral Paul Kaiser, Chief of Naval Intelligence. Of all the men at the table, he was the most nondescript looking. Of average height, with blond hair turning gray, he had the kind of face people often thought they recognized.

In front of each man was a red folder marked in big black block letters, TOP SECRET INFORMATION. Alongside the folder were several sharpened pencils and a pad. In the center of the table, between the men, was a tray with a pitcher of ice water and four glasses.

Kinkade cleared his throat, helped himself to a glass of water, and after he had taken several sips, he said, "We have a problem, gentlemen, which we must dispose of as quickly as possible. All of you have read the information in the folder, some of which came from Captain Boxer's own transmissions to us and some of which comes from our sources in the Soviet Union. Any comments?"

"I for one," Stark said, "am here only to satisfy my own curiosity about the nature of this meeting."

"The purpose of this meeting," Kinkade said, "is to come to some decision about how Captain Boxer should be punished for compromising —"

"If that is its purpose," Stark said, "then I have no business being here." He started to stand.

"Admiral please," Williams said, motioning to him to sit down. "Let's not lose our perspectives."

"By answering the Mayday," Kinkade said, "the Russians were able to photograph the *Shark* on the surface from their satellites and Boxer ran the risk of having the *Shark* destroyed by the *Q-21*."

"The former would have happened anyway," Admiral Kaiser responded. "The *Shark* was disabled and on the surface. That Captain Boxer was able to dive at all and still bring her back to the surface was nothing short of a miracle. As for the latter, the *Shark* was not destroyed. As you know, Mister Kinkade, in our line of work, there's a vast difference between being almost dead and being dead."

"Besides," Stark added with a vigorous nod, "Captain Igor Borodine had to know about the *Shark* as soon as he made contact with her off Torpay."

"Knowing about her and photographing her," Kinkade said, "are two different things."

"You know what kind of information their specialists can derive about her from the photographs," Williams added.

"Then we have the matter of the survivors," Kinkade said. "Just how long do you think they'll keep silent about the *Shark*?"

"I should think," Kaiser said in a soft voice, "That the Company would be able to ... frighten them into silence. A visit from a Company man, or even someone from the FBI, or the National Security Agency should seal their lips forever."

"Admiral, I don't think you understand what you're proposing," Williams commented. "We would be breaching —"

"Let's cut the bullshit," Stark said, living up to his reputation for plain talk. "Tell me what the hell you think you're going to do to Boxer and I'll tell you what my reaction is."

"Remove him from command immediately," Kinkade said.

"No way," Stark answered.

"In my opinion, he's not fit to command the *Shark*."

Stark flushed. "I won't take away his command. Not because you want him removed, and not without him present to defend himself."

Kinkade put his palms down on the table. "Just suppose the President should ask for his removal?" he asked calmly.

"I'd have to tender my resignation," Stark answered just as calmly.

"And I'd have to tender mine too," Kaiser said.

"Bruce," Williams said, "we don't have to act immediately on this. The *Shark* must undergo extensive repairs. There's no harm in waiting until we hear what Boxer has to say."

"I can wait," Kinkade answered. "But I don't like blackmail, even by the navy, and I don't like it when one of my agents is shot up and another agent accounted for but not permitted to contact the Company. I'm speaking about Hayes."

"Boxer is within his rights as captain of the *Shark* to deny anyone access to —"

"My agents have priority to communicate with the Company under all circumstances. Boxer admits that he denied him permission to use the radio."

"Boxer also says," Kaiser said, "that he could not grant permission to Hayes without granting the same permission to everyone else."

"A Company man isn't the same as everyone else," Williams answered. "Boxer should know that."

"Gentlemen," Stark said, "Boxer is a naval officer. He is not one of your Company men. What he did, he did because he was trained to do things that way."

"Then you don't fault him in any way?" Kinkade asked.

"Not sufficiently to remove him," Stark said. "And most certainly not to take that drastic a step without first hearing his reasons for doing what he did."

"Bruce?" Williams questioned.

"I'll wait," Kinkade said. "But I don't care who resigns from the navy; if Boxer's explanation doesn't cut the mustard, then I want him out. Have I made myself clear?"

Stark stood up. "Kinkade, I'm not in the habit of being spoken to the way you just spoke to me. Nor do I have to take it." He moved away from the table. "I don't know why you think you have the right to play God, but you just played the role with the wrong man. Now if you want to get rid of Boxer, you'll have to get rid of me too and Admiral Kaiser as well. You don't seem to understand that Boxer managed nothing short of a miracle. Now I have better things to do than listen to you tell me what you want or don't want."

Kaiser, too, stood up.

"I won't hesitate to put this entire matter before the President," Kinkade said.

"You do that," Stark replied, heading for the door.

"Please, gentlemen," Williams said, "we're letting this difference between us get out of hand. We have other things to consider. The Russians obviously have developed a laser weapon, though albeit a primitive one. We have to address ourselves to that."

"You're right, Thomas," Stark acknowledged and returned to the table.

Borodine was in his quarters listening to a tape of Schubert's Quartet No. 15 in G Major, which he had bought in the United States, when he'd been naval attaché to the Soviet Embassy in Washington. The music held him in its spell, and he was far from his *Sea Savage* when a knock on the door of his cabin instantly brought him back to reality. "Come in," he said, switching off the tape.

Viktor entered. "I have the sound analysis of the American submarine," he said, offering the computer readout tapes to Borodine.

"What do we have?"

"Aside from the usual analysis of its propulsion system, its size and weight, we have definitely established the fact that there are well over one hundred and seventy people aboard. Say, for argument's sake, that forty or so are survivors from the wrecked aircraft, that makes about one hundred and thirty men."

"Too large a crew for a boat as highly automated as she is," Borodine answered.

With a nod, Viktor agreed. "About a hundred too many, given the last radio transmission from Torpay."

Borodine rubbed his beard, which had grown to a respectable length since he had put to sea. "Troop-carrying submarines aren't new," he said. "The Japanese used them during World War Two, but this isn't exactly the same concept, is it?"

"According to our analysis," Viktor said, "she was running slower than she should have."

"Reason?"

"Too much turbulence around her sail ... must have sustained some sort of damage there. Everything else about her appeared to be functioning normally."

"Has engineering finished with the analysis of the laser equipment?" Borodine asked.

"No. But according to our EO, if we had used it a second time we might have had some real trouble with our electrical system. He thinks it fired up too fast, which would explain the sudden dimming of our lights and the loss of power throughout the boat."

"I want a full report on his assumptions and the reasons for them," Borodine said.

"Yes. There is one more thing the EO did say and that was that he would appreciate it if you'd tell Markov not to interfere with the operation of his section."

"That would be like telling the Pope not to be a Catholic," Borodine answered.

Viktor chuckled. "I know exactly what you mean."

"Tell the EO I'll speak to Markov," Borodine said, "though I'm sure I don't know what I'll say that I haven't already said." He handed the computer tapes back to Viktor. "Better make two copies of them."

"You know," Viktor said, "it's strange that we're designed to do exactly what the American sub is designed to do."

"Next time we put to sea we'll be carrying ninety marines. We'll be able to carry out any kind of a hit-and-run operation. But more work has to be done before they come aboard."

"Will Markov always be assigned to the *Sea Savage*?" Viktor asked. "Or will we be lucky and have someone else?"

Borodine smiled. "I hope we're lucky. But then he may be permanently assigned to the *Sea Savage* just as we are."

"That would be too bad," Viktor answered. "Too fucking bad!"

"By the way, pass the word that all hands will have two weeks' leave when we arrive in port. I was thinking of taking Galena to Moscow. It's been several months since we've been there and I know she'd like the idea."

"I wasn't sure about the leave," Viktor said. "But since we have it, I think I'll take Sonya someplace where I can rest and do a bit of painting."

Borodine nodded. Viktor was an accomplished painter and had even taken a first prize in several contests. "I wouldn't mind going off somewhere just to rest, but Galena wouldn't be happy. She really loves the excitement of a big city.

"Sonya is the more country-girl type," Viktor said. "Now and then she talks about living in Moscow, but I know it's only talk."

Borodine nodded. "If I told Galena I was transferred to Moscow, she be packed and ready to go the next minute."

"I'd better get back to the bridge," Viktor said. "The watch will changing soon."

"I'll be up there in a little while," Borodine responded. He waited until the door was closed before switching on the Schubert quartet again.

The *Tecumseh* had left the tropics several days before and now was making her way towards the Strait of Magellan. The sea was rough, lashed by a storm that was roaring out of Antarctica, bringing with it blizzard conditions that even made a ship as large and powerful as the *Tecumseh* labor through the heavy seas.

Though it was twenty-three hundred hours, Boxer had been called to the bridge by Rugger to discuss the weather conditions.

"What we have," Rugger said in his gravelly voice, "is a force ten storm. The barometer is still falling. Now it's twenty-eight point nine nine. And according to the weather satellite pictures, the storm will be with us for the next seventy-two hours."

Ordinarily, Boxer would have left the running of the *Tecumseh* completely in Rugger's hands. But Rugger had called him to the bridge because of the worsening weather.

"I planned to go through the strait tomorrow morning at about zero nine hundred," Rugger said. "But with this kind of sea and visibility —"

"Delay it," Boxer said, "until conditions improve. I don't want to risk grounding this ship in the Strait."

Rugger nodded. "It would be one job to free her, if that ever happened."

"Lay off the Strait for a few days," Boxer said. "As soon as the weather gives the slightest sign of clearing we'll make our run."

"That's fine with me," Rugger answered.

Boxer looked at the radar scope. It was clear. "How far are we from the coast?" he asked.

"Twenty miles, at least."

"Helmsman come to one hundred and ten degrees," Boxer said.

"Coming to course one hundred and ten degrees,' the helmsman said.

"Better tell your officers," Boxer said, "to keep her into the wind at all times. Better hold to ten knots. That should keep us in this vicinity."

Rugger nodded.

"I'll be in my cabin," Boxer said, "if I'm needed, or if you want me to spell you on the bridge."

"I'm going below myself," Rugger said. "My first officer comes up at twenty-four hundred. It doesn't make sense for all of us to be dead tired."

Boxer agreed and left the bridge. It was difficult to walk down the companionway and along the corridor without being thrown from side to side. He guessed the *Tecumseh* was rolling about ten degrees, to say nothing about how much she was pitching and yawing. A ten-degree roll was significant for a ship as large as she. She probably could take another ten degrees before she'd been in any real danger of capsizing, but the combination of roll, pitch, and yaw was putting an enormous strain on her.

Before going to his own cabin, Boxer looked in the rec room: no one was there. He had hoped to find Redfern, have a nightcap with him and talk. Disappointed, he continued along the passageway to his own quarters.

Boxer's quarters were the equivalent of a three-room apartment: a living room, a bedroom, and an office which included everything from radar screens to phone connections to every part of the ship. It was a second bridge from which the *Tecumseh* could be run. The living room was furnished with a sofa and two easy chairs. Each of these pieces were covered with a good grade of leather. On one wall there was a well-stocked bar and a small refrigerator that made two dozen ice cubes at a time.

Boxer went directly to the bar and poured himself a double Scotch. With the drink in his hand, he looked out of the porthole. It was iced over; then he went into the control room and switched on the monitor that permitted him to view the *Shark* from any angle. Despite the heavy roll of the *Tecumseh*, she was secure in a special cradle.

Satisfied, Boxer said aloud, "That's it for tonight." He switched off the monitor, finished his drink, and returned to the bar. He was going to pour himself another, but changed his mind. Instead, he went into the bathroom, brushed his teeth, stripped off his clothes, and then showered. A few minutes later, he walked into the darkened bedroom. He opened the dresser drawer, took out a pair of skivvies, and put them on.

Suddenly, Boxer realized he wasn't alone. Someone was in the room with him! He turned toward the bed. There was sufficient light spilling through the doorway to see Dee. She was resting on a pillow; the blanket was drawn up over her breasts.

"Aren't you going to say something?" she asked.

Boxer remained silent. But his heart was racing.

"Anything... Say anything."

"I need a drink," he said, turning and heading for the bar.

"Bring me one too... I'll have whatever you're having," she called after him.

Boxer poured a double shot of Scotch into the glass he'd already used and an equal amount into a clean glass. This wasn't the first time he'd found a woman in his bed, and if the gods were good to him, it wouldn't be the last. But this circumstance was completely different from the other times; he was aboard a ship he could command if he chose, and this woman was a self-admitted embezzler whom he would hand over to the police as soon as they reached port. Holding a glass in each hand, he returned to the bedroom and handed one drink to Dee. He started to sip his own.

"A toast," she said. "Let's make a toast."

"Listen," he said, "this isn't a social situation. It's not a party. I'm just about ready to tell you to get out of here."

"You're angry," she responded.

Boxer drank.

"Okay, have it your way. No toast," Dee said; then she drank.

"You don't belong here," Boxer told her. "You should be with the rest of the people —"

She shook her head. "No," she said quietly, "you're wrong, Captain. Or is it skipper? That's what your men call you."

Boxer shook his head. "You don't belong here."

Dee finished her drink. "Tonight it's the only place I belong. Do you want me to tell you why?"

"Tell me... I'm listening."

Dee took a deep breath and slowly exhaled. "Aren't you cold standing there like that?"

"I said I was listening," Boxer answered.

"You're not an easy man to speak to when you take an attitude."

"Tell me!" he ordered, growing more and more impatient with her.

"The storm," she said, "frightened me and made me think of what lies ahead for me."

"You'd better go," Boxer said.

"I didn't come here to trade," she said. "I know that's what you're thinking. You're thinking I came here to trade a lay for my freedom."

"Remember, you tried it once. You even offered me most of the money you embezzled."

She nodded. "I do remember."

"It's a no-go situation," Boxer said.

Dee ignored him. "This time I came for me. I need to be loved. No, love is the wrong word. I need to be fucked. It will be a long time before I have the opportunity to have a man caress me again. That's why I'm here." Her voice was barely audible when she finished, but she looked straight at him.

Boxer put his glass down on the dresser, reached around to the living-room control, and dimmed the switch.

"And," Dee added, "you saved my life and I have nothing to give you in return; nothing but myself."

Boxer was at the side of the bed. He drew back the blanket: she was completely naked. The nipples on her pear-shaped breasts were erect.

She moved over to make room for him.

Boxer eased himself down beside her and pulled the blanket over the two of them.

She moved close to him. "You're cold," she said.

Boxer didn't answer. Her body was warm and soft against his.

"When I was a kid in high school I used to dream of having all sorts of adventures," she said. "Like I'd go to Paris and meet a rock star and he'd fall madly in love with me — or a millionaire — and I'd marry him and live happily ever after.

But there was always sex and lots of partying. If my mother or father knew what my daydreams were like, they'd have hauled me off to a shrink. Not that they knew what a shrink was. But you know what I mean. What were your dreams like then?"

"To become a naval officer," Boxer answered. "To travel strange places and to fuck beautiful women."

Dee managed a laugh. "I guess you've done everything you dreamed of doing."

"Probably," Boxer answered.

"Where did you live?" she asked.

"Brooklyn."

"Staten Island," she answered. "A place called New Dorp. I even graduated from New Dorp High School."

"I graduated from Brooklyn Tech," Boxer said, not telling her that Staten Island was the home base for the submarine he'd previously commanded. The less they knew about one another the better off they'd be.

"Yeah, even when I was going to school, Tech was considered a good school."

"How long ago was that?"

"Not as long as you think. I'm twenty-two. I graduated when I was eighteen. A lot has happened to me in the last four years ... a hell of a lot."

Boxer didn't answer.

"A few of my teachers tried to tell us the truth about what the world was like outside of school. But most of us didn't believe them. We were convinced that we could make it the way we always had: by bluffing our way through a situation, by cheating, and if the opportunity came our way, by stealing. I used to go into the local stores and rip off whatever I wanted. If I'd known then what I know now ... well, maybe I'd be in bed with you, but not for the same reason. Not for the same reason," she repeated in a breathy voice.

Boxer was afraid she was going to cry. The one thing he didn't need was a weeping women in his bed. "Listen," he said and paused. He was going to tell her that it wasn't going to work, that he didn't feel very sexy, that it was the wrong time and place. But she suddenly changed her position and he felt her bare breasts against his chest.

"Hold me," she whispered. "Please hold me!"

It was a cry for help ... for pity. Boxer put his arms around her. There was nothing worldly or tough about her now. She was just a frightened woman.

"You know," she said, "I've never really been in love. I've gone to bed with guys because I wanted the same thing they wanted, but I've never really been in love. A few times I thought I was but I wasn't, not really."

Boxer didn't want to hear her life story. "Why don't you try and sleep?" he suggested.

"I can't sleep," she answered. "I want to make love."

"Listen, I'm too tired now," he said. "Depending on the weather I may be called to the bridge again."

She pressed her lips to his.

Boxer felt himself becoming aroused. He kissed her back, moving his tongue into her mouth.

"You'll see," she said. "I'm good. You won't be sorry."

The phone began to ring.

"Not now," Dee cried. "Oh God, not now!"

Boxer eased away from her, and lifted the phone from its cradle on the wall. "Boxer here," he said.

"The snow has stopped," Rugger said. "We've got four miles visibility. I think we should make a run for the Strait. We're in the eye of the storm and it might just get us through the Atlantic."

"I'll be up on the bridge in a few minutes," Boxer said. "In the meantime bring us onto a course that lines up with the Strait."

"Will do, Skipper," Rugger answered.

Boxer put the phone back in its cradle and, sitting up, planted his feet on the floor.

"I'm needed on the bridge," he said. He stood up and padded into the bathroom, where he brushed his teeth, rinsed his mouth, and washed his face with soap and hot water.

When he returned to the bedroom, Dee was sitting up. She was bare breasted and her nipples were erect. "I don't know how long I'll be on the bridge," he said.

"I'll wait," she answered.

"It will probably be —"

"It doesn't matter," she said. "I don't have any special place to go."

"Suit yourself," Boxer answered, pulling on a heavy woollen turtleneck sweater.

"Good luck," Dee said.

"Thanks," he said, kissing her on the forehead. "Thanks."

Boxer switched on the infrared optics and scanned the passageway leading to the Strait. The wind had died, and the sea was placid. Low scudding clouds hid the sky and covered the tops of the cliffs on either side of the channel.

"Once we're inside the Strait, we'll be okay," Rugger said, "unless we have more snow. Then we'll have to feel our way through and that could be very tricky, especially with a ship this size."

Maybe we'd do better to forget about the Strait and go south around Tierra del Fuego," Boxer suggested.

"The weather'd be worse," Rugger answered. "I don't want to put the *Tecumseh* under any more strain than I absolutely have to."

"Okay, we'll go for the Strait," Boxer said. "Helmsman come to course five zero degrees."

"Coming to course five zero degrees," the helmsman answered.

"We'll go through at half speed," Boxer said.

Rugger rang the engine room and ordered half ahead.

Boxer keyed the radar officer. "I don't want to come any closer to the shore than one thousand yards."

"I'll keep a sharp watch," the RO answered.

It took several minutes for the *Tecumseh* to begin to slow down.

Boxer keyed the RO again. "Give me the bearing and range of land off the starboard bow."

"Target bearing four zero degrees... Range six thousand yards."

"Helmsman, come to course three five degrees," Boxer said.

"Going to three five degrees," the helmsman answered.

Boxer peered through the infrared optics again. From the calibration marks on the lenses, he estimated the *Tecumseh* would enter the Strait with almost two thousand yards between herself and the shore on the starboard side. Moving away from the optical system, he took a few moments to fill and light a pipe.

"What we might have to worry about," he said between puffs on the pipe, "is some other ship coming westward. Another tanker the size of the *Tecumseh* would crowd us."

"Suppose we set the fog horn to blow at intervals of say two minutes," Rugger answered.

"Set it for three minutes," Boxer said.

Rugger walked over to the control panel. "Starting three minutes from now," he said, "we'll have two short blasts every three minutes."

Boxer nodded. "It's going to take us about ten hours to go through... That's if we don't run into any problems."

"How about a sandwich and some coffee?" Rugger asked.

"I'll take the coffee," Boxer said.

Rugger rang the galley and asked for two cups of black coffee and a ham and cheese sandwich for himself.

Boxer settled into one of the two captain's chairs and thought about Dee. Strange, now he wanted her and hoped she'd be waiting for him when he returned.

For the next several hours the *Tecumseh* twisted and turned through the Strait. The weather held and several times the clouds gave way to patches of blue sky. But the sun never shone.

No other ship passed the *Tecumseh* but often the sky was filled with hundreds if not thousands of birds.

"Where do they all come from?" Boxer asked.

"Here for the winter, some of them. And the others live here all year round," Rugger said.

Boxer made no additional comment. He was just curious. He enjoyed reading about nature and someday he hoped to be able to devote some time to studying it.

At 0830 hours, Rugger said, "From here on the course is straight into the Atlantic. You get some rest and I'll have my first officer take over for me as soon as we leave the Strait and turn north."

"Okay," Boxer said. "But call me if —"

"I'll call you," Rugger said with a smile. "This ship is your responsibility when you're on board."

Boxer knocked the ashes from his pipe into an ashtray. "See you in a couple of hours," he said. A few minutes later he entered his cabin and went straight into the bedroom. Dee was still there, curled up into a small ball. Boxer undressed and slipped into bed beside her. He put his arm around and cupped one of her breasts in his hand. It was cold. Colder than it should have been with the blanket over her. "Dee," he called. "Dee?"

She didn't answer.

Boxer rolled her toward him. She was dead. The handle of a switchblade knife was sticking out of her chest.

Boxer stood at the foot of the bed; he was dressed now as he had been a few minutes before. Rugger, Redfern, and Cowly were in the room with him. Dee's naked body was covered with the blanket.

"But you were on the bridge with me," Rugger said, "from zero one hundred hours until fifteen minutes ago."

Boxer drew down the blanket and pointed to the knife below her left breast. "Have any of you ever seen it before?"

"It's an ordinary switchblade," Cowly said. "Many of the men carry them."

"We'll have a better idea about the time she was killed after the doctor does an autopsy," Rugger said. "He should be here any moment."

"What was she doing here, Jack?" Redfern asked.

"Waiting for me," Boxer answered.

Redfern raised his eyebrows.

"It's a long, somewhat strange story," Boxer answered, realizing it would sound even stranger to someone else.

"Does anyone know anything about her?" Rugger asked.

"She was being extradited from Australia," Boxer volunteered. "She was being taken back to New York to stand trial for embezzlement. The detective taking her back drowned."

"Oh!" Rugger exclaimed.

Someone knocked on the cabin door.

"Come in," Boxer called.

Doctor Klee entered.

"In the bedroom," Boxer said.

Boxer drew the blanket all the way back exposing Dee's naked body. "Can you give me a fix on the time it might have happened?"

Klee a tall, thin man with a prominent Adam's apple, bent over the corpse and flexed the fingers and toes; then he lifted the eyelid of each eye. He palpated the body on the breasts, the abdomen, and in the groin area. "I'd say about three, four hours ago, but I'll give you a better idea after I do an autopsy."

"How long will that take?" Boxer asked.

"Two, three hours, at the most," Klee said.

"I'll send the body down to the hospital in a little while," Boxer told him.

"Any idea who did it?" Klee asked.

"None. No idea who did it and no idea why anyone would want to kill her."

The doctor looked down at the body. "She certainly was an attractive — I might even say beautiful — woman." He pulled the blanket over her again. "What was she doing in your bed?" he asked, facing Boxer.

"Waiting for me."

The doctor's Adam's apple bobbed up and down as if he were going to speak but he said nothing.

"Doctor, you may go now," Boxer said.

Klee nodded and left.

Boxer didn't care for the doctor's attitude. He had the feeling that the man had more than just a professional interest in Dee.

"I'll have a couple of men come up here with a gurney and remove the body to the hospital lab," Cowly said.

"Make sure they say nothing to anyone about it," Boxer said.

"It's going to be a tough thing to keep under wraps," Redfern said.

"I'm not even going to try," Boxer said. "But I want to tell everyone at the same time. I don't want any rumors aboard. We still have a long voyage ahead of us."

"What are you going to say?" Rugger asked.

"She died of a heart attack," Boxer answered. "She'll be buried at sea."

"Are you sure burying her at sea is wise?" Cowly questioned.

"We'll go through the motions of burying her, but her body will be stored in the deep freezer. The authorities probably will want to examine it when we reach port."

"Even if an autopsy has already been performed?" Rugger asked.

Boxer shrugged. "I'd rather be safe than sorry. As things stand, I'm going to have enough trouble explaining what she was doing in my bed. I don't want to add to that by destroying any evidence."

"Is it possible someone was trying to kill you?" Cowly asked.

"I guess it is," Boxer answered, "though I couldn't begin to guess who or what the reason would be."

"I don't think you should cover this up with a heart attack story, Jack," Redfern said. "I think you should tell it the way it happened. You don't have to say where she was killed. But if you tell it the way it happened, then the rest of us can do some questioning … maybe get a lead on whose knife was used?"

"I think Tom is right," Cowly said.

"So do I," Rugger added.

"Okay," Boxer agreed. "We'll tell the truth … but I still want the body for the authorities."

"I'll go with that," Redfern said.

Cowly and Rugger also agreed to keep the body for the authorities.

"All right," Boxer said, "we'll wait until we have the results from the autopsy before I make a statement about the murder. Cowly get the detail up here to remove the body. For the rest of us, it's the usual routine."

Rugger returned to the bridge.

Boxer and Redfern moved into the living room. Boxer dropped down into one of the easy chairs and filled his pipe. "Stark and the others are going to be angry about this. They're not going to understand why Dee was in my bed."

"I don't think I understand it either," Redfern said.

Boxer puffed on his pipe. "She was there to have sex," he said.

"That much is obvious," Redfern answered. "But why did you have her there?"

"I'll explain exactly what happened."

For the next few minutes Boxer told Redfern what had taken place when Dee had come to his quarters the first time; what they'd said in sick bay, and how he'd found her in bed waiting for him after he'd come down from the bridge the previous night.

"The second call from the bridge interrupted you?" Redfern asked.

"Yes. When I returned six hours later, she was already dead."

"Maybe someone came into your quarters to steal something," Redfern suggested. "She awakened and he killed her."

"Could be," Boxer said. "The only thing I can be sure of is that someone aboard the *Tecumseh* killed her."

The detail arrived with the gurney.

"In the bedroom," Boxer said. He got up and went to the door. "Wrap the blanket securely around her, Cowly," he said.

"Will do, Skipper," Cowly answered.

Boxer watched them lift Dee's covered body onto the gurney and he stepped aside to let them pass.

"Anything else, Skipper?" Cowly asked.

Boxer shook his head. "If you guys don't mind, I'd like to be alone for a while. I'll see you in a little while."

"Sure, Jack," Redfern said. "See you."

"I'll be in the holding bay," Cowly said.

As soon as he was alone, Boxer sat down again in the same easy chair he'd used before. He was physically and emotionally drained. The long hours on the bridge made him yearn for sleep. His eyes burned and he had a foul taste in his mouth.

Suddenly the full impact of Dee's death flooded through his consciousness. She was a woman to whom he had given pleasure a few hours ago and from whom he was expecting pleasure. That she was nothing more than a body on the cold slab of an autopsy table was almost inconceivable. He shuddered, uttered a loud sigh of resignation, and went back into the bedroom.

Boxer checked over his personal belongings and found nothing missing. Then he checked his office. All the equipment functioned properly. But suddenly he realized a stack of paper had been moved from one place to another. Someone had been there looking for something. Redfern had been right, or so it seemed.

Boxer closed the door to the office, locked it, and returned to the living room, where he immediately phoned the ship's security officer.

"Lieutenant Jackson, this is Captain Boxer, I want a two-man armed guard outside my quarters twenty-four hours a day." Even as he spoke, he felt he was acting like the farmer who'd closed the barn door after the horse had run away.

"Aye, aye, Skipper," Jackson answered in his nasal voice.

Boxer put down the phone and began to pace. Suddenly he stopped. Someone aboard the *Tecumseh* was a foreign agent. He let out a long, low whistle, and then he said aloud. "And we don't have a snowball's chance in hell to find out who it is."

CHAPTER 9

"The knife entered the right ventricle at an angle of eight, nine degrees. Death was probably instantaneous," Doctor Klee said. "My best guess is that she was killed about zero three hundred. I put all the other details in my report."

"Thank you," Boxer said, as he took the manila folder from Klee and prepared to leave the medical office.

"Oh, by the way, there were no signs of sexual molestation," Klee said.

Boxer raised his eyebrows.

"I took a vaginal swab and checked it under the microscope. There weren't any spermatozoa. I thought you'd like to know."

Boxer flushed. He definitely didn't like the man.

"I wanted to cover all bases," Klee said. "She might have been raped before she was killed or after."

"Thanks again for being so thorough," Boxer said, as he stood up.

"You have a copy of the report, Captain," Klee told him. "I'm required by Company rules to turn over the original to the Company's chief medical officer."

Boxer nodded.

"Do you want to have a last look at her before she goes into the deep freeze?"

Boxer was about to say no, but the smug expression on Klee's face made him change his mind. "Yes, I'd like very much to see her."

"She's in the lab," Klee said.

Boxer followed Klee into the corridor, then through a door marked Authorized Personnel Only. The air had a heavy antiseptic smell about it.

"She's over there on the table," Klee said.

Boxer walked over to the dissecting table and looked down.

Dee's body was uncovered. She had been opened up from her breast bone to the top of her pubic mound and flapped back; then after the autopsy, the flaps had been closed and crudely stitched together.

"Not in the least bit sexy now," Klee commented, coming alongside Boxer.

"I get the feeling you're trying to tell me something, Doctor," Boxer said, looking straight at him. "But you don't have the guts to come out with it, or don't really know what you want to say."

Klee flushed.

"Forget my rank," Boxer said.

Klee shook his head. "It won't make any difference whether I say it or don't. There are men like yourself who get what they want, even if they don't want it."

"I don't know what the hell you're talking about!"

"Women, Captain. Women." Klee pointed to Dee. "She's a perfect example. I wanted her, told her I wanted her. I was even half convinced that during the time we had left at sea, I'd have her … but she wanted you and now she's here."

Boxer pursed his lips; then in a low voice, he said, "I didn't have her either."

Boxer radioed a full account of Dee's murder to Williams and then, over the ship's MC system, he told everyone on board about her death. "Miss Long," he said, "will be buried at sea at 1200 hours today." He put the mike down and went on deck.

The Strait was already several hours astern of them and they were sailing north. In another day or two, the weather would moderate. But now spume was coming off the tops of the waves and a wind-driven rain was falling.

Boxer looked out toward the rain-obscured horizon. The spume seemed to be whirling from wave crest to wave crest, much the way his thoughts were leaping from incident to incident. He had a clear picture in his mind of what Dee had looked like when he'd reached down and pulled her aboard the *Shark*, then later when she'd come to his quarters and tried to strike a deal with him, and last night when he'd held her naked body in his arms — finally when he'd seen her body on the slab. He would carry that image of her for the rest of his life. He had never seen a dead woman before, much less one with whom he had been intimate. Despite the fact that she was really a stranger, he decided to visit her parents and —

Suddenly something in the water caught his attention. A wake! He wiped the rain out of his eyes and tried to get a better fix on it. But it was almost impossible for him to see it for more than a few seconds at a time. Whatever it was, it seemed to be keeping pace with the ship. Killer whales often did that, but Boxer did not know whether killer whales might be in this area at this time.

He saw the wake again and realized it was being made by a periscope. He left the railing and headed for the bridge. "Rugger," he said, stepping through the door, "we're being shadowed by a sub."

"What?"

"Off the port side, about one zero degrees off the bow."

Rugger trained his glasses on the ocean. "I don't see anything."

"It's there," Boxer said. "I'm sure of it."

"What the hell would it be doing down here?"

"I don't know," Boxer said. "Maybe it was waiting for us. I don't know. I wish to Christ we had sonar gear aboard. At least we'd be able to ID the thing."

"One thing we know for sure," Rugger said, "it isn't one of ours."

"I sure as hell don't like the idea it's shadowing us," Boxer said. "I don't want it to pick up any more information about us than the Russians already have"

"How can you be sure it's one of theirs?"

"I'm not sure," Boxer answered. "But I don't want it following us."

"I don't see that there's anything you can do about it," Rugger answered. "The *Shark* is in no condition to go into action."

"But the minisub can go into action," Boxer answered.

"If you could launch it, yes," Rugger said.

"Flood the bay for the normal launch procedure; then I'll flood the bay aboard the *Shark* and take the minisub out just as if the *Shark* were on her own. Slow the *Tecumseh* down, to about one zero knots would be fine."

"You're going to attack?" Rugger asked.

Boxer nodded.

Rugger went to the electronic speed control and reduced the *Tecumseh*'s speed to one zero knots.

Boxer went to the MC and switched it on. "Now hear this ... now hear this... Mister Cowly report to bay area immediately... Mister Berness report to bay area immediately... All of the *Shark*'s crew report to the bay area on the double... All hands for the *Shark* report to the bay area immediately." He switched off the MC and, turning to Rugger, said, "If I don't make it back, Cowly takes command of the *Shark*. You maintain your command of the *Tecumseh*."

Rugger nodded.

"See you," Boxer said and he left the bridge. By the time he reached the bay area the entire crew was aboard. He keyed Rugger. "We're ready to begin flooding."

"Flooding beginning," Rugger responded.

"Everyone to duty stations below," Boxer said. The men scrambled down the hatchways. The last man dogged them shut.

Boxer went the bridge. "Prepare to launch the minisub," he told Cowly.

"What the hell is going on?" Cowly asked.

Boxer explained about the submarine that was shadowing them. "I'm going after it. You take command of the *Shark*. Hold her steady. When the bay is completely flooded and the doors open, flood the launch bay in the *Shark* and open the doors. I'll take the craft out."

"Just how the hell do you expect to come back?" Cowly asked.

"The same way I went out, with luck," Boxer answered.

"No way. It can't be done."

"Then the craft will be hoisted aboard the *Tecumseh*."

"You know that's impossible in this kind of sea," Cowly said.

"That sub out there can't be allowed to collect any information about us."

"But it probably has," Cowly said.

"That's exactly why I can't let it return to wherever it comes from," Boxer answered.

"What if you should fail and the sub turns on the *Tecumseh*?"

"That's the chance we'll have to take, won't we? Now get Mister Berness up here. He's going with me. Pass the word to arm the sub with everything it can carry. I want to kill that sucker, not wound it."

"Aye, aye, Skipper," Cowly answered.

Fifteen minutes later Boxer was in the control seat of the minisub.

Berness was next to him.

"You'll be the FCO on this mission," Boxer said. "Everything you need to know, you already know, and you have the advantage of having the UWIS screen. All our attacks will be made on what you see on the screen ... and try not to be frightened."

"Skipper, I'm scared shitless," Berness said. "But I'll do the best I can."

"That's all any of us can do," Boxer said. Then he keyed Cowly. "Ready for flooding."

"Beginning flooding," Cowly answered.

Within minutes the entire bay was flooded and the doors opened.

Boxer took a deep breath and slowly exhaled. "Here goes," he said, opening the main valves of the craft's ballast tanks and at the same time easing the power throttle forward to one third ahead.

The small craft began to move. It left the *Shark*.

"We've got one five feet clearance on either side to clear the *Tecumseh*," Berness reported.

"Holding her steady as she goes," Boxer answered.

"Clearing the *Tecumseh*," Berness reported. "Clearing the *Tecumseh*."

Boxer moved the throttle to full ahead. The craft surged forward and began to sink. Boxer eased her over to the starboard side. His plan was to circle around the *Tecumseh* and come astern of the submarine for his attack. "Making three hundred feet," he said, setting the ADC.

"Sweeping the area with the sonar," Berness said. "Have target ... bearing two five five degrees ... range eight hundred yards ... speed two two knots."

"Tell me when you get her on the UWIS," Boxer said, maneuvering the minisub toward the target.

"Have her on the UWIS," Berness said. "Switching off sonar."

"Make a tape of her sound," Boxer said.

"Tape being made."

"What does she look like?" Boxer asked.

"World War Two type," Berness answered. "But she is shadowing the *Tecumseh*."

"Stand by to attack," Boxer said. "We'll go in visually. Arm all torpedoes. Set them for sound ID."

"Torpedoes armed. Recording target's sound into computer memory."

"Fire when ready," Boxer said.

"Fixing FC problem into computer," Berness said. "Computer indicates firing two salvos of two torpedoes, separated by a forty-second interval. Optimum range five hundred yards. Our depth okay. Our speed okay. Will fire at five hundred yards."

Boxer radioed the *Tecumseh*. "Everything going five by five."

"Ten four that," the *Tecumseh* commented.

"Five five zero yards," Berness answered.

"Six hundred yards and closing fast," Berness reported. "Beginning countdown. Five nine zero yards ... five eight five yards..."

Boxer saw the submarine. They were diagonally below it. "She's still at periscope depth," Boxer answered.

Suddenly there was the familiar ping of the sonar.

"They've spotted us; they're diving."

"Ten seconds to firing time. Sonar switched on target info being fed through master FC computer to torpedoes."

Boxer was pleased that Berness was handling the situation so well. He was calm and almost matter-of-fact about it.

"Three seconds to firing... First salvo away!"

The sudden loss of weight caused the craft to rise. But the ADC system immediately brought it back to its present depth of three five zero feet.

The torpedoes streaked toward their target. The two struck it at the same time.

The force of the explosion rocked the minisub.

"Second salvo away!" Berness exclaimed.

Within seconds another explosion aboard the submarine rocked the minicraft.

"Target has heeled over on its starboard side and has broken in two," Berness reported. "Several bodies are in the water."

Boxer keyed the *Tecumseh*. "Target destroyed. Prepare to retrieve us."

"Roger that," Rugger answered.

"Let's go back to the ship," Boxer said, turning toward the dark shape of the *Tecumseh*'s hull.

It took better than two hours for the minicraft to finally come to rest in the *Shark* and another hour to pump the water out of the *Shark*'s bay and out of the *Tecumseh*. It was well past 1600 hours before Boxer could leave the *Shark* and hold the funeral service for Dee.

He stood on the windswept deck and said, "I did not know Dee very well, or very long, and I cannot say anything about the kind of life she led." Then he recited the Twenty-third

Psalm and ended with, "We commit her body to the deep. May she rest in peace."

Byron Hayes came over to Boxer and said, "That wasn't much of a funeral service."

"I did the best I could," Boxer answered. "Now if you'll excuse me —"

"You said she was murdered but you didn't say how or where," Hayes said.

"If I had wanted you to know, I would have told you," Boxer said.

Hayes nodded, turned around, and walked away.

Boxer went down to his quarters and poured himself a double Scotch. He drank it in two swift gulps; then he went into his bedroom. Since that morning all of the bedding had been removed, including the mattress, and the bed had been freshly made by the steward.

Boxer pulled back the cover and dropped down on the bed. He kicked off his shoes and put his hands behind his head; then he closed his eyes and hoped that sleep would come quickly.

The phone rang.

He reached for it and said, "Boxer here."

"Skipper," Cowly said, "that sub was ID as Chinese."

"Are you sure?" he said, wide awake again.

"Absolutely. Sold to them by the French," Cowly said.

"What were they doing in this part of the world?"

"Better still, why were they shadowing us?"

"If you come up with an answer," Boxer said, "save it until I'm awake. Now I want to get some sleep."

CHAPTER 10

As the days passed, the *Tecumseh* sailed north into the tropics and finally into the North Atlantic, where it was already late spring. The sea was calm and the sky a lovely azure blue.

Much of the conversation between Boxer and the other officers was about the Chinese sub. No one could come up with a reason why she was so far from home.

Redfern summed the situation up one evening at dinner when he said, "It was in the wrong ocean. If it had been anywhere in the Pacific, or even the Indian, there wouldn't be any question about what it was doing, but in the South Atlantic, a day or so off the Strait ... well, that raises questions."

"Maybe the Company will have the answer," Cowly said.

"Maybe," Boxer answered, looking at Berness, who hadn't joined in the evening's conversation or, now that he thought about it, the conversations about the submarine on previous evenings. He waited until Berness left the table and followed him out into the corridor. "I'd like a word with you, Mister Berness," he said, coming up alongside the man.

Berness stopped and looked questioningly at him.

"Let's go up on deck," Boxer said.

"Sure, Skipper," Berness answered.

Boxer filled his pipe and lit it; then he asked, "Is anything bothering you?"

Berness cast his eyes downward. "It's personal, Skipper."

Boxer blew a cloud of smoke out of his mouth. He decided to take a direct approach. "You're lying," he said.

"Skipper —"

"It has something to do with that Chinese sub, doesn't it?" And before Berness could answer, Boxer said, "It had to be destroyed."

"But I saw the bodies on the UWIS," he said in a choked voice. "I saw it break up ... and I keep seeing those bodies, twisting and turning in the water every time I go to sleep." His hands were clenched over the ship's railing. "I keep telling myself what you told me: the sub had to be destroyed. Then a voice from somewhere inside me asks, 'Did it really have to be destroyed? Couldn't we have warned it? Couldn't we have avoided killing all those men?'"

Boxer ran his hand over his beard. "All of us have heard that same voice," he said softly. "All of us who hear it ask those same questions. These last weeks I have heard my voice ask about the mission, about the men we killed on Torpay. We could have told the Russians we knew about the base and demand they dismantle it. But given the nature of American–Soviet relations, what do you think their answer would have been? I'll tell you what it would have been. They'd say — not in so many words of course, but the meaning would be there nonetheless — we could take a flying fuck for ourselves. There really wasn't anything we could do, except destroy that base. There was no other way of neutralizing it."

"I understand that, Skipper," Berness said.

"That sub was gathering information about us," Boxer told him, "information that one day some other Chinese sub might use against us. I couldn't allow that to happen. I don't know how long she was shadowing us. She might have followed us through the strait, or maybe she picked us up a few minutes before I saw the wake from her periscope. Either way, I couldn't risk having her go back to China with any information about us. We destroyed her so that we might survive. Think about that."

"I'll try," Berness answered.

"Don't just try. Do it. Think about surviving. We're in the business of death. You either have to make peace with yourself on that score, or find another line of work."

"I want to remain with the *Shark*," Berness said.

Boxer nodded. "You're a good officer and will be a better one if you understand why we do what we do. I'll admit that sometimes it is hard as hell to understand it."

Berness managed a smile. "I'll come to terms with it, Skipper."

"I'm sure you will," Boxer answered, putting his hand on Berness's shoulder, though he wasn't at all sure Berness would. From experience, Boxer knew that some men couldn't accept the fact that they were professional killers. Boxer knocked the bowl of his pipe against the palm of his hand and dropped the ashes into the water. "You think about what I said," he told him.

"I sure will, Skipper," Berness answered.

"Good night," Boxer said.

"Good night, Skipper," Berness replied.

Boxer divided his time between Redfern, with whom he played ball on deck, and Rugger on the bridge.

Boxer discovered that Rugger was an old Company hand in Asia for several years after the fall of Nam.

"I sailed everything from a junk to an old coal-burning freighter along those coasts," Rugger said in his gravelly voice. "Even had a few scrapes with Chinese pirates in the South China Sea."

Boxer laughed. "I'm impressed. And here I thought you were new to the game?"

"Only new to this particular game," Rugger answered. "The *Tecumseh* is the biggest ship I've commanded and in one respect, the strangest. All it is, is a mobile drydock for the *Shark*."

"And the *Shark* isn't anything more than a means to transport Tom's men," Boxer said.

"Jack, the *Shark* is much more than just an underwater bus."

Boxer nodded. "I guess I was trying to play down how spectacular she really is. Only the *Q-21* comes anywhere close to her."

Rugger nodded and placed his hand against the wall. "I feel the same way about this lady here," he said.

Boxer nodded. There was nothing more either of them could say about their ships.

The more time Boxer spent with Rugger, the more he liked him. The man was many-sided. To Boxer's astonishment, he discovered that Rugger was a painter of some repute.

"I've had one-man shows in New York, Washington, and London," he told Boxer one afternoon, as the two of them walked the length of the ship.

"Seascapes?" Boxer asked, figuring the man would paint what he knew best.

Rugger laughed. "A few. But mostly nudes and landscapes with twisted old trees in them. The more tortured the trunk and branches the happier I am."

Boxer nodded. "How about the nudes, do they have to be tortured and twisted to make you happy?"

"Not on your life," Rugger answered. "The human body is beautiful and that beauty deserves to be painted."

Boxer agreed.

Then Rugger said, "A man should be able to leave something behind, when he goes, something more than his children — something that is totally his, even if it's a brick wall."

Boxer thought about that for a few moments before he said, "A kind of immortality, isn't it?"

"No, not really. It's a statement about oneself. It's saying this was part of a man... Maybe not the most important part, but nonetheless part of him that was unique, different from all other men and different from all other artists. Haven't you ever felt that way?"

Boxer shook his head. Rugger was thinking in areas that he had always avoided.

"Maybe I'm all wrong," Rugger said. "But I get one hell of a kick doing what I'm doing."

"I should think so," Boxer teased, "especially with the nudes."

"I've slept with a few," Rugger said matter-of-factly. "More since my wife and I split up. When they're in bed they're like any other women. But the magic occurs when they pose; then they become even more beautiful."

They reached the *Tecumseh*'s bow and turned around.

"Come down to my cabin after dinner," Rugger said, "and I'll show you some of my sketches. I even have one of Miss Long. I went down to see her in the hospital and asked her to pose for me."

"In the nude?"

Rugger nodded. "She came to my cabin the first night she was out of the hospital. She had a lovely body ... lovely."

"Did you —"

Rugger held up his hand. "No. I wasn't interested and she wasn't interested. She just posed."

Suddenly Boxer's radio began to beep. He lifted it to his face and said, "Boxer here."

"Skipper," Cowly said, "we've got a problem."

"What is it?"

"Better get down to sick bay on the double" Cowly said. "Out."

"Roger that," Boxer answered.

"Something is going on in sick bay," Boxer said. "I'm wanted there."

"Then let's get going." Rugger answered.

The two of them ran the length of the ship and hurried down three staircases and into the sick bay.

Cowly was there with three other officers from the *Shark*.

"Better ask the doc," Cowly said.

Boxer had to take several deep breaths before he could ask, "Where is he?"

"Inside surgery."

Boxer grimaced. Not too many days before he had viewed Dee's body there and the memory of the way it had looked came full blown into his brain.

Suddenly the door opened and Doctor Klee walked in. He looked straight at Boxer. "Mister Berness hanged himself."

Boxer staggered; he felt as if he had received a blow from a giant fist.

"If Cowly hadn't found him, he'd be dead," Klee said.

Boxer heaved a deep sigh of relief.

"I just gave him a sedative," Klee said. "He has a broken neck and a broken mind. He'll be in a psychiatric hospital for a long, long time."

Boxer looked at Cowly. "Where did you find him?"

"I went to his quarters to ask him if he wanted to play a few rounds of poker. He's — was — a good player. He was hanging from one of the beams in his cabin. I cut him down and carried him here."

"Do any of you know why he tried to take his own life?" Klee asked.

"Whatever it was," Cowly said, "he kept it to himself."

The other officers agreed with Cowly.

"I'd like to speak to him," Boxer said.

"Make it fast," Klee told him. "He'll be going to sleep very soon."

Boxer started toward the door.

Klee followed him.

"I'll see him alone, Doctor," Boxer said, mustering all the authority he could into his voice.

"You're the skipper," Klee answered, putting up the palms of his hands. "The patient is all yours."

Boxer nodded and left the room. He stopped to take several deep breaths before he went into surgery.

Berness was lying on a bed behind a screen.

Boxer went directly to his side.

Berness forced his eyes open. His lips puckered and tears streamed down his face. "Couldn't handle it, Skipper. Those bodies wouldn't go away."

Boxer put his hand on Berness's forehead. "They'll go away now."

"Don't think so," Berness answered. "Don't think so. My dad always said that every man has his pack to carry, and that pack is full of things he wishes he hadn't done." He began to weep openly. "I'm sorry, Skipper... I really am. My pack is filled with twisting, turning Chinese bodies. Sometimes I can actually feel them, I think I can actually hear them. How does a man scream when he's drowning underwater? How can he scream?" He grabbed hold of Boxer's hand. "What's going to happen to me now?"

"You'll be sent to a hospital and —"

"The funny farm, eh?"

"You'll be helped," Boxer said.

"I should have died." Berness wept. "I should have died. It would have been better for my folks, my girl … everyone. And better for me."

Boxer had no words of comfort, except to tell him to sleep.

"Sleep," Berness repeated and closed his eyes. "Sleep and never wake up… that would be merciful." He took several ragged breaths and was asleep.

Boxer hurried out of surgery and back into Klee's office. "He's asleep now," he said.

"Learn anything?" Klee asked.

"Nothing," Boxer lied. He wasn't going to expose Berness's weakness in front of the other officers. Sometime in the next few days, he'd tell Klee everything he had to know about the cause of Berness's crack-up.

"An unsolved murder and now an attempted suicide … to say nothing of the storms and the destruction of something or other a few days ago… What was destroyed, Skipper?"

"I'll be in my quarters," Boxer said. He turned and left the sick bay. He was in no mood for Klee or, for that matter, anyone else. He wanted to be alone. No that wasn't exactly true. He wanted to be with Gwen.

"Jack?"

Boxer stopped and turned.

Rugger was coming up to him. "Now is a good time to look at my sketches," he said.

"I'd rather —"

Rugger took hold of his arm. "I've been just where you are now," he said. "And I'm doing for you what someone once did for me. The worst place you can be is in your quarters alone."

"Maybe you're right," Boxer said.

"I know I am," Rugger answered. "Come. You'll have a couple of drinks and I'll tell you old Nam stories while you criticize my sketches."

"In the mood I'm in I'll probably say they're all lousy."

"That's the chance I'll have to take isn't it?"

Boxer nodded and went along with him.

CHAPTER 11

When the *Tecumseh* was 200 miles off Miami, a coded radio message from Admiral Stark ordered Boxer to report immediately to him.

Boxer packed his gear quickly, said his goodbyes to the officers and men of the *Shark*, and told them they'd meet in Norfolk; then he went out on deck and bid goodbye to the people he and the men of the *Shark* had rescued.

They crowded around him. The men slapped him on the back. Several of the women wept, and two of them promised to remember him in their prayers.

Boxer thanked all of them and with his gear in hand he started toward the waiting helicopter.

"Hey, Skipper, hold it a minute!"

Boxer turned and saw Rugger running after him.

"I have something for you," Rugger said, puffing up to him. He held out a mailing tube. "I thought you'd like to have this."

"The sketch of Dee?" Boxer asked, taking the proffered tube.

Rugger nodded.

Boxer smiled. "Thanks," he said. "I intended to ask you for it the next time I came aboard."

"This saves you the trouble," Rugger answered.

The two men shook hands, and Boxer boarded the helicopter for the flight to Miami's international airport, where a Company jet was waiting to fly him to Washington.

Two and a half hours after Boxer left the *Tecumseh*, the Lear jet on which he was traveling landed at Dulles Airport, taxied up to the side of a hangar, and stopped a few feet from a waiting limousine, complete with a uniformed CPO driver who took his nylon valise and his shoulder bag and stowed them in the trunk.

Boxer settled in the back seat. The Virginia countryside was in full bloom. When he had left, several weeks before, it had been in the grip of winter.

The drive to naval headquarters took forty-five minutes.

The CPO opened the limo door and said, "I'll be here when you're finished, sir."

Boxer got out and looked at the man, who was about twenty-four, wore government-issue, white metal-framed glasses, and had two service stripes on the right sleeve of his uniform. "Have you been assigned to me?" Boxer asked.

"Aye, aye, sir," the man answered.

"What's your name, chief?"

"Paul Zweky, sir."

"Okay, Paul, since we're going to be together for a time, let's get something straight ... no more sirs. Skipper will do just fine."

"Aye, aye, Skipper."

Boxer nodded and went into the building. He knew his way to Stark's office and looked forward to seeing Cynthia Lowe, the admiral's aide. She was one of the women with whom he had something going. The other was Tracy Kimble, a reporter for the *Washington Globe*, and the third was Kathy Tyson, whom he knew less about than the other two.

Boxer walked rapidly through the warren of corridors and rode two different elevators to reach the floor where Stark's office was located. When he finally stood in front of Cynthia's desk, she was too busy to look up until he said, "Will you please tell Admiral Stark that Mister Boxer is here to —"

Her head bobbed up. "Jack?"

"Me," he answered with a broad smile. She had lovely blue eyes, and an exciting body which he knew intimately.

"I had a dream about you a few nights ago," she said.

"I hope it was worthwhile."

Her cheeks reddened.

"You'll have to tell me about it... How about tonight?"

"You have the key to the apartment," she answered in a low voice.

"Yes, I do. Do you want it back?" he teased.

"I'll tell the admiral you're here," she said, ignoring the question.

Boxer nodded.

Stark's office was Spartan. An admiral's flag was on the left side of the desk. On the walls there were pictures of famous ships. Some were paintings, others prints from the days of sail or from World War Two. A large window framed a portion of the sky and a good-size piece of ground now green with new grass. Boxer remembered the first time he'd looked out that window; the sky had been gray and the ground barren.

A cigar sticking out of the right side of his mouth, Stark crossed the room to greet him. "Just been going over your last report. Tough about Berness ... a real tough one. Just after you left the *Tecumseh* I ordered him removed. He should be arriving at the naval hospital in Bethesda a few minutes from now."

"He should never have been a submariner," Boxer said.

"The screening isn't perfect," Stark commented.

The two men walked to the desk. Stark sat down behind it and Boxer alongside and to the Admiral's right.

"Cigar?" Stark offered.

Boxer took one from the humidor.

Reaching across the desk, Stark handed him the device with which to clip the end. "I could use a drink. What about you?"

Boxer took a moment to light up before he answered, "I never turn down a good cigar or an offer of a drink."

Stark did a double take; then he smiled. "You're a lot more relaxed now," he said, leaving the desk and going to the bar on the other side of the room. "Not like the first time you were here."

"I'm already out of the navy," Boxer said.

"Give a man a little power and he goes crazy," Stark answered. "Scotch or vodka, I forgot which one?" he asked.

"Vodka now," Boxer answered. "On the rocks, please."

Stark returned and handed Boxer his glass.

"To the future," the Admiral toasted.

"To the future," Boxer echoed; then he drank.

Stark settled himself behind the desk again, rolled the cigar to the other side of his mouth, and said, "You did a fine job on Torpay."

"My men did a fine job. Hicks did a fine job. Me? Well, I just happen to have the world's best crew and the best sub ever built."

Stark nodded. "Still, you did go along for the ride, so to speak."

"Can't deny that," Boxer replied.

"All right," Stark said. "Now that we've got the bullshit out of the way, I can tell you, Jack, you're in deep shit. Kinkade is screaming for your balls. He says —"

"I don't give a fuck what he says," Boxer answered.

Stark said, "Bring the bottle over here and pour another drink for us."

Boxer nodded, went to the bar, and brought the bottle back. "Say when," he said, reaching across the desk to pour vodka into the admiral's glass.

"Two fingers would do me fine," Stark said.

"Two fingers it is."

Boxer then poured his own drink. "This time," Boxer said, lifting his glass, "let's skip the toast and just drink."

Stark nodded. "Kinkade" he said, "has demanded a formal hearing."

"He's a fucking idiot!" Boxer exploded, leaping to his feet.

"Aren't you going to hear why?"

Boxer went to the window and looked down on the large patch of green grass. "Because I went after the survivors of the downed plane," Boxer said.

"That and the fact that you wouldn't let one of his agents make contact."

Boxer turned. "What the fuck would you have done?"

"Made the same mistakes you did," Stark answered. "Does that answer satisfy you?"

Boxer returned to the chair and sat down. "Has Kinkade read the report about the Chinese sub?"

"The last I heard from him is when you reported Miss Long's murder. He's been out in the field somewhere and that somewhere could be anywhere in the fucking world."

"How does Williams stand on all of this?"

"He's less bloodthirsty than Kinkade. But he thinks the hearing will clear the air."

Boxer leaned back in the chair. "When will it be?" he asked resignedly.

"You're going to have to stand by for it. As quickly as possible, I hope. I want to get this matter out of the way."

"That's something I'll drink to," Boxer said, lifting his glass and finishing the vodka.

"Is there anything you didn't put in the report, anything not on the operating tapes?" Stark asked. "Anything that Kinkade might be able to beat you over the head with, should it surface during the hearing?"

Boxer hesitated for a few moments.

"Better let me know, whatever it is," Stark said.

"The place where Dee was murdered might give him a fit," Boxer said, surprised that Klee hadn't mentioned it in his medical report.

Stark raised his eyebrows. "Where?"

"In my bed," Boxer answered.

"That will sure as shit buy you a big fucking problem," Stark said. "One way or another, Kinkade will find out about it. As it is, he holds you responsible for the fact that a murder was committed aboard the *Shark*."

"The circumstances were extraordinary. I could explain them to you, if you want me to."

"Don't bother. I'll probably have to hear your explanation at the hearing. But believe me, if Kinkade could find a way to blame the murder on you, he'd do it."

"That bad?"

"That bad," Stark said. "Now is there anything else I should know?"

"I can't think of anything."

"I'm damn glad of that," Stark said. "Damn glad! Now why the hell don't you get out of here and do whatever it is you want to do."

"The *Shark* will be going into dry dock. I'll be busy with that for a while. I asked for Monty and Pierce to be assigned for the repairs."

"They'll be there. I'll let you know when she's in dry dock. I assume I can contact you at the usual places?"

"Yes," Boxer answered.

The two men stood up.

"You know," Stark said, "that Chinese sub you sank had been spotted off the West African coast a few days before you got her."

"By whom?"

"You know I can't answer that," Stark said. "But I will tell you our sources say that she was certainly on an intelligence-gathering mission. By the way, so far her government doesn't know she's missing."

"Even if they did know it, they wouldn't acknowledge it, at least not to the rest of the world."

"You're right there," Stark answered.

The men walked to the door.

"Thanks for being so candid with me," Boxer said. "I really appreciate it."

"You're a good officer," Stark said. "Maybe a bit too far from the usual mold for some people's taste, but if you weren't, I wouldn't have given you command of the *Shark*, regardless of how many times the computer at BUPERS came up with your name."

"Thanks for being in my corner," Boxer said.

They shook hands.

Stark opened the door and Boxer left the office. A moment later he was standing in front of Cynthia's desk. "I'll see you at your place."

She looked up at him, and smiling, she said, "If you pick up a couple of steaks and the fixin's, I'll make dinner. I'd rather spend the evening at home than go out to a restaurant."

Boxer nodded. "Anything else you want me to pick up?"

"Nothing I can think of now."

"See you," Boxer said and walked away from the desk. Several minutes later, he was back in the limo on his way to Cynthia's apartment, where he'd probably stay for a few days, before checking into a hotel.

Boxer fished his pipe out of his pocket, filled and lit it. Stark was turning out to be more than just his CO, he was fast becoming a good friend and that was something Boxer never would have expected, either from the man's reputation, or from their first meeting after the collision between the *Sting Ray* and the *Mary-Ann*.

On the way to Cynthia's apartment, Boxer stopped at a large supermarket and bought steaks and the vegetables necessary to make a salad; then he went into a package store and purchased a bottle of a Bordeaux.

"Will you give me a hand with these packages?" Boxer asked Paul, when they stopped in front of the building where Cynthia lived.

"Sure thing, Skipper," Paul answered. "I'll take your gear from the trunk."

"Thanks," Boxer answered.

The two rode the elevator together to the sixth floor. Boxer unlocked the door and said, "Drop my gear down anywhere. How about a drink?"

"I'm still officially on duty," Paul answered.

"You're not. I won't be needing you until tomorrow morning about, oh, ten-thirty, or so. What are you drinking, sailor?"

"A shot of anything that goes down smooth," Paul answered.

Boxer went into the kitchen, opened the closet over the sink, and found a bottle of Chivas. He poured a shot for himself and one for Paul.

"Thanks, Skipper," Paul said.

Boxer nodded and drank.

Paul handed the empty glass to him. "See you in the morning."

Boxer walked him to the door and opened it for him. "Don't get itchy if I'm late."

"I have nothin' to do but drive you, Skipper," Paul said. "Thanks for the drink."

Boxer closed the door and walked back into the apartment, which consisted of a living room, a dining room, and a kitchenette. Reproductions of famous paintings were on the walls, the same ones that had been on them the first time he'd been in the apartment. Then he hadn't known any of them. But now he not only knew the names of all the paintings, he also knew the names of the artists who had painted them.

Boxer brought the two empty shot glasses back to the kitchen and washed them; then he went into the bedroom and phoned his parents to tell them he'd be visiting them in a few days. After he spoke to them, Boxer called Gwen at the studio where she was filming another episode for the TV series, *Another Universe*.

"I'm terribly sorry," her secretary said, "but Miss Holcomb is on the set and won't be finished with the day's shooting for several hours. Is there a number where she would be able to reach you?"

"No," Boxer answered. "Just say her ex-husband called." He hung up. He was disappointed; he wanted to speak with Gwen. He had hoped to see her and John when he went to New York to see his parents.

"Hell," he said out loud, "I want to sleep with her again!" They had spent the night together just before he had left on the mission. That had been the first time in almost a half a year that he had made love to his ex-wife.

Boxer shook his head, not to deny he was still in love with Gwen, though it was almost three years since they had been divorced, but rather to deny the possibility that the relationship now existing between them was hopeless.

To busy himself, Boxer returned to the kitchen and prepared the salad from the vegetables he had bought. When the salad was ready, he coated each of the steaks with a mixture of mustard and catsup and placed them in the refrigerator. Then he helped himself to a bottle of beer and went into the living room. Boxer turned on the TV and found an old flick to watch. He stretched out on the couch. Within a few minutes his eyelids had become too heavy to keep open, and sighing deeply, he allowed them to close.

Suddenly, Boxer felt something brush gently over his lips. He opened his eyes and found himself looking up at Cynthia's smiling face.

"When I came home, I found you asleep and decided to surprise you." She moved just far enough away for him to look at her. "Do you like my surprise?" She was nude.

"That's like asking a thirsty man, if he'd like a cool drink of water," Boxer said, reaching for her.

She went willingly into his arms. "Are you hungrier than you are thirsty, or more thirsty than you are hungry?"

He drew her face down to his and, kissing her on the lips, eased his tongue into her mouth, while his hands gently squeezed her breasts.

The two of them suddenly began to roll off the couch.

"I was afraid something like that would happen." Cynthia laughed, as she went down.

"Never gave it a thought," Boxer said, following her and landing not too gently on top of her.

"Now what my lover man? Do we pick ourselves up and break this marvelously romantic spell?"

"And do what?" Boxer asked.

"We have three options, as I see it. We can continue and try to recapture the magic; we can pick ourselves up and head for the bedroom and try again; or we can pick ourselves up, have dinner, and wait until the magic strikes again."

"Are you sure the magic will strike again?"

"Certain ... absolutely certain," she answered. "I have ways of making it strike again."

"What do you want to do?" Boxer asked.

"You're my guest," she answered. "I'll do whatever you want me to do."

"Passion is passion, but man does not live by passion alone. Some food would certainly increase and sustain his passion."

"Then if you'd be so good as to get off me and help me up," Cynthia said with feigned dignity, "I'll see to putting some food on the table for you."

Boxer stood up, reached down, and with one swift movement, pulled Cynthia to her feet.

Heading for the bedroom, she said, "I'm going to put a robe on."

"Don't," he said. "I like you just the way you are."

"Come on, Jack."

"Remember, I'm a guest!"

She shrugged.

"Have it your way," she said as she padded, barefoot, into the kitchen. "I'll put the steaks in the microwave; they'll be done in five minutes. You want soup?"

"What kind?"

"Vegetable, chicken with noodle, or minestrone ... all fresh out of a can."

"Vegetable sounds fine," Boxer said, fixing his shirt and zipping up his fly. "I'm going to wash."

"You have time for a quick shower, if you want one. I put out extra towels for you and a terrycloth bathrobe. It's on the bed."

"Thanks," Boxer said, going into the bedroom. What he loved most about Cynthia was her thoughtfulness. Of all the women with whom he'd had sex, she was the only one who would wake him the way she had, or think of putting out a terrycloth robe for him.

Boxer stripped and showered. Within five minutes he was back in the living room. "Fits," he said, drawing the robe's white cowl over his head.

"No fair," Cynthia protested. "I'm bare-ass naked and you look like some damn religious nut."

"That's what makes it sexy as hell," he said, going behind her, placing his hands on her breasts, and drawing her back against him.

She let herself be taken. "It's your beard," she told him in a throaty voice, "that makes you look so satanic."

"And here I thought it was my eyes," he said, nuzzling the left side of her face and flicking his tongue against her ear.

"Those too," she answered.

She turned and looked at him over her shoulder. "I didn't put the steaks up yet and I can shut the gas off under the soup."

Boxer eased his hands down her naked body.

She trembled. "Do you still want to eat?" Cynthia asked.

"Not food," Boxer answered. Scooping her into his arms, he carried her into the bedroom and deposited her gently on the bed; then he stripped off the terry cloth robe and let it fall on the floor.

CHAPTER 12

The day was gray and a cold wind was blowing out of Siberia the morning the *Q-21* entered Vladivostok's harbor. Lieutenant Popov had the CONN, while Borodine stood, frowning, on the bridge. Earlier, just after he had ordered the *Sea Savage* to surface, he had received a message from Admiral of the Fleet Gorshkov to report without delay to him in Moscow. Without delay meant just that. He'd have just enough time to tell Galena he was leaving for Moscow, and he knew she wasn't going to like that. He didn't like it. After this cruise, he desperately wanted to spend time with Galena, to make love to her, and to have her make love to him. But there was nothing he could do but obey.

"The harbor isn't too busy this morning," Viktor said, looking at him. "Except for the gulls; they're always busy."

Borodine wasn't even aware that Viktor had joined them topside. "I'm ordered to report to Moscow immediately," he said.

Viktor shook his head. "Markov's work?" he asked.

Borodine shrugged. "No reason given, just the order to report immediately."

"How's Popov doing?" he asked, dropping his voice to a whisper before speaking.

"So far we haven't run into anything," Borodine answered. "He's following the book and is keeping us on the right side of the channel."

"Are you going to let him take us dockside?"

"Might as well," Borodine answered. "He's got to lose his cherry sometime. This is as good as any. The wind might make it a bit tricky, but a little sweat wouldn't hurt him. It'll teach him that very few things are the way the book says they are."

"That's for sure!" Viktor commented.

For several minutes, the two men said nothing. Then a large tanker slid past them, outward bound and riding high in the water. The three officers on the *Sea Savage*'s bridge and the men on the tanker waved to each other.

"It's a good bet she's going to Libya or Iraq," Viktor said; then he added. "Not bad duty on a ship like that, with women in the crew."

"I've been thinking about the *Tecumseh*," Borodine said. "The more I think about her, the more certain I am that she's the *Shark*'s mother ship."

"I'm talking about women, or at least I'm trying to," Viktor said, screwing up his face, "and you tell me that you've been thinking about the *Tecumseh*. I hope to get a good lascivious conversation going between us, and —"

"You talk a good game when it comes to women," Borodine said, "but I don't think you play as good as you talk."

"That's because you're a married man and have never been out at night with me," Viktor answered with a smile.

Borodine smiled, "You had better announce to the crew that liberty will commence at fourteen hundred hours today. All those applying for transit permits to other parts of the country must clear their requests with Captain Markov. Those staying in port will follow the usual rules and regulations. Remind the crew they must say nothing about the *Shark* to anyone."

Popov saluted and Borodine returned the salute.

"First thing, I'm going to do," Viktor said, "when I get ashore, is —"

Borodine held up his hand. "Spare me the details of your sexual desires."

"I was going to say," Viktor laughed, "that I was going to get into a hot tub and stay there for an hour or two. You can't imagine how much I've thought about having a nice hot tub." Then with a laugh, he added, "Of course it would be nicer, much nicer, if there happened to be a beautiful woman in it."

"You're impossible!" Borodine exclaimed. "I'm going below. I've got to leave for Moscow sometime this afternoon."

The government car pulled up in front of Borodine's house. He and his wife Galena lived in a small, yellow brick house at the end of Pushkin Street. Their house was exactly the same as all the other houses on that street, or, for that matter, in the area nicknamed the Kremlin by the people of Vladivostok because the houses were occupied only by government people.

Each two-story house was situated in the center of a small plot of land. The lower floor consisted of a small kitchen and a living room; the upper part had two rooms of equal size and a bathroom. The rooms were painted white, and curtains were hung on the windows. Each house had a small garden in front and a small vegetable patch in back. Borodine, like a great many men who went to sea, enjoyed working in the garden.

"I'll be out shortly," Borodine told the young woman driver. "Then we'll go straight to the airport."

"Aye, aye, Comrade Captain," she answered smartly. "My orders are to remain with you until dismissed." She looked back at him and smiled; then she got out of the car and opened the door for him.

Borodine strode up to the door, unlocked and opened it.

Galena ran down the steps and into his arms.

He kissed her fiercely on the mouth. She had a slight apple taste and smelled sweet, like roses.

"Oh, how I've missed you," she sighed. "Come upstairs and—"

"I must go to Moscow," Borodine said.

"When?"

"Now," he answered. "There's a flight leaving at fifteen hundred hours."

"I'll go with you!"

"This is a military plane," he said. He didn't want to tell her that it was a bomber that was going on a routine, long-distance training mission.

Galena stepped away from him, and shaking her head, she said, "I hate everything about this place — everything. And now you're going away again."

"I'll be home as soon as I can," Borodine answered.

"So, what will that mean? You'll be home for a day. A week. For how long?"

He opened his hands. "Please," he said, "don't become upset."

"I am past being upset. I am angry, hurt, and frustrated. I hate this place. I hate the life I lead. I hate the people I'm forced to live next to, and most of all I hate what you're doing." By now she was screaming.

Borodine was sure that the neighbors could hear everything she said and that one of them would surely report them to the local KGB representative. Every section in the development had one.

"Please Galena, I —"

"I hate it," she screamed. "I live in fear that someday you won't come home, that someday a government official will come and tell me something has happened to you."

Borodine said nothing. He couldn't assure her that it wouldn't happen.

"Igor… Igor… Igor." She wept and threw herself into his arms. "I love you. I can't bear these separations. I want to live like a normal woman."

He held her tightly and kissed her forehead. "I'll bring you something beautiful from Moscow," he said, trying to placate her. "Tell me what you want?"

"Only you," she whispered. "Only you." She looked up at him. "I want you so much," she said in a low, urgent voice.

"I'll be home in a few days," he said, knowing he couldn't be sure of that, that he might be kept in Moscow for weeks, or months, depending on why he was being called there in the first place.

Galena moved away from him. She shook her head. "You just don't understand."

"I do … I really do. But there's nothing I can do about it. You know that."

"I don't know that," she suddenly shrieked. "I only know that I'm sick to death of the life I'm leading. There's a better way of living. Maybe the other wives here don't know it, but I know that. The way we lived in the United States —"

"Shut up. Shut up!" Borodine shouted. "What do you want to do? The neighbors have ears and the way you're screaming —"

"I don't care. I don't care anymore," she shouted.

"We'll settle this when I come home," Borodine said sharply. "Now I have to go."

"Then go!"

Borodine hesitated. Never before had he left Galena without holding her in his arms and telling her how much he loved her. But now he was too angry and too upset to make any movement toward her.

"You said you have to go; then go!" she yelled.

Borodine nodded, did a military about-face, and left the house, slamming the door behind him. He strode to the car without looking back over his shoulder.

"The airport," he said to the driver who stood at attention alongside the open door of the car.

"Aye, aye, sir," she answered.

Borodine settled into the rear of the car. He was furious with Galena and just as furious with himself for not being more forceful with her. He had spoiled her. He regretted having taken her to the United States. He should have let her stay with her parents, but three years would have been an intolerable length of time to have been separated from her.

Borodine dug into his coat pocket and pulled out a pack of cigarettes. He took one, lit it, and let it dangle from the right side of his lips. He hated arguing with Galena and seldom did. Very few things were worth arguing about. But this time she had pushed him too far. "Much too far," he said aloud.

"I'm sorry, Comrade Captain," the driver said, glancing back at Borodine, "I didn't hear you?"

"I asked how far to the airport," he lied.

"Another twenty kilometers, at least," she answered.

"Thank you," Borodine said, noticing that she was looking at him in the rear-view mirror. He wondered how much of his argument with Galena she had heard. Probably all... Suddenly, he felt very uncomfortable, as if he had been caught in some very private act. He had been. An argument between a husband and wife is a private matter.

Borodine stubbed out the cigarette he was smoking and lit another one. He wasn't going to let himself be intimidated by the driver. "What's your name, sailor?" he asked.

"Luba Baku," she answered.

"Where are you from?" Borodine asked.

"Stalingrad," she answered.

"How long have you been in the navy?"

"Three years."

Borodine puffed vigorously on his cigarette. He had run out of questions.

"We'll be at the airport in about five minutes, Comrade Captain," Luba said.

"Thank you," Borodine replied and stubbed out his cigarette. He was still angry with Galena and found himself wondering what would happen if one of the neighbors did report her to the KGB, or if the house was wired. It could be and he wouldn't know it was.

The airport came into view. It was huge, serving both military and civilian aircraft. There were signs along the road cautioning drivers about low-flying aircraft, though Borodine couldn't understand what a driver was supposed to do if he saw a low-flying plane. He considered posing the question to Luba. After all, she was a navy driver and might know the answer. But he decided against it.

A few minutes later, Luba stopped the car in front of the operations building, got out, and opened the door for Borodine.

"You may return to the base," he said.

"Perhaps, Comrade Captain, I should wait a few more minutes until you are sure that your flight will leave," Luba suggested.

He nodded and walked into the building. A few minutes later Borodine was involved in a heated dispute with Lieutenant Sergei Fyodor, the transportation officer.

"I know you were supposed to leave this afternoon," Lieutenant Fyodor said. "But the plane you were to be on will not leave for another ten hours."

"My orders are to be in Moscow —"

"Comrade Captain, there's nothing I can do … absolutely nothing. I have taken the liberty of calling the admiral's office to inform him about your delay."

"Are you certain there isn't another flight?"

"Absolutely," Fyodor answered.

Borodine looked at the clock on the wall behind the transportation officer's desk. It was fourteen hundred hours. "The plane is scheduled to leave at midnight, is that right?"

"As things stand now, yes. But you know that could change."

"I'll be here at midnight," Borodine said, "and then I want a plane to take me to Moscow. I don't care if I have to fly a thousand miles out of my way. Do you understand, lieutenant?"

"I understand, Comrade Captain," Fyodor answered.

Borodine nodded, turned away from the desk. He walked swiftly out of the building and to the car. "The flight has been delayed for ten hours," he fumed and dropped down in the rear seat.

Luba got into the car, and easing it away from the curb, she asked, "Do you want me to return to your home, Comrade Captain?"

"Yes … no," Borodine said. "No … just drive."

"Where?"

"Wherever you want to," Borodine answered gruffly. "Wherever the hell you want to!"

"Aye, aye, Comrade Captain," Luba said.

For an instant, Borodine thought she was laughing at him. He glanced up at the rear-view mirror. She wasn't even smiling. Still there was something in the sound of her voice that suggested laughter. He lit a cigarette and looked out the window. The drizzle had stopped but it was still a gray day.

Borodine became aware that they were slowing down. "Where are we?" he asked.

"About fifty kilometers south of the city," Luba answered. She stopped the car in front of a two-story building. "It's a country inn," she explained. "Serves a delicious combination of Russian and Oriental food."

"You've been here before?"

She nodded.

Borodine realized the question was stupid. How would she have known where it was and the kind of food served if she hadn't been there?

"I thought you might be hungry," Luba said.

Borodine nodded. "The last time I ate was at zero five thirty this morning."

Luba got out of the car and opened the door for Borodine. "I'm sure you'll find the food very good," she said, accompanying him inside.

Borodine stopped just inside the door. It took several moments for his eyes to become accustomed to the dim light. The main room was large. Huge, blackened rough-hewn timbers supported a low, equally rough wooden ceiling, the chinks of which were filled with dried clay. A large fire blazed in the stone hearth set into the wall opposite the door. The room was filled with long wooden tables and chairs instead of those of the usual size. There was sawdust on the floor, and two small windows, high up on the right wall, were so begrimed with soot that the gray light passing through them was several shades darker on the inside than it was on the outside.

But the smell of food was so delicious that Borodine found himself inhaling deeply and salivating. He turned to Luba and said, "From the looks of it, we're the only ones here."

"It's early," Luba answered, glancing at her watch. "By seventeen hundred it will be hard to find a place to sit. Besides those who come here from the city, a good many local people come here to eat and drink."

Borodine accepted the explanation without comment, and as he started for the table closest to the fireplace, he suddenly became aware of a small, wizened man standing a short distance from him. "Who is he?"

"Ubaki," Luba said. "He and his wife Kuppia own the inn." Borodine motioned to Ubaki.

"It is a pleasure to see you again," Ubaki said, smiling up at Luba.

"This is Comrade Captain Borodine," Luba said, introducing Borodine.

"A pleasure to have you visit my humble inn," Ubaki said, bowing deeply from the waist.

"The pleasure is mine," Borodine answered. "Comrade — I mean Luba has praised your food to me."

"May my food be equal to her praise," Ubaki said. "Please choose the table you desire."

"The one near the fireplace," Borodine answered.

"I will have your coats, please?" Ubaki said.

Borodine quickly slipped out of his greatcoat and helped Luba with hers.

Ubaki gestured toward the table. "I will bring wine and vodka. The food here is simple, Comrade Captain. There's soup and there are raw fish of various kinds and three different meat dishes. You may taste of all three, or none as you choose."

Borodine nodded and gently taking hold of Luba's arm, he steered her to the table. "You will dine with me," he said.

"Is that an order, Comrade Captain?" Luba asked.

"No. It's a request," Borodine answered.

"Then I'll dine with you," Luba responded.

"Would you prefer to sit with your back to the fire or facing it?" Borodine asked.

"Facing it," she answered.

"Please sit," Borodine said, settling himself on the bench facing her. He looked around, smiled and said, "This would have been the last kind of place I'd have imagined myself to be in today. Chances are, even if I knew it existed, I'd have passed it by."

Luba nodded understandingly. "What really matters," she said with a smile, "is that you're now here and I'm certain, once you've tasted the food, you'll return."

A bent woman as wizened as Ubaki came to the table carrying a wooden tray on which stood two hand-fired gray goblets for the wine and two small glasses for the vodka, a large carafe of red wine and one of brown vodka. "The vodka," she said, placing a goblet in front of Borodine and one in front of Luba, "is very cold." She smiled broadly, showing her toothless gums. "I will bring the soup, when you call for it."

"Thank you, mother," Borodine said politely.

She placed the two carafes on the table. "Enjoy your food and drink," she said, moving slowly away.

"That was Kuppia," Luba said.

"I guessed as much," Borodine said; then he asked, "Vodka or wine?"

"Vodka, please."

Borodine poured vodka for Luba and himself. "To a good future," he toasted, lifting his glass. Suddenly, he found himself very much aware of Luba. Until that moment he had scarcely looked at her, but with the fire casting its reddish light over her, he realized she was a beautiful woman with long honey-colored hair, a small mouth, red lips, and dimpled cheeks. The regulation dark blue skirt and jacket didn't hide her totally feminine body.

"Is anything wrong?" Luba asked, flushing under his stare.

"I'm sorry," Borodine said. "I know this is hard to believe, but until a few moments ago, I had no idea what you looked like."

"You had other things to occupy you," she answered.

"Still do," he said. "But let's drink."

They touched glasses and drank.

After three more vodkas, Kuppia brought two bowls of piping hot soup to the table. "That will warm your bones," she grinned.

"It's so thick I can stand my spoon up in it." Borodine laughed. He knew it was a combination of beans and vegetables, generously larded with meat and bits of bacon — perhaps, even bits of sausage — but the overall taste was absolutely unique.

Luba unbuttoned her jacket.

Borodine found himself looking at her breasts.

"You're staring again," she said.

Borodine flushed and apologized. He glanced at his watch. He still had seven hours before flight time — seven hours to spend with Luba, unless he sent her away.

"Tell me, Comrade Captain, do you like being aboard a submarine?"

Borodine nodded and noticed a few more customers had sat down at the benches.

"I was at sea on a destroyer and an icebreaker," she said. "I liked the destroyer better. But the captain of the icebreaker was nicer to sleep with. He was gentler."

Borodine poured himself another vodka and offered to pour one for Luba.

"I'll switch to the wine," she said and, picking up the carafe of wine, filled the goblet.

Kuppia came back, with the raw fish, done Japanese style.

"This is delicious, isn't it?" Luba asked.

"Absolutely," Borodine answered; then he asked, "Have you a boyfriend." He guessed she had many.

"Not anyone steady," she answered, popping a round filet of fish into her mouth. "I'm not ready to think seriously about marriage, and a steady boyfriend means a routine. You know what I mean, don't you?"

Borodine didn't exactly know what she meant, but he pretended that he did and nodded vigorously.

"I hate it when love becomes routine," Luba commented.

Borodine had no comment.

Kuppia brought three meat dishes to the table. One was a stew; the second, braised lamb shank; and the third; roast pork. Each was incredibly seasoned with a combination of herbs that defied description but excited the palate.

"A place like this in Moscow would make a fortune," Borodine commented.

"Is that where you were born?" Luba asked.

"Yes. My father is an engineer and my mother a schoolteacher."

"Any brothers and sisters?"

"None," Borodine answered.

"I have three brothers and three sisters. I'm in the middle. One of my brothers is in flight training with the air force; the other two are factory workers."

Between the two of them, they completely devoured the three meat dishes.

"The dessert is simple … just babka and a choice of tea or coffee," Luba explained.

Borodine asked for tea when Kuppia returned to the table.

"I'll have coffee," Luba said.

A few minutes later they sat in front of empty cups and Borodine said, "I can't remember a time when I had such delicious food. Now what I could really do is go to sleep for a few hours."

"You still have time, Comrade Captain, to go home and sleep," Luba said.

Though the expression on her face remained the same, Borodine caught a challenge in the tone of her voice. And he rose to it. "No, I don't want to go home," he said.

"What do you want to do, Comrade Captain?" she asked.

Borodine took a deep breath, reached across the table, and taking hold of Luba's hands, he said, "Sleep with you!"

She smiled broadly. "And I with you, Comrade Captain."

"Here?"

"Here," Luba answered.

Borodine caught Kuppia's eye, and when she came to the table, he said, "Mother I'd like to have a room upstairs for a few hours."

She nodded. "I will tell my husband."

By the time Borodine and Luba left the table to go upstairs, several people were waiting to be seated.

Ubaki held a lantern in his right hand.

Borodine and Luba followed the old man up a narrow flight of steps and along a short hallway.

"Your room, Comrade Captain," Ubaki said, opening the door.

Borodine took the lantern from him. "Thank you," Borodine responded.

"I will summon you at twenty-two hundred hours," Ubaki said.

"No later," Borodine cautioned.

Ubaki nodded and left them.

Borodine gestured to Luba to enter and, following her in, held the lantern aloft and looked around.

The room was as rustic as the downstairs. A single old-fashioned, highly polished brass bed took up almost the entire space. Folded at the foot of the bed was a large goose-down blanket and at the head were two goose-down pillows. There was a wicker chair in one corner, and against one wall stood an old dresser with a mirror attached to it. A fireplace was built into the other wall. The flames from the fire cast a reddish light over everything in the room. The window was curtainless, but there was a white shade on it.

Borodine closed the door behind him and, crossing the room, looked into the bathroom that had an ancient but usable tub supported by four cast-iron eagles, a small sink, and a commode. Everything in both rooms was spotlessly clean.

Borodine placed the lantern on the dresser and turned it up. "What do you think?" he asked Luba, knowing that if Galena were with him, she would have been unhappy with the room.

"It's what I expected," Luba answered, "only much cleaner."

Borodine nodded and took a deep breath. This was his first time alone with a woman other than Galena since she had agreed to marry him over seven years ago.

"Is anything wrong?" she asked.

"No… No," he answered, feeling stupid. He wanted a cigarette, but was afraid his hands would tremble.

"Well, here we are," Luba said.

"Yes."

She smiled at him.

"I think I'll open the window," Borodine said.

"Comrade Captain —"

"My name is Igor."

"Igor, we don't need the window open," Luba said. "We need another piece of wood on the fire; then we need to —"

"I'll put the wood on the fire," Borodine said, moving quickly across the room to the hearth. He placed a log across the andirons, and when he stood up and turned, Luba was standing directly in front of him.

Her blouse was unbuttoned and the bare tops of her breasts were plainly visible.

She reached down, took hold of his hands, and placed them on her breasts. "Don't be nervous," she said in a whisper.

He wanted to deny that he was; but instead, he slid her blouse off and, reaching around to her back, undid her bra and eased it down, uncovering her full, high breasts.

Borodine placed his hands over her bare breasts. They were firm and warm.

"Do you want to undress me, Igor?" Luba asked, sultry now.

For a moment, he couldn't find his voice; then he said, "I'm all thumbs when it comes to hooks."

"You didn't have much trouble with my bra," she teased.

"Luck," he answered, aware of the bizarre conversation they were having.

Luba stepped away from him, unzipped her skirt, and let it drift to the floor; then she deftly stepped out of it. She took off her shoes; and hooking her thumbs in the waistband of her white half-slip, she pushed it down over the flare of her hips, letting it fall to the floor.

"You want to do the rest?" she asked.

Borodine started for her.

She put up her hands. "No ... first you undress."

Borodine nodded. He took off his jacket and tie, and hung them on the bathroom doorknob. His shirt and undershirt followed. He removed his shoes and stockings; and then his pants, which he folded and carefully draped over the top of the bathroom door. He faced her and asked, "Now?"

She nodded and extended her arms toward him. "Now there's no rank ... no navy. Now we are just a man and a woman."

Borodine went to her and embraced her, kissing her passionately on the mouth.

When Borodine came back to reality, he glanced at his watch. At the very most fifteen minutes had passed since they had gotten into bed. But in that fifteen minutes, he had experienced such intense physical pleasure that it would be a long time before he'd forget it. He pushed the hair out of her face and kissed her passionately on the lips.

CHAPTER 13

Boxer flew up to New York to see his parents and, hopefully, to spend some time with Gwen and his son John, although he hadn't been able to speak to Gwen, even after five phone calls, and he was beginning to get a very pronounced feeling that she didn't want to talk to him. He also wanted to pay a visit to Dee's parents.

He took the first Eastern flight out of Washington in the morning and planned to spend two or three days in the city. The actual flying time should have been forty-five minutes, but because of a storm moving up the coast from Cape Hatteras, where it had developed during the night, the plane spent almost two hours in the air. It was so severely buffeted by the winds that many of the passengers became ill.

Because of the storm, the plane was diverted to Newark Airport, in New Jersey, though it was supposed to land at La Guardia.

During the plane's final approach, it was raining so hard that Boxer, who occupied a window seat, couldn't see anything outside and only knew they were down when the wheels slammed into the concrete runway and he was almost thrown from the seat despite the fact that he was wearing a safety belt.

From Newark, he and three other passengers shared a taxi into New York, where he stopped to phone his parents. "I'll be at the house in about an hour or so," he told his father.

"In time for lunch?" he heard his mother inquire in the background.

"Tell Mom I'll be there for lunch," Boxer said. After he spoke to his father, he phoned Gwen at the studio.

"I'm sorry Mister Boxer, Miss Holcomb is on the set and —
"

"Listen," Boxer said, "you tell Miss Holcomb that I'm in New York and I'll be at the apartment at six tonight."

"But —"

Boxer was more than irritated: he was angry. "But nothing. Just give her the message."

" Miss Holcomb is leaving for Mexico City at eleven o'clock tonight," the secretary said. "She just won't be able to see you until she returns."

"I'll be at the apartment," Boxer answered and hung up. Absolutely no one could get him as angry as Gwen did when she wanted to be difficult. He left the phone booth and started to walk toward Fifth Avenue on Forty-second Street.

The cab had taken Boxer and the other three men to the Port Authority Terminal on Eighth Avenue and Forty-second Street. The cabbie would not be persuaded to go anywhere else in the city, claiming that he didn't know the streets. But Boxer was sure the man was really afraid to drive in the city. He couldn't blame him: traffic was always heavy and always snarled.

The rain had stopped and Forty-second Street was soon filled with people, most of whom were sleazy-looking types.

Boxer walked slowly, trying hard not to be angry or disappointed. But he was and he saw no point in trying to convince himself that he wasn't.

Several times he was approached by women, who were selling themselves, or by men who were selling drugs, watches, and other items that probably had been stolen. Not once did Boxer have to speak. All he had to do was look at them and the sellers, whether prostitutes or drug dealers, turned away.

Suddenly Boxer spotted an open bar. Though it was only 1100 hours, he decided he could use a drink.

Boxer settled on a stool close to the door and took a few moments to look around. There were two men in a booth and two at the bar. The place smelled of sour beer and last night's cigarette smoke. The barkeep, a short, pudgy man, wore a dirty white apron.

"Whatta yer drinkin', mister?" the barkeep asked.

"Scotch — no, better make it vodka on the rocks," Boxer said. The barkeep started to move away.

"Make it Stolichnaya," Boxer said.

"Don't carry that Russian shit," the man said. "Drink American."

"Then make it Finlandia," Boxer told him.

The barkeep came back to where Boxer was seated. "Drink American," he said, "or don't drink here."

"Just give me a vodka on the rocks," Boxer said.

"Shit man," the barkeep said, "you ain't doin' me a favor by drinkin' here."

"Shit man," Boxer answered, "I don't have to drink here!" And he started to stand up.

"You got some kinda problem, mister?" one of the men at the bar asked.

Boxer didn't look at the man but he saw his reflection in the mirror behind the bar. He was a tall, rangy man with a pinched face.

"Dis guy is probably a communist," the barkeep said.

"Is dat so!" the rangy man said, advancing toward Boxer.

"I don't want any trouble," Boxer said, turning around.

"You shoulda thought of dat before youse came in here," the rangy man answered.

Boxer took a deep breath.

"Now," the rangy man said, "youse goin' ta learn da hard way." He put his hand into his pocket and brought out a switchblade knife. "Maybe if you lose some blood you'll remember ta drink American next time."

"You're making a mistake," Boxer said. "Now put away the knife and go back to your stool. I'll even buy you a round."

The man grinned at him. "Mister, when I get done wid you, you ain't goin' ta be buying anyone anything. You goin' ta be in da hospital gettin' yourself sewed together."

Boxer eased to the left of the stool.

The man slashed at him.

Boxer waited until the blade almost cut him; then he grabbed hold of the man's hand and stopped it. "Drop the knife," Boxer said, bending the man's hand back. "Drop it!"

"Fuck you!" the man answered, struggling to be free.

Boxer forced the man's hand back.

He screamed in pain; then his fingers opened and the knife fell from his hand.

Boxer kicked the knife away, let go of the man's hand, and with a quick chop to the side of his neck, he dropped him to the floor.

"I told you," Boxer said, "you were making a mistake." He looked back at the barkeep. "Your friend is going to have a hand and neck that will hurt for a while. Tell him next time I come in and he pulls a knife on me, I'll kill him."

The barkeep's jaw dropped.

"I didn't hear anything," Boxer said.

"Sure, sure I'll tell 'im," the barkeep answered.

Boxer nodded. He walked out of the saloon, knowing that he was lucky. Had he not known how to take care of himself, he would have wound up in the hospital.

He walked up to Seventh Avenue, hailed a cab and gave the driver his parents' address; then he settled back and tried to relax before he saw his mother and father.

By 12:30, Boxer was at the small, white table in his mother's kitchen having lunch with her and his father. The sliding door leading to the deck was open.

"You look wonderful," his mother had said. "But tired."

Boxer nodded. "I've had a great many things to keep me busy over the past few weeks, but now the *Tecumseh* will be in Norfolk for a while and so will I."

"Then we'll have the chance to see more of you?" his father asked.

"I won't promise anything," Boxer said, "but I'll certainly try." He did not like to make a promise and then go back on his word because the proverbial "something" came along.

His mother was a petite woman, with green eyes and finely chiseled features, who looked at least ten years younger than her sixty-two years. She frowned but said nothing.

Boxer looked questioningly at his father.

"That was fine chicken salad," his father said. "But I couldn't eat another morsel of it."

"What about you?" his mother asked, looking at her son.

"Not me," Boxer answered. "I'm stuffed."

Mrs. Boxer brought coffee and blueberry pie to the table. "I baked it last night," she said. "I had a feeling you'd be coming to visit us soon."

"That I'll eat," Boxer answered.

After the coffee and pie, Mrs. Boxer asked, "Have you seen that lovely Miss Tyson again?"

Boxer smiled. "Come on, Mom, give me a chance. I'm only back a few days."

"Are you going to see Gwen?" his father asked.

"I don't know," Boxer answered. "I've tried calling and I can't get through."

"What do you mean?" his mother asked.

"I don't think she wants to talk to me," Boxer said, facing the situation honestly. "I don't think she wants to see me."

"But why?"

Boxer stood up, fished out his pipe, and lit it before he answered. "Before I left, we spent the night together and —"

"And?" his father urged.

Boxer looked at his mother. She was frowning. His eyes went to his father. Between them there was more than just the father-son relationship. His father was his best friend.

"Maybe it's none of our business," his father suggested.

"I think," Boxer began, "that we can still have a sexual relationship but ... but I don't think Gwen wants to be part of my life."

"And you still love her?" his mother asked.

"I never wanted to divorce her," Boxer answered. He turned, opened the screen door, and walked out onto the wooden deck overlooking the small yard.

The two Lombardy poplars and the red Japanese maple were already fully leafed, as were all of the other bushes. Along both sides a colorful variety of tulips and begonias looked as if they were ready to bloom.

Boxer felt his father's hand on his shoulder.

"I'm sorry about you and Gwen," his father said. "I guess some marriages just aren't meant to be, but I'd have to admit that I was hoping yours would come together and —"

"So was I, Dad," Boxer said. "So was I."

For a while neither of them spoke; then his father said, "Let's go down into the yard. I have something to show you." Boxer nodded and walked down the steps.

His father led him to the far end of the yard and said, "Mom would never tell you, but I think you should know."

"Know what?" Boxer asked, removing the pipe from his mouth.

"I have bone cancer."

Boxer stiffened.

"Don't ask if I'm sure," his father said. "I'm sure."

It was Boxer's turn to put his arm around his father's shoulders.

"And don't say anything," his father said.

"I wasn't going to," Boxer answered, clearing his throat before he spoke.

"I thought you should know," his father said. "It's going to be very hard on your mother as time goes on. She's going to need your moral and emotional support... I have provided for everything else."

Boxer nodded.

"When the time comes for me to go," his father said, "don't let the doctors keep me alive."

"You know I wouldn't do that," Boxer answered.

"I know you'll take care of everything else," his father said.

"Yes," Boxer responded.

"I think we'd better go back into the house," his father suggested.

"I'll be along in a few minutes," Boxer told him. "I'd like to stay out here and enjoy the garden."

"Sure," his father said. "Sure, I understand."

Boxer arrived at Gwen's apartment exactly at 6 P.M. The maid opened the door, nodded, and said, "Miss Holcomb will be with you in a few minutes."

"Where's John?" Boxer asked.

"He's been living at his grandmother's for the past two weeks," the maid answered.

Boxer said nothing. He walked into the living room and found it completely refurnished in high tech, which he didn't like at all. He spotted the bar and helped himself to a shot of Scotch. He went to the terrace, opened the door and stepped out. From it, he could see down into the East River where a freighter was making its way north, toward Long Island Sound. But the view also included the upper harbor and parts of Brooklyn and Queens.

Boxer heard movement behind him, turned, and saw Gwen. She was standing in the doorway, dressed in a lovely blue pants suit and a matching light pink blouse.

"You're not easy to speak to," he said, stepping toward her. "I called you five times."

She moved back into the living room.

Boxer followed her. He knew it was going to be one of those meetings. If that was what she wanted, that was what he was prepared to give.

"I don't want to see you again," Gwen said.

"That's fine with me," Boxer answered. "But the court has given me visitation rights with my son."

"You may see him whenever you can," she answered.

Boxer went to the bar and poured himself another drink. "Here's to the lucky man," he said raising his glass, "or is it men?"

"Don't be a bastard!"

"Tell me, Gwen, what happened between the last time we saw each other and now?"

She turned away. "I met someone," she said. "Someone who can give me what I want."

"Will you tell me what that is?" Boxer asked, angrier than he previously had been. "Do you know what you want? Do you really know?"

"I know I don't want to discuss it with you," she shot back at him.

Boxer shook his head. "After the last time, I thought we had something going between us again. That just goes to show, to use a cliché, how wrong a fellow can be." He set his glass down on the bar.

Gwen said nothing.

"Not even a goodbye kiss?"

Gwen remained motionless.

"A handshake then?" he asked, instantly regretting that he had asked.

"No," she answered. "Not even that. I think you had better go."

Boxer pursed his lips and nodded. This wasn't his day. First that stupid fracas in the bar, then finding out his father was dying of bone cancer, and now this — the end of his relationship with Gwen. "You know I love you," he said.

"I don't want to hear it," she answered stridently.

"What about John?" Boxer asked.

"Once I'm married, he'll live with me and Phillip. I told you, you can see him any time you're in. Just give me a few hours' notice."

"I can't give you notice if you don't have the courtesy to speak to me."

"That won't happen again," Gwen said. "This time was different. I didn't want to see you now."

"What the hell is so different about this time?"

"I'm going to be married in Mexico," she said, shouting the words at him.

Boxer was too stunned to answer.

"That's why I didn't want to see you. I knew that if I spoke to you, you'd want to see me. Now you're here. Okay, I told you what I would have told you after the fact. I didn't want you to spoil it." She went to the bar and poured herself another drink.

Boxer took a deep breath and slowly exhaled.

"I'm sorry," she said. "But there really wasn't an easy way to tell you."

Boxer nodded. "I hope you'll be happy," he said. "I really do."

"Thanks," she answered, managing a smile.

"Is he in show business too?"

"God, no. He's an interior designer. He redid my entire apartment."

"I should have guessed," Boxer said, looking around again. He still didn't like what he saw, but he decided to say nothing about it.

"I think it expresses more about what I am than the previous furnishings," she said.

Boxer wasn't going to comment on that.

"I guess there's nothing more for either of us to say." Gwen looked directly at him.

"Nothing more," Boxer agreed. "I'll call you when I want to see John," he said; then he turned and walked to the door.

"I'll have the maid see you out," Gwen said.

"No need to... I can open the door myself," Boxer answered. A few moments later, while waiting for the elevator, he used a handkerchief to wipe the tears from his eyes.

Boxer remained with his parents for two days. Never once did he mention to them that Gwen was getting married again. His father was particularly fond of her and would have been very upset if he knew about her second marriage. He had hoped that his son and daughter-in-law would remarry. Nor did Boxer speak to his father about his illness. But he did spend time working in the garden with him.

"You know," his father said, after Boxer put two bags of topsoil down, "I can't tell you how much pleasure this garden has given me. For the past few years, it has been like a good friend." Then with a sad smile he added, "If it's not taken care of after I'm gone, it will quickly go to weed."

"As long as mother lives here," Boxer said, "I'll see that it's taken care of."

His father nodded but didn't say anything more.

The few times that Boxer left the house and especially when he went to see Dee's family in Staten Island, he had the feeling that he was being followed. But he couldn't make anyone out and attributed it to his extremely low emotional state. Not only was it no longer possible to remarry Gwen, now his father was dying ... and he still had to face a Company hearing.

The afternoon Boxer rode the ferry over to Staten Island, he was very depressed and didn't look forward in the least to meeting Dee's family. But he felt he owed her memory something.

Boxer hailed a cab at the terminal and told the driver to take him to 46 Apple Street. Though he had been stationed in

Staten Island when he'd commanded the *Sting Ray*, he had never gotten to know the place.

"Just where is Apple Street?" Boxer asked the driver.

"New Dorp," the man answered.

Boxer accepted the answer without comment and a few minutes later found himself standing outside a two-story one-family home located approximately in the middle of the block on a street that ended near the water. He had called before coming and knew that he was expected.

He walked up the steps, and as soon as he rang the bell, the door was opened by a good-looking young man who was dressed in a white shirt and brown tie, brown slacks, and a tan buttoned-down sweater, although it was a sunny day with temperatures in the high seventies.

Boxer could see the resemblance between Dee and the young man. The dark complexion and black eyes were unmistakably the same. But unlike Dee's eyes, which had been full of sparkle, this young man's eyes were vacant.

"I'm Captain Boxer," Boxer said.

The young man opened the door wider. "Please come in," he said.

Boxer nodded and walked into the living room, where a large-boned man of middling height was standing. He was dressed in black slacks and a black shirt. Boxer glanced at one of the walls. It was completely covered with a mirror that reflected the three of them.

"Dad," the young man said, "this is Captain Boxer."

Boxer shook the man's hand.

"I'm Dee's father," he said. "That's my son Darrel."

Boxer shook Darrel's hand.

"My wife," Mr. Long said, "is upstairs. She didn't sleep very well last night and has a headache. She gets bad headaches."

158

Boxer nodded sympathetically.

"You want coffee?" Mr. Long asked.

"No thank you," Boxer said.

The three of them stood in the center of the living room; neither of them said anything.

Boxer was sorry he had bothered to phone and even sorrier that he had made the trip from Brooklyn.

"Dee," Mr. Long said, ending the silence, "was a good girl."

"I'm sure she was," Boxer answered.

"Everybody liked her. Isn't that right Darrel?"

"She got mixed up with the wrong company," Darrel said.

"He should be a priest," Mr. Long said. "He never liked Dee's friends. Said they were no good. But he doesn't know anything about life."

"I'm going to be the president of this borough," Darrel said.

"He worked last summer in city hall," Mr. Long said. "Everybody liked him there. They said he should go into politics."

Boxer didn't know what to answer.

"He has letters from the President and the Vice President," Mr. Long said. "He writes to them all the time."

"That's nice," Boxer answered, wondering whether Mrs. Long was like her husband and son.

"Before Dee started to travel," Mr. Long said, "I warned her about traveling. I said, 'The best place is home.' That's what I said."

"Were you a friend of Dee's?" Darrel asked.

Boxer nodded.

"I told you Darrel, he was a friend of hers," Mr. Long said. "Everybody liked Dee."

"How did you know her?" Darrel asked.

"I was master of the ship that rescued her and some other passengers," Boxer said. He had no intentions of saying anything about the *Shark*.

"You know she was coming home for her mother's birthday," Mr. Long said.

Boxer did a double take.

"That's the kind of daughter she was," Mr. Long said. "She was making that big trip just to be here for her mother's birthday."

"Yes," Boxer agreed, "she was that kind of woman."

"I told my wife," Mr. Long said, "that you must have liked Dee a lot to come all the way out here to tell us you met her."

"But —"

"The next time I see her," Mr. Long said, "I'll tell her you paid us a visit. She'll like that."

"My sister shouldn't have canceled her visit," Darrel said. "She should have come home for my mother's birthday."

"She really did try," Boxer said, realizing that her father and brother couldn't accept Dee's death, much less the kind of life she had led, or they weren't put together too tightly. Maybe the latter was the cause of the former?

"You know when she was a teenager," Mr. Long said, "she'd change her clothes three, sometimes four times a day. She had thirty pairs of jeans and just as many pairs of shoes."

Boxer nodded.

"See Darrel, he dresses just like his uncle … always wears a tie. Dee is like my sister, just like her."

"I'm afraid," Boxer said, "I'll have to be going. I have to be back in Brooklyn soon."

The three of them moved toward the door.

"It was nice of you to come and tell us all about Dee," Mr. Long said, extending his hand.

Boxer shook it.

"Thank you for coming," Darrel said, also offering his hand. "Next time you come, I'll show you letters from the President and Vice President."

"That'll be very nice," Boxer answered.

Darrel opened the door and Boxer walked out of the house and back into the real world. Later, when he was on the ferry going back to Manhattan, Boxer realized Mr. Long and Darrel would probably tell their neighbors about his visit, twisting and embellishing it until they were convinced that he had come to tell them how wonderfully Dee was doing in Australia and how beautiful she looked. The image of Dee's naked body lying on the lab table sprung into Boxer's mind. He pushed that sad picture from his thoughts and walked out of the cabin to stand in the wind.

Boxer returned home at 1700 hours and was told by his mother, "A Miss Cynthia Lowe called and said she was being TDY'd to Mare Island and was leaving immediately."

"Thanks, Mom," Boxer said and tried to call Cynthia at the apartment, but she wasn't there.

Boxer walked over to the screen door and looked out at the back yard. His father was working on his knees at the far end.

"How did your visit go?" his mother asked.

"Strange people," Boxer said.

"Oh!"

Boxer turned to face her. He hadn't told her or his father anything at all about the mission. "Just strange people," he said again. Then he asked. "How is Dad doing?"

"Not too badly," she said.

He went up to her and putting his arms around her, he said, "You can't know how much I love the two of you."

She smiled up at him. "I think we know," she said. "I really do think we know."

Boxer kissed her on the forehead.

"Now that you've told me what every parent wants to hear," she said, gently pushing against his chest, "let me go so I can make dinner for us."

Boxer released her. "What's for dinner?"

"Can't you smell it?"

Boxer sniffed the air. "Baked leg of lamb," he said.

"With baked broccoli."

Boxer licked his lips.

"You looked just the way you did when you were a small boy." His mother laughed.

"How's that saying go: 'You can't make a boy a man, but you can never take the boy out of a man.'"

She raised her eyebrows.

"Well, it's something like that," he answered.

"I wouldn't swear it was anything like that," she answered, beginning to set the table.

"Here, Mom, let me do that," Boxer said, taking the plates from her.

"You know," his mother said, going to the oven and opening it, "your father and I would feel a lot better if you — if we — were sure you're happy." She pulled the roast leg of lamb out of the oven and held it up for Boxer to admire.

"A thing of beauty!" he exclaimed.

"Are you happy?" she asked, carrying the roaster to the countertop, where she transferred it to a large plate.

"If you mean am I happy with what I'm doing, I'd say on a scale of one to ten I'd rate it about eight and a half. Maybe nine."

"You know what I mean," she said returning to the oven for the broccoli.

"As far as my personal life goes," Boxer explained, "I have moments of happiness."

"I know you have a lot of women," she said, transferring the broccoli to a serving dish. "But that's not what I mean and you know it."

"Mom, I can't make happen what doesn't happen of its own accord," Boxer said, completing the last place setting. "But when I do find —"

"Someone you want to marry, you'll tell me. But until you do, you don't want to be bugged by questions. Right?"

"Absolutely right," Boxer said, moving out of the kitchen and into the living room.

"Dinner will be ready in about five minutes," his mother called. "I want the lamb to breathe before it's cut."

Boxer didn't answer. He drifted over to the window and looked out. Across the street was a black car. Two men were sitting in it. His feeling had been right: he was being followed. The two men in the car were Company men.

For a moment, Boxer was furious with Williams and Kinkade. But his anger only lasted for the few moments it took him to realize the men were there as much to protect him as to give the Company a report about his daily activities. He couldn't fault the Company for wanting to protect its property as much as possible.

"Dinner!" his mother called from the kitchen.

"Good," Boxer answered, "I'm starved."

His father slid open the screen door, just as Boxer came into the kitchen.

"I have to wash my hands," Boxer said.

"So do I," his father added.

A few minutes later the three of them were seated at the round table.

"Why don't you carve?" his father asked, looking at his son.

Boxer hesitated. It was the first time his father had asked him to carve.

"Go on," his father said. "I'll only make a mess of it."

Boxer nodded and picking up the carving knife, he ran his finger along the blade.

"I sharpened it myself this morning," his father said.

"It feels as if it would be able to cut paper," Boxer commented, as he picked up the large fork and dug it into the leg of lamb to steady it.

"It does cut paper. I tried it," his father answered.

Just as Boxer was about to make the first cut, the phone rang.

"I'll get it," Mrs. Boxer said, leaving the chair and walking over to the wall, where the phone was. She lifted the receiver. "Yes, Captain Boxer is here," she said, after a few moments. "It's for you," she said, looking at her son.

Boxer set the knife and fork down on the platter, left the table and took the phone from his mother. "Boxer here," he said.

"This is Williams," the voice on the other end said.

"Yes?"

"Are you armed?" Williams asked.

"What?" Boxer's voice went up several decibels. He glanced at his parents; they pretended not to have heard.

"I asked if you were armed," Williams said calmly.

"No."

"From now on you must remember to carry a piece at all times," Williams told him.

"Is that why you called me?" Boxer asked, annoyed that he had been disturbed at dinner. Sometimes the people working for the Company could do the weirdest things at the weirdest times.

"There's a car across the street from your parent's house," Williams said.

"Yes. I have seen it. There are two of your men in it."

"They're not our men" Williams said.

"What the hell are you talking about!" Boxer shouted. "If they're not yours —"

"They're KGB," Williams answered.

"What are they doing here?" Boxer glanced at his parents.

"They want you," Williams said.

"You're crazy!"

"We received word that they were going to attempt to kidnap you," Williams said. "Our people said the order came from the top man in Moscow to kidnap you, or kill you, whichever is easier."

"When?"

"I should think sometime within the next hour or so," Williams said.

"What the hell would they do with me?"

"Get you out of the country and then sweat you until they found out all about the *Shark*."

"I'm a sitting duck," Boxer said.

"Not exactly," Williams answered. "There's a four-man team in a UPS truck up the street. One man has left the van and is on his way down to you. He will come to the door and hand you a package. Inside the cardboard container you will find a small, modified Uzi. You will also find a radio by which you'll be able to coordinate your activities with those of the team. If possible take the two men alive. But if they put up any sort of a fight kill them. Do you understand?"

"Yes."

"There's one more thing," Williams said.

"What is that?"

"Admiral Stark wants you to report back to him as soon as possible."

Boxer knew better than to ask why. "I'll take an early flight out tomorrow morning."

"A late flight tonight," Williams said. "Be in his office by zero nine hundred tomorrow."

"I'll be there."

"Sorry for the trouble," Williams said.

"So am I," Boxer answered and hung up. For a moment, he didn't move; then he returned to the table and said, "I want the two of you to go upstairs, and don't go anywhere near the front bedroom."

"But why?" his mother asked.

"No questions now," Boxer answered. "Just do what I ask."

The doorbell rang.

"I'll get it," Boxer answered. "Now go upstairs." He waited until his parents were on their way up the steps before he opened the door.

The man handed him a package and a slip of paper to sign. "So far," the man said, "they don't have any idea we're here."

Boxer nodded, thanked him, and retreated into the house closing the door behind him. He tore open the cardboard box, took out the machine gun, loaded it, and switched on the radio. "This is Boxer," he said.

"Hear you ten by ten," a man answered.

"Can anyone else hear us?" Boxer asked.

"We're being scrambled through equipment in the van."

"Have you guys any ideas?" Boxer asked.

"Nothing that wouldn't wind up in shooting," the man answered.

"Any idea when they plan to come for me?"

"Like Mister Williams said, 'Soon,'" the man answered. "The time they try to make the snatch has been left up to them."

"We can't wait for them to move," Boxer answered.

"Agreed."

"Suppose you crash into them?" Boxer suggested.

"Then what?"

Instead of answering the question, Boxer said, "I want you to come down the street and, almost in front of them, stop; then make a U-turn. While making the U-turn, back into them. That way they won't be able to leave, unless they go into reverse and swing around the truck. But the truck is big enough to block most of the width of the street. Then I want the driver to get out and start arguing with them. Two of the other men slip out of the van and come up behind them. By this time I'll come out of the house and have the Uzi trained on them. If they're smart, they'll realize they've been had and won't put up a fight."

"What about the driver?" the man asked. "He'll be in the most dangerous position of all of us."

"I'll tell him when to hit the deck," Boxer answered.

"What if they grab him and use him as a shield?"

"That's a risk we'll have to take," Boxer answered. "I hope it won't happen that way. But if it does, then we'll have to rush them."

For several moments the man didn't speak; then he said, "We roger that."

"Good."

"We're beginning to move down the hill now," the man said.

"Good luck," Boxer said. He switched off the radio and moved to the side of the window, where he could observe what was happening without being seen.

The truck was coming down the hill. It rolled to a stop a few feet in front of the black car, blocking it from Boxer's view. Then it moved beyond the car, started to go into reverse, stopped, and pulled forward. It stopped and went into reverse again. Then it backed into the front of the black car, crashing into its left fender.

The truck stopped. The driver got out and immediately started to curse the man at the wheel of the black car.

Boxer took a deep breath, exhaled, and with the back of his arm, wiped the sweat from his forehead; then he opened the door on a crack and looked out.

The driver was shouting at the men in the car.

"Just move the damn truck," the man behind the wheel said. "Move it out of the way."

"I'm not moving anything," the truck driver yelled. "You want to move. You move."

Boxer flung the door open. "Now!" he shouted, running toward the car, with the machine gun at his waist.

The driver hit the deck.

The man behind the wheel, flung open the door, drew his gun, and pulled off two rounds.

Boxer squeezed the trigger. The Uzi bucked. But he held it down. The man in front of him gripped his stomach and fell to the ground.

Two of the Company men put several rounds into the side window.

"Don't shoot," the KGB man shouted. "Don't shoot!"

The truck driver got to his feet. 'We'll take it from here, Captain."

Boxer nodded and looked around. Almost everyone who lived on the street was outside now. He was about to speak when two police cars rushed up the street with their sirens screaming and their red lights flashing.

They came to an abrupt halt and the cops came out of the cars with their revolvers drawn.

"Drop those guns," a burly sergeant ordered.

Boxer dropped the Uzi to the ground.

"No need for that," the truck driver said. "Tell your men to put up their guns."

"Drop your gun," the sergeant ordered. "I'll count to three. If they're not all down in the gutter, my men will shoot. One … two…"

"Put the weapons down," the driver said.

"Good now put your hands over your heads," the sergeant said. "And all of you get against the van," he said.

Three more squad cars came racing up the street and stopped. A uniformed captain and several detectives got out of the cars.

"One dead and one alive," the sergeant said.

"Cuff them," the captain said, "bring them down to the station house. Did you call an ambulance for the —"

"Better not put the cuffs on them," Boxer said.

The captain walked over to him. "And who the fuck are you?"

"Captain Jack Boxer," Boxer answered. "These men were under my command."

"Your command, eh?"

"Captain," Boxer said. "This is a CIA operation. Just take the dead man away and tow the vehicle to a safe place. I'm sure the Agency will want to go over it."

"Just who the fuck are you trying to bullshit?"

"Call this number," Boxer said. "Get on your radio and get yourself patched into a phone. Speak to the man at this number."

The captain frowned.

"I'm only trying to save you some trouble," Boxer said.

"Has anyone searched these men?" the captain asked. "What the hell is in the truck?"

One of the cops opened the back of the van. "Holy shit, it's full of electronic gear and weapons!"

"Call that number," Boxer said.

The captain went back to one of the radio cars and picked up the mike.

Boxer looked toward his house. His mother and father were standing in the doorway, holding tight to one another and looking very frightened. After this, he'd have to give them a more accurate explanation of what kind of work he was doing since he'd left the navy.

The captain returned. "Release them," he said.

"Get the people inside their houses," Boxer told him.

"You heard him," the captain said, "get the people off the street." Then to Boxer, he said, "A tow truck is on its way up, and an ambulance."

Boxer nodded.

"Is there anything else you want?" the captain asked.

"Keep the press away from my father and mother," Boxer said. "I don't care whether or not they speak to anyone else on the street, but I don't want them bothering my parents. My father is ill and I don't want him pestered."

"We'll keep a couple of men here for the next few days," the captain answered.

"Plainclothes."

"You got it," the captain answered.

"Thanks," Boxer said.

The captain saluted Boxer. "I really did think you were bullshitting me," he said.

Boxer nodded and, smiling, said, "When it comes to using guns, I never bullshit." He returned the salute and walked across the street to where his mother and father were standing. "Come inside," he said gently. "And I'll explain everything at dinner."

CHAPTER 14

Boxer cabbed it out to La Guardia Airport for the last shuttle flight to Washington. He arrived a half hour before take-off time and went into the bar for a drink.

He ordered a vodka on the rocks. This was not one of his better visits home. Nothing about it was good.

Boxer picked up the vodka and drank.

"Buy a woman a drink?"

Boxer turned around and found himself looking at Kathy Tyson.

"I thought it was you when you walked into the waiting area," she said.

Boxer gestured to the stool alongside his. "What are you drinking?"

"Whatever you are."

"Vodka on the rocks."

Kathy nodded.

"Another vodka on the rocks," Boxer ordered.

Kathy took a cigarette out and Boxer lit a match and held it to the cigarette. "What are you doing here?" she asked, blowing smoke through her nose. "I know. You went to see your parents."

"Right," he answered.

"And how are they?"

He almost told her about his father but instead he said, "They're fine. My mother asked after you."

"She's a dear," Kathy commented.

"And what brings you to the big city?" Boxer asked.

"Shopping," she answered with a smile. "New York is the only place where a woman can buy clothes with any style."

"I wouldn't know about that," Boxer said.

The bartender brought Kathy's drink and set it down in front of her.

"I came back to Washington a few days ago," Boxer said. "I was going to call you as soon as I got myself squared away."

Kathy nodded, lifted her drink and said, "To all the things we intend to do but somehow don't."

"Really, I was," Boxer said.

"You don't owe me anything," she said, after taking a sip of her drink.

"I was going to call your answering service," he told her.

"Well, now you don't have to," she said.

Boxer finished his drink and ordered another.

"You look down," Kathy said.

"This has not been the best visit home I ever had," Boxer answered. "But I guess that's the way it goes sometimes."

Kathy nodded.

A short while later they boarded the plane together and sat next to one another. Within minutes after take-off, Kathy snuggled against Boxer. Her red hair was just below his chin and she smelled of lilac perfume. She breathed easily. Her right breast intermittently touched his chest. He put his arm around her shoulder, rested his head against her's and dozed.

"Ladies and gentlemen we are making our landing approach to Washington's International Airport," the stewardess announced. "Please fasten your seat belts and obey the No Smoking sign when it comes on."

Boxer opened his eyes and raised his head.

"I was having such a wonderful dream," Kathy said, straightening up and pushing her hair back into place.

Boxer removed his arm from her shoulders. "Tell me about it. I can use a nice dream, even if it's someone else's."

She looked straight up at him. "We were in bed together and we were making love," she said.

Boxer took hold of her hand and squeezed it.

"I really did think we had something going," she said softly, her green eyes focused on him.

He nodded. "You're not too far wrong," he answered.

"Still carrying the torch for your ex?"

"That's all over."

"Is that another reason why —"

"No questions, Kathy. I don't want to talk about it. Okay?"

"Sure. Okay … really, it's okay."

Boxer nodded and looking past Kathy to the window, he saw the white shaft of the Washington Monument come into view. The plane banked to the left; then to the right again; made a half turn and started down.

"Spend the night with me," Boxer said.

"Yes," Kathy answered. "I have a place — a two-room suite in the Watergate Hotel."

Boxer nodded.

"I thought you'd have enough sense to carry a piece," Stark said, puffing on cigar.

"I never carried a weapon."

"Now is not never," Stark cut in.

Boxer said nothing. If Stark was going to give him a reaming, nothing short of God's intervention would stop him. He sat back and waited for the admiral to continue.

"In a few days, a week at the most, you'll be going off on a new assignment," Stark said.

Boxer leaned forward. "The *Shark* —"

"The *Shark* will be ready by the time you need it," Stark said. "It will be ready, or some heads will roll."

"Ready with the modifications that I want done?" Boxer asked.

"Ready to do this job," Stark answered.

"What is it?"

Stark reached over to the humidor, snapped open the top, and extending it toward Boxer, he said, "Have one?"

Boxer took a cigar, cut the tip, and lit up.

"I can't tell you what the deal will be," Stark answered. "I can only tell you what you must do and a few other things."

Boxer realized that Stark was angry, but not at him. The admiral's anger was directed against others.

"You agree to a joint cooperation," Stark said, "and suddenly the CIA are in charge."

"I know what you mean," Boxer answered.

"How the hell could you know what the fuck I mean?" Stark exploded. "You don't know what the fuck I mean; you can't possibly know what the fuck I mean."

Boxer said nothing.

"The only one who knows what the fuck I mean is me," Stark said. He got up and went to the bar. "You're a vodka man, aren't you?" he asked.

"Yes," Boxer said.

Stark returned with two glasses in hand, each liberally filled. He gave one to Boxer. "You're to fly to Cannes and report to Sanchez aboard the *Mary-Ann*."

Boxer was on his feet.

"Sit down!" Stark snapped.

"You want me to report to Sanchez?"

"I'm ordering you to report to that fuck," Stark said, dropping into the chair behind the desk.

"What the hell for?"

"You'll receive further orders when you're aboard the *Mary-Ann*."

"Great... Sanchez will be my CO. That'll be just fucking great!"

"I don't like it when anyone swears in my presence," Stark said. "I don't like it at all. Do you fucking understand that?"

Boxer nodded.

"The *Shark* will be repaired, so that she can deep-dive again," Stark said. "All other modifications will have to wait. The *Mary-Ann* will rendezvous with her, though I don't know where or when."

"When she does will Redfern's people be on board?"

"Yes. All of your people and all of Tom's were removed from the *Tecumseh* yesterday. Tom should be home by now. But they'll be back aboard the *Shark* when you meet her. Aboard her will also be Commander Steven L. Bush."

"Just what the fuck — Sorry... Fuck it! I'm not sorry. I want to know what the fuck is going on?"

"Captain Bush will be aboard to observe and learn."

"The hell you say!" Boxer exploded. "He'll be aboard to spy." He was on his feet and pacing rapidly back and forth.

"Kinkade wanted him there," Stark said. "He's there instead of you having to go through a hearing."

"I'll take the hearing, thank you."

"You'll take Bush," Stark said, "and that's an order."

Boxer sat down; then he got up, walked to the bar, and poured himself another two fingers of vodka.

"He'll command the *Shark* until you go aboard."

"The men aren't going to like that. Remember they already know him, and when they left the *Sting Ray* none of them told him why they were being transferred off. As far as he knows, they all resigned."

"I will speak with him," Stark said.

"Why him?"

"Kinkade wanted someone who'd go by the book."

"Then he should have taken the fucking book and had it made into a man."

Stark looked at him; suddenly he threw back his head and roared with laughter. "That's not half bad," he said, still laughing. "Not half bad."

"You tell Bush the goddamn men aboard the *Shark* are special and —"

"I'll tell him," Stark said.

"What else?"

"The hearing will take place when you return," Stark said.

"Even if Bush gives Kinkade a good report?" Boxer said sarcastically.

"I want the hearing," Stark told him. "The hearing will clear the air about your actions, about how Miss Long was murdered, and also about how much discretion a mission commander has."

"Dee — Miss Long — was murdered by —"

"A mole," Stark said. "You know it and I know it. But sooner or later Kinkade and Williams have to believe it."

Boxer put his empty glass down. "So I still stand a chance of being knocked out of the ball game?"

"It's a tough game." Stark answered, lighting the stub of his cigar again. "A fucking tough game."

"How long do you figure before we rendezvous with the *Shark*?"

"Three weeks, a month at the outside," Stark said.

"And all that time I have to be aboard the *Mary-Ann*?"

Stark nodded. "It shouldn't really be that hard. Think of it as a vacation."

"What's his role in the mission?"

"Don't know ... but Kinkade does."

Boxer lit his cigar again. "This isn't going to be easy for me to take."

"Never said it would be," Stark answered.

"Anything else I should know?" Boxer asked.

"Only that the Chinese sub you destroyed had been spotted off West Africa, more precisely off southwest Africa by the Russians and they chased it off."

"How do you know that?"

Stark grinned.

"Okay. So you know that. Are you sure it was the same sub. If there was one, there could have been two?"

"No chance. The ID was by the spy in the sky. It surfaced at night to recharge its batteries. We got some very good photographs of it."

"What the hell was it doing?"

Stark shrugged and shook his head. "We don't know."

Boxer frowned.

"We do know that the Chinese are blaming the Russians for its loss," Stark said. "And that means they'll go looking for a Russian sub and make every effort to sink it."

Boxer nodded. "Anything else I should know?"

"I can't think of anything, except that from now on you're to be armed at all times," Stark said.

Boxer was about to object.

"That's an order, Captain, not a request."

"Aye, aye, sir," Boxer answered.

"You're really becoming a wise-ass, aren't you?"

"Yes, sir," Boxer answered. "I think so."

Warm, spring sunlight was being reflected off the Kremlin's golden domes, and the people Borodine passed on his way to Naval Headquarters were smiling. The time he'd spent with Luba was never far from his thoughts, though it now was a full seventy-two hours since he had left her. Sometimes it seemed to him that he could actually smell her body, though they were separated by thousands of miles. And since he had made love to her, he seemed to sense that other women were interested in him, or more precisely, looked at him differently.

Borodine passed the guards at the entrance to Naval Headquarters. They saluted him and he returned the salute. A few minutes later, he stood in front of the desk of Admiral Gorshkov's aide, a young severe-looking woman, who held the rank of a captain-lieutenant and who spoke in a clipped manner. Though Borodine had been ordered to report immediately, he had already spent three days in Moscow without seeing Gorshkov.

"The admiral will see you," the woman said, as soon as Borodine gave her his name. "Sit down, please, Comrade Captain," she said, gesturing to a chair against the far wall.

"Thank you," Borodine said politely and walked toward the chair, where he might have to sit for several hours before being asked to enter the admiral's office.

Borodine sat down and with nothing to focus his thoughts on, he thought about Galena. Their argument most certainly had led him to commit adultery with Luba. Not that he had stopped loving Galena, but she had been his wife long enough to know that an order was an order, especially if that order came from Fleet Admiral Gorshkov. His experience with Luba was, if nothing else, refreshing, and it most certainly provided a balm for his feelings. But despite his intense physical reaction to Luba, he did not love her, and he knew she did not love him. Between them it was only sex and — He looked across the room at the captain-lieutenant and wondered how she would be in bed? He had often heard men say that the severest-looking women, were the best in bed. But he did not have sufficient experience to deny or confirm what he had heard. Though not a virgin when he'd married at age twenty-five, his sexual encounters had been limited to prostitutes and

—

"Comrade Captain Borodine?" the admiral's aide called.

Borodine was on his feet immediately.

"The admiral will see you now," she said, gesturing to the door to her right.

Borodine thanked her and, walking up to the door, knocked politely.

"You may go in," the woman said.

Borodine opened the door and entered the admiral's office.

Gorshkov looked up from the papers on his desk. He was a dignified-looking man in his late sixties, with a full head of very white hair and a walrus-like mustache.

Borodine saluted smartly.

Gorshkov returned the salute, gestured to the chair alongside the desk and said, "I'm pleased to see you, Comrade Captain Borodine."

Borodine nodded but said nothing.

"I have a memo from the KGB complaining about your attitude, command decisions, and several other things," Gorshkov said, tapping a sheet of paper with his stubby fingers. "What have you to say about the complaints?"

"They're probably all true," Borodine said, feeling the muscles in his back tense.

Gorshkov regarded him for a moment; then he said, "Would you have made similar complaints against a fellow officer acting as you had?"

"If I were Comrade Captain Markov, yes," Borodine answered.

"And if you were not Markov, but yourself?"

"No," Borodine answered. "I would have understood, or at least I would have tried to understand, why the Captain of the *Q-21* acted as he had."

Gorshkov ran the fingers of his right hand over his mustache; then he said, "You will remain in Moscow for the next few weeks. During that time you will report to my aide, Comrade Captain-Lieutenant Irena Glazunov. She will have your daily schedule. In a few weeks we will begin a clandestine salvage operation off the southwest coast of Africa, where we hope to recover a billion dollars' worth of gold. The *Sea Savage*, as you call the *Q-21*, will be sent to transport the gold from the undersea salvage base to Murmansk. This time you will have a hundred handpicked and specially trained marines on board."

The tension in Borodine's back eased. He moved slightly forward.

"The gold was carried by a Portuguese treasure fleet that had been en route from India to Portugal in the early part of the sixteenth century, sixteen eighteen to be exact. A storm sank the entire fleet. But recently — well, let's say that we found out where that gold is and intend to salvage it. The operation cannot take too long. We don't want to be discovered doing it and the sea in that part of the world is very difficult. Our oceanographers tell me that there are huge undersea storms there and that there are even more violent ones on the surface, violent enough to give even a supertanker difficulty."

"How long do you expect the entire operation to take?" Borodine asked.

"Not more than a week," Gorshkov answered.

"Will Markov sail with me again?"

"Yes."

"He will, no doubt, send in another report about me," Borodine said.

"I am sure he will," Gorshkov answered. "But I don't expect lightning to strike twice in the same place." Then with a smile curling his lips, he added, "Another Mayday would be highly improbable and you answering it would be even more improbable. Isn't that so?"

"It would be improbable for the situation to occur again," Borodine answered.

"That was my point with the head of the KGB," Gorshkov said.

Borodine nodded. He did not need any further explanation from his CO. The KGB was looking over his shoulder and he'd better watch his step if he did not want to be in real difficulty with them.

"Based on your report," Gorshkov said, "the laser gun was declared effective, but I ordered it removed for further development. We need one with a greater range and one that will not, when fired, cause a sudden drop in the ship's operating power. Such a drop in a chase could spell the difference between a successful kill or a successful escape."

"Absolutely," Borodine said.

"Do you have any questions?" Gorshkov asked.

"None ... except..." Borodine hesitated.

"Go on, ask."

"May I bring my wife to Moscow?" Borodine asked.

"Makes little sense to do that," Gorshkov answered. "You'll be too busy to pay any attention to her."

Borodine accepted his CO's answer without any show of emotion, but he was upset. And he knew Galena would be very upset.

Gorshkov shook Borodine's hand. "You did well, Igor. Very well."

"Thank you," Borodine answered.

"While you're in Moscow," Gorshkov said, "we'll have drinks together."

"It would be an honor," Borodine answered. "A real honor."

CHAPTER 15

Four weeks to the day after his meeting with Stark, Boxer was on his way to Cannes. Rather than fly out of Dulles International Airport, which was closer to Washington, he left from Kennedy in New York so that he could spend the day with his parents. The change in his father was becoming more and more apparent and it made Boxer realize that his father was running out of time.

Kathy had come up to New York with him several times and she was with him now as he rode out to Kennedy from his parents' house.

"I'll take the helicopter to La Guardia and the shuttle flight from there," she said, in answer to Boxer's question about how she'd return to Washington.

The cab swung onto the Belt Parkway. Because it was an off hour the cab sped along.

Boxer took hold of Kathy's hand. "Listen," he said, "when I get back, there are a few very important things I want to talk to you about."

She lifted his hand to her lips. "I think I know what they are."

His eyes held hers for a few moments; then he said, "I hope my father lasts until I return."

"He's very weak," Kathy said.

Boxer nodded, let go of her hand, and turned toward the window. His vision was blurred and he fought down the sob that leaped up into his throat from the depths of him. He felt Kathy's hand on his shoulder and bent his cheek against it.

"Would you like it if I visited your folks while you're away?"

"Very much," he answered, facing her. "And so would they. They're very fond of you."

"And I'm fond of them."

Boxer sat back, fished out his pipe, filled and lit it.

"Have you any idea how long you'll be gone?" Kathy asked.

For a moment, he almost wanted to tell her the truth. But then he said, "No. I will join the *Tecumseh* in Marseilles. My orders will be waiting for me. I suspect we'll go to the Persian Gulf area and buy oil on the spot market."

"I'll miss you," Kathy said. "This past month has been wonderful."

"For me too," he said, feeling a sudden stirring in his groin.

The cab turned into the long highway approach leading to the terminal.

Boxer leaned forward and said to the cabbie, "I'm leaving from TWA."

"TWA it is," the man answered.

"When does your flight leave?" Kathy asked.

"About an hour ... but there's no need for you to wait," Boxer said. "Besides, I hate airport goodbyes."

"So do I," Kathy said.

The cab pulled up in front of the TWA terminal. It was supposed to look like a bird in flight, but somehow it just looked peculiar.

Boxer turned to Kathy, took her in his arms, and kissed her, passionately on the lips. "Remember," he said in a low voice, "we have important things to talk about when I come back."

"There's no chance of me forgetting," Kathy whispered, just as ardently.

Boxer let go of her, opened the door, and left the cab. Within moments he'd paid and tipped the cabbie; then he gave his valise to a skycap, blew Kathy a kiss, and walked into the terminal without looking back, though he very much wanted to.

Before Boxer went through the metal scanning device, he summoned the police officer on duty and handed him the Company permit for his revolver.

"What kind is it?" the cop asked.

"Snub-nose thirty-eight," Boxer answered.

The cop nodded, turned off the machine and waved him through.

A few minutes later Boxer boarded the jet. He occupied a window seat in the first-class section of the aircraft.

The take-off was delayed an hour, and by the time the plane was actually airborne, the highways below were crowded with homeward-bound traffic.

Boxer placed his seat in the reclining position and settled back, knowing he would be awakened, if he fell asleep, by an attentive stewardess when dinner was served. He closed his eyes and let his thoughts range where they would. He didn't want to think of the mission, mainly because he didn't want to think about Sanchez. The last time they had met he had put him through a glass window and now — if he had learned nothing else about the Company, he had learned that its ways were strange and mysterious.

Boxer didn't want to think about his father's coming death, but he couldn't stop himself. It would be one of the most difficult experiences he'd have to undergo. More difficult, in many ways, than his divorce from Gwen had been. Boxer pursed his lips and felt his throat tighten. *There will be time enough for that*, he silently told himself. *Time enough to cry*. He opened his eyes, put his seat into the upright position and looked out of the window.

Below him, he could see the whalelike shape of Long Island and to the north, across Long Island Sound, the southern reaches of New England.

The captain came on the PA system. "Ladies and gentlemen this is Captain Walker. On behalf of TWA and the entire crew welcome aboard TWA Flight Two Forty-four, from New York to Paris. Our flying time will be six hours and forty-two minutes. Our cruising altitude will be forty-four thousand feet. The weather in Paris is clear; the temperature is sixty-five degrees. Thank you and enjoy your flight."

"Excuse me?"

Boxer looked up at the stewardess. She was a petite blond, with an engaging smile.

"Would you care for a drink?" she asked.

"A vodka on the rocks, please," Boxer answered, noting from the name tag over her right breast that her name was Judy.

She nodded and went to the bar to pour the drink.

Boxer turned toward the window just as Cape Cod, shaped like a flexed arm, came into view, reviving memories of times spent there with his mother and father. He was sixteen the summer he lost his virginity. Lost wasn't really quite accurate. As Boxer remembered the incident, he was more than willing to give it up. He smiled.

"Your vodka." Judy smiled down at him and extended a small tray. "I brought some crackers and cheese with your drink. We'll be serving hors d'oeuvres in a while."

Boxer nodded. "Are they any good?" he asked.

"Very."

"Then I'll have some," he said.

She moved away and started to speak to another passenger.

Boxer looked out of the window again. Cape Cod was now diminishing astern, but the memories of the times he'd spent there were splashing themselves across his brain. There he and his father had walked along the beach, talking about everything from politics to astronomy. There they had gone out drinking together, not as father and son but as two friends. And most important, there he had come to understand his father and to truly love him. Boxer took out his handkerchief and blew his nose in it; then he swallowed most of his drink.

At forty-two thousand feet, it takes the sun a long time to leave the western sky. Down below the ocean was covered with night, and night was ahead and around them. But in the west, the sky remained red and orange until well after 2100 hours.

Boxer had several of the hors d'oeuvres, including several with anchovies, which made him very thirsty. When dinner was finally served, he ordered broiled red snapper but ate very sparingly, though he did drink several glasses of Cabernet Sauvignon, which was better tasting than he thought it would be.

After dinner, he got up to stretch his legs and go to the bathroom; then he returned to his seat, prepared to sleep until the plane landed. Except for the overhead reading light that was on several rows in front of where Boxer sat, the main cabin lights were dimmed. He closed his eyes, aware now of the flight attendant's soft laughter that came from the galley area behind him. He took several deep breaths and —

The laughter ceased and the captain's voice came over the PA. "I'm sorry to disturb you," he said. "But this plane has been hijacked and will be landing in Paris only to fuel before going on. Please cooperate. Do whatever you are told to do."

Boxer had opened his eyes the moment he had heard the captain's voice.

Suddenly the lights in the cabin came up to their full brightness.

A man holding a glass jar moved toward the cockpit, opened the door and said something Boxer couldn't hear.

Another man wielding a knife herded the stewardesses away from the galley to seats.

Boxer caught Judy's eyes and nodded to the empty seat next to him.

She sat down.

The man with the knife took his place at the open curtain that divided the first-class section from the rest of the aircraft.

Boxer leaned toward Judy. "Are you all right?"

She nodded. "Just scared."

"Don't let it bother you," he said. "So am I." Then he half stood and looked around. "There're only two of them," he commented sitting down again.

"That doesn't make me feel any better," Judy answered.

Boxer could see that she was very, very frightened. But he also figured that he was the only passenger aboard armed with a gun. He doubted that the two skyjackers had one between them. "Listen," he said to Judy, "I have a gun and I might be able to get those bastards."

Judy's eyes widened with fear. "You're crazy," she whispered. "If you fail, they'll blow the plane up"

"Then we won't fail," Boxer said, forcing a smile to show how confident he was. "I want you to unbutton your blouse. Show most of your breasts. Sooner or later those characters are going to want coffee and something to eat. You're going to bring it to one of them. The rest I'll do."

"If you shoot one of them and miss, you could put a hole in the plane and —"

"I know what the risk is," Boxer answered. "But I won't miss. Believe me, I won't."

"I'm really scared now."

"You'd be a fool not to be. But between the two of us, we can get them."

Judy hesitated for several moments. "Okay. Okay, I'll do it. When do you want me to unbutton?"

"Now," Boxer answered.

Judy unbuttoned her blouse to the second button.

"More," Boxer said.

She undid another button.

"That's good. Now separate the blouse. Expose as much of your breasts as possible."

"This okay?" she asked, turning the front of her blouse into a plunging neckline.

"Good. Very good," Boxer answered, looking at her breasts, which were held loosely in place by a thin, white bra. Suddenly he realized that he couldn't risk involving her in his plan as he had previously thought. He would have to come up with another idea... Something that would be less dangerous to her.

"You're staring at me," Judy said.

"Sorry," Boxer answered. "I was just thinking."

"I bet," she answered.

"No ... really I was."

"Now what do we do?"

"Wait," he answered.

"By the way, since we're going to do something stupid together, I'd like to know your name."

"Jack Boxer," he answered.

"Well, Jack, I have to be honest with you. I think we have as much chance of doing anything as a snowball has in hell."

Boxer wasn't listening to her. He realized that the longer they had to wait, the less he would be able to depend on Judy. He had to do something soon, or forget about doing anything. Suddenly, he knew exactly what he was going to do.

"Why don't you move closer," Boxer said, "and let me play with your breasts." Before she could answer, his hand was on them.

"What the hell are you doing?" she shouted.

"C'mon baby," he said loudly, "just a little squeeze."

"You bastard," she yelled.

Suddenly there was a rapid exchange between the two skyjackers.

One of the other male passengers started to stand.

The man with the knife came running down the aisle and punched him in the head.

Judy struck him across the face.

Suddenly the man with the knife was standing over them. "What the hell are you doing?" he shouted.

"Only having fun," Boxer said, letting go of Judy's breasts.

"Take your hand off her," the man ordered.

"Go away."

The man leaned forward. "Let go of her," he growled.

"Make me."

The man standing by the cockpit said something, and the man with the knife answered.

"Let go of her," the man with the knife said, "or I'll —"

Boxer reached behind himself and freed the .38 from its holster. "You can't do anything to me," he said.

The man jerked the knife toward Boxer's face. "Next time, I'll cut you. Let go of her."

"There's not going to be a next time," Boxer said, whipping the gun out and pushing it into the man's neck. "Move and I'll kill you. Judy, take the knife."

She hesitated.

"Take the knife," Boxer commanded. "We don't have much time."

She reached up and disarmed the man.

"Now call your friend over here," Boxer said, pushing the gun's muzzle hard against the man's neck.

The man shook his head. "Call him yourself."

"Okay, you want to hang tough; then we'll see just how tough you can hang. Move back slowly. I'll follow you. Do anything other than what I tell you to do, and I'll kill you. Now start to move." Boxer followed the man out into the aisle.

The man standing near the cockpit started to shout.

"Shut up," roared Boxer. "I have your friend here. Put that jar down, or I'll shoot him."

"You wouldn't risk it," the man answered.

Boxer squeezed the trigger. A thunderous explosion filled the cabin.

The man dropped to the deck.

Boxer faced the man in front of the cockpit and squeezed the trigger again.

A second explosion tore through the cabin.

The man dropped backward.

Boxer ran to him and ripped the glass jar out of his hands and tore the wires out of the plastique. It was over!

The room Captain-Lieutenant Irena Glazunov led Borodine to was located in the third subbasement of the building. There he met Comrade Captain Third Class Fyodor Allexeyev, a short, balding man who wore thick glasses and had a high-pitched voice. Allexeyev immediately got down to business, and pointing to a table on which there were several large interconnected cylinders, he said, "What you are looking at, Comrade Captain Borodine, is a model of the undersea base which will be used to salvage the gold."

Borodine glanced at his escort, but she ignored him.

"These three cylinders are exact models of the real station. The first one," Allexeyev said, pointing to one of the cylinders marked with a red circle, "is the living station for your work crew."

"My work crew?" Borodine asked. "I was not told —"

"The marines you carry on the *Q-21* will be used for the salvage operation as well as for any defensive action, should the need arise. Those are the admiral's wishes."

Borodine acknowledged the information with a nod.

Allexeyev continued. "The actual area can support fifty men. That includes sleeping, eating, and the necessary equipment for waste disposal."

"At what depth?" Borodine asked.

"It has been designed and tested to operate at one thousand feet," Allexeyev said. "But the salvage operation will take place at a depth of three hundred feet, which is well within the operational parameters of the station." He proceeded to remove the top of the cylinder, exposing the mock-up of the station's interior. "You can see that we have provided for everything needed by the men."

"What provisions have been made for an emergency escape?" Borodine asked. There was something about this man that rubbed him the wrong way.

"The men would have to go to the third unit," Allexeyev said, pointing to the cylinder with a yellow circle on it. "This one has the necessary flooding compartments. Access to the sea takes approximately ten minutes. The decompression time is three hours."

"What is the middle cylinder for?" Borodine asked. So far he was not impressed with the undersea station, or his assignment.

"Storage space for tools, food, and eventually the gold," Allexeyev said.

"Open it please," Borodine said.

Allexeyev removed the top half of the cylinder.

Borodine looked down. It consisted of nothing but bins and racks for food and tools. "I want an escape hatch in the bulkhead nearest the living quarters," he said.

"What?" Allexeyev asked.

"Have an escape hatch installed in the bulkhead nearest the living quarters," Borodine said.

"But it's not needed," Allexeyev said. "It's not needed at all. I designed this —"

"Have you ever worked under the sea? Have you ever been under the sea?" Borodine didn't wait for an answer. "You haven't. I have spent a good part of my life under the sea. Things happen down there that you can't even begin to understand."

"I will speak to the admiral about your request," Allexeyev said.

"I don't care who you speak to," Borodine answered. "Just put that escape hatch where I want it."

Allexeyev turned very red. "May I continue, Comrade Captain Borodine?"

"Yes. But before you do, let me remind you that when the salvage operation begins, I am responsible for the lives of my men. You're not. No one else is. I take that responsibility very seriously. Now you may continue."

Allexeyev began the first of what was to be many detailed explanations of how each section of the undersea station worked.

Every morning Borodine reported to Captain-Lieutenant Glazunov. She escorted him to, and remained in, the room while Allexeyev gave his lecture on the undersea station. Though she was there for the entire lecture, she was so unobtrusive that Borodine forgot about her as soon as Allexeyev began to speak.

At the end of the third day Allexeyev gave Borodine three large books containing detailed drawings and operating instructions for each of the cylinders. And on the tenth day, before Allexeyev began his lecture, he said, "Your request for an escape hatch in the bulkhead closest to the living quarters has been approved by the admiral."

Borodine nodded at Glazunov, who seemed not to notice. But he was sure she had. And at the end of the session, as they were riding the elevator up to the lobby, he said, "Comrade Captain-Lieutenant, did the admiral ask you about my differences with Comrade Captain Allexeyev over the escape hatch?"

"He did," she answered forthrightly.

Borodine nodded.

"He asked me what I thought, and I told him that I thought your men should be given every chance to escape from the station should something unforeseen happen."

"Thank you, Comrade Captain-Lieutenant," Borodine said.

The following morning when Borodine reported to Glazunov, she said, "Comrade Admiral Gorshkov has asked to see you before you go for your daily briefing." Then she picked up the phone and informed Gorshkov that Borodine was there. "Go right in," she said, looking up at Borodine and for the first time smiling at him.

Borodine smiled back and opened the door to Gorshkov's office. The admiral was wreathed in cigar smoke.

"Sit down, Igor," Gorshkov said. "I have a few important things to tell you. Would you like a cigar?"

"Yes, thank you."

Gorshkov held a light out to Borodine. "An attempt was made to kill Captain Boxer by our people. It was a stupid move and ended in disaster. The Americans now hold one of our people."

"Can't anyone control the KGB?" Borodine asked, moving back into his chair and blowing smoke up toward the ceiling.

Gorshkov shrugged, but he didn't answer the question. Instead he said, "An attempt was made to hijack the plane on which Boxer was traveling and he killed one of the hijackers and wounded the other."

"Our people?" Borodine asked.

"Not that time. Our people don't think the hijacking had anything to do with Boxer. He just happened to be on the plane on his way to Cannes, with a few hours layover in Paris. The press made quite a hero out of him."

"He's that all right," Borodine answered.

"The CIA has managed to squash any news about his exploits in the Pacific," Gorshkov said.

"I should think they would have."

"One of our agents was among the people Boxer rescued," Gorshkov explained. "Unfortunately he killed a woman."

"What?"

"Captain Boxer has what might be called a large sexual appetite. The woman was in his bed aboard the *Shark* when she was killed."

"What has this to do with me?" Borodine asked.

"Just information about the man whom you might meet again someday. The more you know about him, the more you'll be able to figure out how he thinks, and when you know that, you'll be in a better position to deal with him."

"I can't argue that," Borodine answered.

"Now for some news that I'm sure will make you very happy," Gorshkov said.

Borodine was certain he'd be told that Galena was going be allowed to come to Moscow.

"Comrade Major Alexander Petrovich will command the marines aboard the *Q-21*."

Borodine smiled broadly. "He's a very good man," Borodine said.

"That's why he was recently made a colonel," Gorshkov said. "He and his men will join the *Q-21* in about ten days. That's when they finish training."

"When will I rejoin the *Q-21*?" Borodine asked.

"A week later. She'll be in Kronsdat by then," Gorshkov said. "Your first officer, Viktor Korzenko, will have sailed her there."

"That will be excellent experience for him," Borodine said.

"I thought so too," Gorshkov said.

Borodine sensed the meeting was coming to an end.

"I still want to have dinner with you," Gorshkov said. "But I don't have a free evening for days."

Borodine nodded. "I'm honored that you have even remembered it," he said respectfully.

"You'd better go to your briefing," Gorshkov said, "or Allexeyev will become unstrung. He's a stickler for details, and about time."

The two men shook hands, and then, closing the door softly behind him, Borodine left the admiral's office.

Glazunov was waiting for him. "I trust you had a good meeting with the admiral," she said, as they walked to the elevator.

"A very good one," Borodine answered.

Boxer boarded the *Mary-Ann* at 0300 hours and was immediately escorted to Mr. Sanchez's quarters, which were as elaborate as Boxer had suspected they would be. They were what Boxer would call Cathouse Special, complete with a king-size bed and a ceiling mirror, both of which were visible through the open bedroom door. Though he couldn't see anyone, Boxer was sure there was a woman in the bedroom.

Sanchez, dressed in a blue silk smoking jacket and ascot, got up from the couch to greet him. "Welcome aboard," Sanchez said, extending his hand.

"This is not a social call," Boxer said icily. "I am here because I was ordered to be here. Any relations we have with each other will deal with my mission."

Sanchez lowered his hand and looked at Boxer for several moments without saying anything. Then with a nod, he said, "As you wish, Captain. But for my part I offer you the hospitality of the *Mary-Ann*. You may, if it pleases you, reject part or all of the offer. That is entirely up to you."

Boxer nodded. "I'd appreciate being shown to my quarters. I am very tired and would like to sleep. At ten hundred hours tomorrow, I want to be briefed."

"Yes, Captain," Sanchez snapped out.

Boxer glared at him.

"I saw you on TV earlier. You are very much the hero of the hour."

"I want to go to my quarters," Boxer said sharply.

"Of course," Sanchez answered, and walking over to a panel of buttons, he pressed one of them. Almost immediately, a member of the crew entered the stateroom. "Take Captain Boxer to his quarters," Sanchez said.

"Will you please follow me, Captain," the man said.

Boxer nodded.

"Pleasant dreams," Sanchez called after him.

Boxer gritted his teeth. He walked out of the stateroom without answering, or looking back. He was afraid that if he had stopped to do either, he would have thrown Sanchez against the wall of the cabin, just as he had once thrown him through the window of a restaurant. If ever he hated a man, he hated Julio Sanchez.

A few minutes later Boxer was installed in a luxurious stateroom of his own, complete with king-size bed and ceiling mirror, a six-foot color TV, a VHS, and a small library of tapes.

Boxer stripped, showered, and climbed into bed. Using the remote control, he switched on the TV. Most of the stations were off the air but on one was a wrap-up of the day's news, including some shots of him as he deplaned at Orly. He was able to understand enough French to know that the commentator said that he was certainly a courageous man and a lucky one.

"More lucky than anything else," Boxer said aloud as he switched off the TV and the lights. He slid down on his back, and closing his eyes, he hoped that sleep would come quickly. But he knew it wouldn't. Meeting Sanchez was enough to make him angry, very angry. All the details of the crash between the *Sting Ray* and the *Mary-Ann* came rushing into his head. He could even smell the stink of the burnt flesh of the men trapped in the engine room.

"And this bastard is still around," Boxer said aloud. He pursed his lips, switched on the night-table lamp and padded into the living room. At the bar he poured himself a double Scotch.

From the porthole of the stateroom, Boxer could see the lights of Cannes and those of several of the other large yachts moored nearby. He moved away from the porthole, finished the drink, and returned to bed. Switching off the light, he closed his eyes. This time he knew he'd fall asleep.

At precisely 1000 hours, Boxer and Sanchez faced each other across the deck in Sanchez's private study. The walls were lined with shelves of books and decorated with paintings and antique photographs that ran the gamut from nudes to pastoral scenes.

"Before we begin," Boxer said, "I have some ground rules to lay down."

"Oh?"

Boxer looked straight at Sanchez and said, "I hate your guts, but my orders are to work with you. I'll do that as long as you obey my orders. The moment you do something contrary to my wishes, I will arrest you and take command of this vessel."

"You must be joking," Sanchez said.

"Try me," Boxer answered. "Just try me!"

Sanchez got up and walked to the other end of the study. For several minutes he stood and looked out of one of the portholes, then he returned to the desk, sat down, and said, "You're not an easy man to work with."

Boxer didn't answer.

"What are your ground rules, Captain?" Sanchez asked.

"All of the crew, including your captain come under my command for the duration of the assignment."

"Agreed."

"The use of any and all drugs is prohibited to the crew and the guests alike. Anyone guilty of breaking that rule will be confined to quarters until he or she can be removed from this vessel."

"Some of the people on board need —"

"I don't give a damn what they need," Boxer growled. "No drugs are to be used."

Sanchez nodded.

"Now we can begin to discuss the assignment," Boxer said.

Sanchez fitted a cigarette into a gold cigarette holder, lit it, and said, "Through my contacts in the Soviet Union I have learned that they are going to salvage the gold from a Portuguese treasure fleet that went down off the southwest coast of Africa in the first part of the seventeenth century. The fleet was on its way home from India"

"I know all that," Boxer said impatiently. "What is the position of the salvage operation?"

Sanchez pressed a button on the desk. The wall behind him slid open, revealing a huge map of Africa. "The exact position is twenty-seven degrees, three minutes north latitude, and twelve degrees sixteen minutes east longitude. That would put it about there," Sanchez said, using an electric pointer that marked the location with a red light.

"That's off the Skeleton Coast," Boxer said, "and is in the path of some of the worst weather in the world."

"You didn't think it would be easy, did you, Captain?"

Boxer didn't answer; instead, he said, "Tell me how they're going to do it?"

"My sources tell me they've developed an undersea work station, consisting of three large cylinders attached to one another. These will serve as the work station and storage area for the gold when it is recovered. On the surface a fishing fleet will keep watch."

"Armed?"

"Of course," Sanchez said, nodding his head.

"Then my men must attack the work station?"

"That's the idea," Sanchez answered. "We let the Russians do all the work; then we come in and take it."

"Just like that," Boxer said, snapping his fingers. "You think they'll give it up without a fight?"

"There's certain to be some fighting," Sanchez admitted. "But we have the element of surprise."

"And they have the gold," Boxer said. "They'll fight to keep that gold. They'll fight hard to keep it."

"We'll fight harder," Sanchez responded.

"Just what do you mean by we?"

"Your men of course," Sanchez said.

"You bet your ass it will be my men. Now tell me where the *Mary-Ann* will be?"

"Anyplace you want her," Sanchez said. "Mister Kinkade wants the gold put aboard the *Mary-Ann* as quickly as possible. We don't want to look suspicious. We're just another pleasure-cruising yacht on our way to nowhere."

"In those waters at this time of the year?"

"In any waters at any time of the year," Sanchez answered, unable to keep the anger out of his voice.

Boxer smiled. "I'll tell you where I want to be after I've had a chance to study the coast and the adjacent waters. I assume you have maps of it and the undersea terrain?"

"Yes," Sanchez answered.

Boxer nodded. "Oh, by the way, have you informed your captain that he and his entire crew are under my command?"

"I did," Sanchez said.

"Good; then you won't mind telling them to stand by for an inspection at thirteen hundred hours. I want to make sure everything is ready for an open ocean voyage."

"I can assure you it is," Sanchez said.

"I don't give a damn for your assurances, Sanchez," Boxer said. "Have the crew ready for inspection at thirteen hundred hours. That's an order."

Sanchez flushed and said, "I'll see that they're ready."

"Can you tell me how you found out about this Russian salvage operation?"

"You know you have no need to know," Sanchez answered.

"Suit yourself," Boxer said and started to stand.

"I didn't say I wouldn't tell you. Sit down."

Boxer dropped down into the chair.

"There is a world-famous photogrammetrist by the name of Boris Donskoi, who has been feeding the West information for some years now and recently he was asked by a friend to help him interpret some undersea photographs. One thing led to another and this friend admitted that he was trying to find a lost Portuguese treasure fleet. Well, Donskoi was able to make certain measurements and managed to locate it. There's much more to it than that, but it was Donskoi who passed the information to us."

"Interesting," Boxer said. "This Donskoi must be quite a man."

"He's a character," Sanchez said. "He's handed us a great deal of information."

"And the Russians don't know about his double life?"

"He's given them some very good work, including identifying the *Shark* as you took it down the Mississippi. He was the one who spotted the moving piece of land and it was Captain Borodine who made the final ID."

"I'm impressed," Boxer said.

Sanchez smiled.

"You don't happen to know what the insides of the three cylinders look like?"

Sanchez shook his head. "If there was more time, I might have been able to obtain more information about them. But — "

"We'll make do with what we have and what we learn when we're out there," Boxer said.

"Sometime today a friend of yours will be joining us," Sanchez said.

"Tracy?"

Sanchez nodded. "She doesn't know you're on board. I'm sure she'll be delighted."

"Anyone else?"

"Byron Hayes," Sanchez answered.

"Keep him out of my way," Boxer said, "or I just might use him for shark bait."

"I expect we'll be ordered to sail in a day or two at the most," Sanchez said.

"Have one of your men bring the maps and other information to my quarters."

"I'd much rather you use them here. This cabin is yours to use for as long as you want it. Here are the keys. Make sure it is locked when you leave."

Boxer took the keys and pocketed them.

"Not even a thank you," Sanchez chided.

Boxer nodded and said, "Thank you."

"Lunch will soon be served. Will you join me and my other guests?"

Boxer was about to refuse the invitation, but changed his mind and said, "Yes, I'll join you."

While Borodine was in Moscow, Galena's letters to him were little more than formal notes, and even the three times he spoke to her on the telephone, she seemed more distant than the thousands of miles that separated them. But there was nothing Borodine could do to change the situation between them until he returned from his assignment. To keep himself from thinking too much about his personal life, he spent long hours in his room memorizing the material Allexeyev gave him, and when he grew weary of that, he walked around Moscow. Gorky Park was his favorite place, especially in the late afternoon, or during twilight when the sky to the west was smeared with red or orange.

Borodine recognized that something very different was happening to him. Much of it was taking place in his head. He thought a lot about his experience with Luba. Though there was nothing emotional about their going to bed, the pleasure she gave him was so intense that frequently, during his walks, he would look at a strange woman and find himself wondering if she could provide the same pleasure.

Borodine considered going to various cafés where he might be able to meet a woman who'd be willing to spend the night, or at least a few hours, with him. But he wasn't much good at that kind of casual arrangement when he was single, and he didn't think he'd be any better at it now that he was married and terribly lonely.

Then late one afternoon, when he was walking in Gorky Park he suddenly saw Glazunov. He would have avoided her, but she recognized him and waved.

He went up to her and said, "I didn't know you came here."

"Now and then," she answered. "My rooms are on the other side of the park, and when the weather is nice, I enjoy walking to them."

Borodine nodded and fell in beside her.

They walked for some distance without speaking; then suddenly Borodine said, "I haven't had any dinner yet, Captain, and I was wondering if you would join me?"

Glazunov stopped and, looking straight at him, answered, "Yes. But first I want to go home and freshen up. Would you mind waiting for me?"

Borodine shook his head. "Not at all."

They continued to walk through the park in silence, and a few minutes later came out on the other side of it.

"I live two streets from here," Glazunov said.

Borodine realized the buildings were rather old, but they were kept in good repair. A few minutes later, he followed her up four flights of steps and along a dimly lit hallway to the door of her apartment.

She unlocked the door and opened it. "Please," she said, gesturing to him to enter. "The light switch is on the wall to the right."

Borodine reached over and flipped the switch.

"Two rooms and a private bathroom," Glazunov said. "And part of one room is also the kitchen."

Borodine looked around. The apartment was very small. Each room was no more than three by four meters. The bedroom had a window but the combination living room and kitchen had none. Still, small as the apartment was, it was furnished and decorated with taste.

"I'll try not to be too long," Glazunov said. "There's vodka in the refrigerator and glasses in the cabinet above the sink." She went into the bedroom and closed the door behind her.

Borodine removed his jacket and placed it on the back of a chair. He poured himself a vodka and sat down on one of the four kitchen chairs placed around the small square table.

"Have you found the vodka?" she called from behind the bedroom door.

"Yes," Borodine answered.

"There are few magazines in the living room."

"That's all right. I'm fine just the way I am." And he was. For the first time since he'd come to Moscow, he felt relaxed. It was almost like being at home.

He finished his vodka and was about to pour another, when the bedroom door opened and Glazunov walked out. She wore a white, somewhat threadbare, terry cloth robe. Her black hair, held in place with a simple red ribbon, cascaded to her shoulders. The robe clung to her body the way her uniform never did.

"I just want to take a quick shower," she said.

Borodine was on his feet. Suddenly he had her in his arms and was kissing her passionately.

"I didn't ask you here to make love to me," she said, when he stopped kissing her.

Borodine let go of her and dropped his hands. "I'm sorry," he apologized. "I'll go if you want me to."

She frowned. "If it's not the bed, it's nothing?"

Borodine began to stammer. "I didn't think Captain —"

"You may call me Irena. There's no need to —"

"You're right," he said. "There's no need to be so formal. My given name is Igor."

"I don't want you to go," she said. "And I don't want you to make love to me. That's not true either. I do want you to make love to me. But not now."

Borodine took her in his arms, hoping to convince her.

"You're a married man," she said. "I will not come between you and your wife."

Again he let go of her and walked to the other side of the table.

"Would it make you feel better," she said, "to know that I'd even like to fall in love with you, if it were possible. But it's not possible, is it? Not without me being hurt and I don't want to be hurt, Igor. Do you understand that?"

"Yes, of course I do."

"I want to be very good friends. Do you think that's possible?"

"Yes," he answered in a very low voice. "Yes, Irena, it's possible."

Then she reached across the table and took hold of his hand. "Don't be hurt or disappointed. Trust me. This way neither one of us will have anything to feel guilty about."

Borodine nodded and poured himself another drink. "To our friendship," he toasted.

"I'll drink from your glass," Irena said.

Borodine drank; then he handed the glass to her.

"To our friendship," Irena said; she drank.

"Go have your shower," Borodine told her. "I'm getting very hungry."

"Yes, so am I," she answered.

During the next two days Boxer divided his time between studying the maps of the South Atlantic and sightseeing in Cannes. And except for joining Sanchez and the other guests aboard the *Mary-Ann* for dinner, he avoided them. He even absented himself from the two parties that Sanchez gave.

The maps he studied did not make him feel very good about the mission. The area where the salvage was to take place was an undersea plain with no place to hide. He was worried about what kind of ASW devices the trawlers on the surface would have? If they were very sophisticated, his mission would be that much harder and might necessitate their destruction.

Late in the afternoon on the third day, Boxer saw Tracy and Byron Hayes come aboard. She was as startlingly attractive as he had remembered. She wore a white linen suit that accentuated her svelte body and a wide-brimmed straw hat hid most of her strawberry blond hair.

She saw him looking down, flashed a broad smile, and waved.

Boxer waved back. Because he had spent most of his time in Washington with Kathy, he hadn't bothered to call her when he had been there. Besides, the last time they had been together they had argued.

Sanchez came alongside Boxer, and with a grin on his face, he said, "She's a fine-looking woman, isn't she, Captain?"

Boxer turned to him. "That's something we both know," he answered.

Sanchez nodded. "Will you be joining us for dinner?" he asked. "I'm sure Tracy would appreciate your company."

"No, I have some things I want to do," Boxer said.

"Suit yourself," Sanchez said and added, "Oh, by the way we sail at twenty-two hundred hours. Word came over the radio a few minutes ago."

"And did our rendezvous point with the *Shark* come also?" Boxer asked, somewhat annoyed by Sanchez's attitude.

"No."

"Now if you'll excuse me," Boxer said, "I'll go ashore and take care of a few things."

"Certainly," Sanchez answered, stepping aside.

Boxer hurried off the *Mary-Ann* and headed straight for the Hilton Hotel, where he sat down in the lobby and wrote three letters: the first was to his son, John; the second was addressed to his father, though it was for both his parents; and the third went to Kathy. After he'd mailed the letters, he walked around the streets, enjoying the sights and sounds of the city; then he found a small bistro and had a wonderful dinner of bouillabaisse with freshly baked bread and a liter of local white wine. When he returned to the *Mary-Ann* the guests were gathered on the after deck, but he went straight to the bridge.

"I will take her out of the harbor," he told Sanchez's captain.

"As you wish," the man replied, obviously annoyed.

"That's right," Boxer answered, "as I wish."

By the time Boxer received clearance from the harbor master, another hour had passed; then it took an additional thirty minutes to ease the *Mary-Ann* away from the dock, turn her around, and head out to sea.

When the twinkling lights of Cannes lay well astern of them, Boxer turned the command of the bridge back to the captain of the *Mary-Ann* and left the bridge. Most of the guests were still up, enjoying a nightcap in the saloon. For a moment, he considered joining them. But then he decided to maintain the distance he had already put between himself and them. After all, he was aboard the *Mary-Ann* because he had to be, and they were aboard because they wanted to be.

A short time later, he was in his own cabin enjoying a vodka on the rocks and preparing to go to sleep. Finally, he climbed into bed and switched off the light. He was pleasantly tired and slipped quickly into a restful sleep.

Something, or someone was blowing into his ear. He opened his eyes. There was just enough light in the room for him to see Tracy. She was naked.

Grinning, she said, "I'll bet you thought you were dreaming."

Between them there was nothing more than lust and antagonism mixed in equal proportions. She had been one of Sanchez's guests when the *Mary-Ann* had struck the *Sting Ray*. Writing about that disaster and about him, she had managed to go from a society columnist to a full-fledged reporter with her own by-line.

"Are you going to sleep here?" Boxer asked.

"Yes. I intend to get what I want while the getting is good," she answered.

CHAPTER 16

Borodine held the *Q-21* at periscope depth. "The trawlers are there," he said, moving away from the eyepiece to let Viktor have a look.

"I count four," Viktor said, making a three-hundred-and-sixty-degree sweep of the area.

"Two more should be close by," Borodine commented.

"Shouldn't they have located us by now?" Viktor asked.

"About five minutes ago according to the COMMCOMP," Borodine replied.

"That sky is steel gray," Viktor said.

Borodine nodded. "Lower the periscope, Viktor. We'll cruise around for a while. Maybe everyone topside is asleep, or drunk."

Viktor pressed a button and the periscope retracted into its well.

Borodine frowned. "I don't like it," he said. "I don't like it in the least. Those trawlers are supposed to provide the work area with cover."

Viktor shrugged. "You already know my opinion about most surface units," he said.

"I should," Borodine answered. "It's the same as mine."

Borodine switched from the automatic navigation system to the manual. "Helmsman," he said, "keep the present course for five minutes; then make a one-hundred-and-eight-degree turn; hold that course for five minutes and return to your former heading for five minutes."

"Aye, aye, Captain."

"That should provide our surface friends with more than enough time to ID us, don't you think?"

"Major Petrovich," Borodine said over the MC system, "please report to the bridge."

"I'll bet you five Rubles Markov comes along with him," Viktor said.

"Would you expect him to do anything else?"

"It would make life more interesting if he wasn't so damn predictable," Viktor answered.

Petrovich came up to the bridge. He was a solidly built, fair complexioned man, with blond hair, a strong jaw and a bull neck. He had started his military career in the ranks at the age of eighteen when he'd joined the Naval Marines.

"Are you and your men ready?" Borodine asked.

Petrovich nodded.

"Captain," Markov said, coming up to the bridge, "is anything wrong?"

"The surface units haven't ID'd us and we've been in their scan area for the past ten — no, twelve — minutes."

Markov frowned.

"Have you located the work station?" Alexander asked.

"Not yet. There's a possibility that it hasn't been put down," Borodine answered.

Suddenly there was the familiar ping of the sonar signal striking the hull of the *Q-21*.

"Well, well," Borodine commented, "someone is finally awake up there." He keyed the COMMO. "Send a standard ID signal."

"Aye, aye, Captain."

Borodine switched on the MC. "All hands, stand by ... stand by!" He hit the klaxon button once. "Prepare to surface ... deck detail exit through hatches one and five... Bridge detail stand by... Going to manual control... Diving planes up zero five degrees..."

"Diving planes up zero five degrees," the DO repeated.

"Blow forward and aft ballast," Borodine ordered.

"Target ... one four six degrees ... range six thousand yards ... speed one eight knots," the SO reported. "Second target, one four eight degrees ... range, six thousand five hundred yards ... speed sixteen knots."

"ID both targets," Borodine said, guessing they were the two missing trawlers. He kept his eyes on the large depth gauge. The *Sea Savage* was forty feet below the surface.

"Targets ID ... both trawlers ... one, the *Ural* ... two, the *Kishky*," the SO officer reported.

"Blow main ballast," Borodine ordered.

"Blowing main ballast," the DO repeated.

The air rushing into the ballast tanks made a hissing sound. Borodine watched the depth gauge. The needle swung rapidly to zero. "Surface," he ordered over the MC. "Surface. Deck details out; bridge detail out." Then he said, "Viktor take the CONN down here until I'm topside; then join me." He hurried through the open bulkhead door, leading to the steps inside the sail. Moments later he was on the outside bridge. "I have the CONN," he said to Viktor over the phone.

The *Sea Savage* had surfaced two hundred yards from the nearest trawler. Already the men on aboard the ships were crowding the railings to look at the submarine.

After an exchange of signals, Borodine was informed by the squadron commander, Captain Georgi Danilov, that they were ready to put the sea station in place and begin the salvage operation.

Borodine summoned Alexander and Markov to the bridge. "We're going to have a conference with Captain Danilov,"

Borodine said, suppressing his rage. "I want the two of you there to hear exactly what I tell this damn fisherman." Then to his communications officer, he said, "Signal Captain Danilov that I'm coming aboard his ship."

"Aye, aye, Captain," the CO answered.

A few minutes later the *Sea Savage* hove to alongside the trawler, *Kishky*.

"Get bow and stern lines out," Borodine ordered.

Men aboard the trawler threw lines to the deck details on the *Sea Savage*.

"Secure lines," Borodine said; then keying the engine room, he told the EO, "Keep her steady as she goes."

"One zero two zero revs," the EO answered.

Borodine fed the figure into the COMMCOMP. "One two zero revs will do fine," he answered.

"Aye, aye, Captain," the EO answered.

A Jacob's ladder was put over the side of the trawler.

Borodine summoned Viktor to the bridge and gave the CONN to him; then he quickly climbed the Jacob's ladder, with Alexander behind him and Markov last.

Danilov, a tall, thin, bearded man, stepped forward to greet Borodine and introduced himself.

Borodine nodded and waited until Alexander and Markov were alongside him before he introduced them. After the handshaking, he said, "Your quarters, Captain."

Danilov gestured toward the cabin.

A few minutes later they were seated around a plain wooden table.

"A drink?" Danilov offered.

"How soon can you launch the undersea station?" Borodine asked, ignoring the man's offer.

"Any time you want it launched," Danilov answered, frowning.

"Launch it now," Borodine said.

"But it's sixteen hundred hours; we won't have much daylight left."

"Then you'll work under floodlights," Borodine said. "I want the station launched now. I also want you to understand that your ships are here to protect my men, more accurately Major Petrovich's men. That means your men will man the ASDW equipment and weapons twenty-four hours a day. Do you understand that?"

Danilov's ears turned very red.

"It took you people over twelve minutes to search and find the *Sea Savage*. That's too long. From now on, your people will drill every day. You will have your SO officers organize training drills. Is all this clear, Captain?"

"I am not responsible to you," Danilov answered. "I have no orders —"

"I don't give a damn about your orders," Borodine said. "Your ships are here to support me. Follow my orders, or I promise you, you'll be pushing papers around some prison."

"But you haven't got the right —"

"Complain about it when you return to port," Borodine said. "But now I'm taking the right. You ask one more question about my authority, I'll arrest you and put your second in command."

Danilov switched on the PA system. "All hands ... all hands stand by to launch undersea station... Stand by... Master divers report to main diving officer." He switched off the system, looked at Borodine, and asked, "Are you satisfied, Captain?"

"It will take a lot more than that to satisfy me, Captain," Borodine said. "And to make sure I will be satisfied, Captain Markov will remain aboard your ship until this operation is completed."

Markov's jaw went slack.

Pleased that he had taken him by surprise, Borodine said, "It is your responsibility to see that the surface ships protect the undersea station."

"Aye, aye, Captain," Markov answered.

Borodine nodded, then stood up. "Major," he said, "let's return to the *Sea Savage*. I want to be below when the undersea station is assembled."

"It will take most of the night," Danilov said lamely.

"Then we will begin salvage operations tomorrow morning," Borodine said, as he stood up. Looking at Markov, he added, "I'll have your gear transferred before we dive."

"Thank you, Captain," Markov answered.

Borodine left the cabin and hurried down the Jacob's ladder to the deck of the *Sea Savage*. When he was back on the bridge, he exploded with laughter.

Petrovich, too, laughed.

"Viktor," Borodine said, "I just killed two birds with one stone, as the saying goes." And again he laughed.

"He scared Captain Danilov shitless, and then he palmed Markov off on him," Alexander explained. "Markov won't be with us for the duration of this operation."

"How did you manage to do that?" Viktor asked, looking at Borodine.

"It just came to me, while I was talking to Danilov and I did it."

"Well, good for you!" Viktor said.

Borodine signaled his CO. "I want a special channel kept open with Captain Danilov," Borodine said.

"Aye, aye, Captain," the CO answered.

"Viktor, we'll go down to the bottom. That's three hundred feet; then Alexander and I'll go out and take a look around."

"Just the two of you?"

"I'll take about six other men," Borodine said. "I want to make sure those capsules are set down correctly."

Viktor nodded.

"It will take at least two hours to decompress when we re-enter the *Sea Savage*."

"I'll have the chamber brought up to pressure for you," Viktor answered.

Borodine looked around. The sky was still gray but the wind was down. "Deck details," he said over the MC, "cast off fore and aft lines... Clear the deck!" He keyed the EO. "Give me ten knots," he said, "starting now."

"Aye, aye, Captain. Ten knots."

Borodine waited until the *Sea Savage* pulled several yards in front of the trawler before he said, "All hands prepare to dive!" He sounded the klaxon twice. "Bridge detail go below!" He was the next to last man off the bridge. He looked back over his shoulder and saw the chief dog the hatch cover. Moments later he sat down in front of the COMMCOMP. "I have the CONN," he announced.

"All systems on manual," Viktor said.

"Switching systems to autocontrol," Borodine said.

"Systems on automatic," Viktor responded.

Borodine set three hundred and fifty feet into the automatic dive control system. The DIVCONTSYST did the rest, including the flooding of the ballast tanks and the actuation of the fore and aft diving planes.

"Making one hundred feet," Borodine announced over the MC.

"DC," he said, keying the damage control officer, "check all systems."

"Systems go," the DC reported.

"Making two hundred feet," Borodine announced.

Slowly the *Sea Savage* began to level out.

Borodine watched the AUTODG: the rate of descent was decreasing. The diving planes were being brought into a null position.

"Making two five zero feet," Borodine announced. "Two seven five feet ... coming to three hundred feet ... all engines stopped!"

"Engines stopped," the EO answered.

The *Sea Savage* eased down on the bottom and stayed there.

"A perfect landing!" Borodine exclaimed, smiling at the other officers on the bridge. He keyed the COMMO. "Are those channels open yet to the surface?" he asked.

"Get me Captain Danilov," Borodine said.

Moments later Captain Danilov answered.

"We're on the bottom," Borodine said. "Commence your operation... Put the station in place."

"Aye, aye, Captain," Danilov answered.

"Out," Borodine responded; then to Viktor he said, "I think we'll get more cooperation from Danilov than we'll know what to do with."

"That's good," Viktor answered. "It's even better that Markov will be on his back and not on ours."

"Yes," Borodine said. "That's very good." Then he added, "Better start things moving for the dive outside."

"Everything is ready," Viktor said. "All you have to do is put on your scuba gear and walk out through the dive chamber."

Borodine, Alexander and six of Alexander's marines moved to the right of the *Sea Savage*, where regular divers were already moving high intensity lights into position. They worked efficiently, if not quickly.

Borodine took his men over the site. Pieces of wreckage were strewn over a wide area. Here and there they saw bits of barnacle-encrusted metal.

Alexander pointed to a large cylindrical object which once had been a cannon, and said, "I wonder what its range was?"

"Probably not more than ten to fifteen meters, if that," Borodine answered.

Suddenly one of the marines found a human skull, with the mandible missing.

"Put it down," Alexander said. "And let him sleep where you found him."

The man placed the skull back in the white sand.

The bright lights were beginning to attract fish of every description, including sharks. Borodine pointed to them and said, "We'll have the men work in groups of three. One man will look out for sharks and killer whales. Sharks can be dealt with, but as soon as a killer whale is spotted the men are to retreat to the station."

"I'll pass the word," Alexander said.

Borodine moved into the shadowy world beyond the reach of the yellow circles made by the high-intensity lamps.

Alexander and the marines followed him.

"The undersea maps show this bottom to be as flat as this for hundreds of miles in every direction," Borodine said. "I asked one of our specialists why it's so flat and he told me it was a plain that extended out from the African coast. But I've seen undersea plains before and none of them looked as if they had been worked on by earth movers; yet this one does."

"Captain," Danilov said, "the first section of the station is on its way down."

"Very good," Borodine said.

"Why the concern about the terrain?" Alexander asked.

"I don't understand it. There's not even a boulder in sight and there aren't many large rocks."

"So?"

"Something happened down here that we don't know about," Borodine said.

"Any ideas?" Alexander asked.

"None," Borodine answered, turning back toward the lighted area. There he waited until the first capsule was down and set into place, before he returned to the *Sea Savage* and three hours of decompression.

Borodine lay in the bunk with his eyes closed. The topography of the bottom bothered him. He pursed his lips. Something had to have scoured it clean, leaving only a thin cover of sand. Something that the experts didn't know anything about, or if they did know, they purposely had not given him the information. Whatever the reason, he was more than just concerned: he was worried!

Even though Tracy was aboard the *Mary-Ann*, Boxer maintained his distance from the rest of the guests. But late one afternoon, after Boxer and Tracy had finished making love, Tracy asked him to go to the evening cocktail party with her.

"I'd rather not," Boxer answered.

"It would make me happy," Tracy said. "The only time I ever get to see you is in bed and then we don't spend any time talking."

"Not much," he admitted.

"You bastard!" she exclaimed and began tickling him.

Boxer squirmed and wriggled. He was very ticklish. "Okay," he laughed. "Okay, I'll go to the damn cocktail party…"

At 1700 hours Boxer and Tracy joined Sanchez and the other guests on the after deck of the *Mary-Ann* for the evening cocktail party.

"So this lovely young woman has been able to get you to join us," Sanchez said, with a large toothy smile. "The power of women," he said, "is beyond reckoning."

Boxer smiled back but said nothing, though he wondered if Tracy and Sanchez still slept together. But he realized that even if they did, it was none of his business. He didn't have any real emotional ties to her.

"Excuse me," Sanchez said. "I see one of my other guests is motioning to me."

Boxer nodded.

"He's such a dear," Tracy said. "You'd be surprised how generous that man can be."

"In my dealings with him thus far I haven't seen that side of him," Boxer answered.

"In another second," Tracy chided, "your back will arch and you'll begin to growl."

"That obvious?"

She nodded.

"Let's get a drink," Boxer said, folding her arm around his.

"Good idea," she answered.

Boxer quickly discovered that Tracy knew everyone. And everyone was "a dear," or "charming," or "so very chic." Finally he had had enough and said, "No more introductions. I don't want to meet another person."

"But darling —"

"No more introductions," he said sternly.

"But these people are my friends," Tracy objected.

"With all due respect to you," he said, "most of them are worthless parasites, who never have done a day's work in their lives: honest or dishonest."

She smiled up at him. "Hicks said you were something else when you got your temper up."

"What?"

"Hicks … remember him? I went to see him in the hospital. He thinks if there ever was a skipper next to God, you're it."

Boxer suddenly felt chilled.

"I asked him what made him change his mind," she said. "But he wouldn't tell me." She pouted. "He was in some kind of a terrible automobile accident in Brazil of all places. He's pretty badly banged up. The steering column went through his chest."

Boxer breathed more easily. He knew Tracy well enough to know that if she had had the slightest inkling of what really had happened to Hicks, she'd go after it like a shark after prey until she got what she wanted; then she'd write about it, regardless of who or what that might endanger.

"There's Byron!" she exclaimed, waving to him before Boxer could stop her. "I flew over with him."

Boxer finished his drink, as Hayes came toward them. "Now there's a man who's really interesting," she whispered.

"Not to me," Boxer answered.

"Well, well, well," Byron said, looking at Boxer, "if it isn't the skipper himself."

Boxer said nothing.

"I can't imagine what you're doing here," Hayes said.

"Like yourself," Boxer answered, "I'm a guest of Sanchez."

"Strange that you're here, considering how much you hate him."

Again Boxer remained silent.

Hayes turned to Tracy. "Ask him about Dee Long," he said.

"There's nothing to ask," Boxer said. "She died aboard my ship."

"She was murdered aboard your ship," Hayes said.

"That's right; she was murdered aboard my ship."

Hayes smiled. "Come on, Skipper, there's more to it than that."

"More than what?" Tracy asked.

"Ask the skipper here," Hayes answered and he walked away.

"What the hell was he talking about?" Tracy answered. "Who was Dee Long?"

Boxer shook his head. "Let it alone, Tracy, just let it alone. Let's go," he said, "I could use another drink."

"Just what is going on between the two of you?" she asked, following him across the deck.

"Nothing."

"Then why are you so angry?" she pressed.

Boxer stopped short. "No more questions," he said loudly enough for almost everyone on deck to hear."

"But —"

"There are no buts on this one," he said. "No buts at all!"

"Is that an order?" She asked defiantly.

He was sorely tempted to say that it was. But instead, he said, "It just doesn't concern you."

"It might concern my readers."

Boxer took a deep breath and slowly exhaled. "Let's not argue about it."

"That's fine with me. I wasn't the one who started the argument."

"Okay," Boxer said. "I just don't want you asking me a lot of questions about something that doesn't concern you in the least."

"There you go telling me what concerns me," Tracy said.

"It happened to me aboard my ship," Boxer answered.

"Why was Miss Long murdered?"

Boxer shook his. "It was a mistake for me to come out here," he said; then turned around and walked away

"You're walking away, just like that?" she shouted.

Boxer didn't even look back.

"You're a bastard, Jack Boxer," Tracy yelled. "A bastard!"

Boxer returned to his cabin, poured himself a double Scotch, and drank it; poured another and drank that one too, before he was able to lose some of his anger.

On the very night of Boxer's argument with Tracy, she had a steward move her clothing out of his cabin. And for the days that followed he kept more to himself than he previously had. But on the evening of the eighth day, Sanchez summoned him to his office.

"There will be a special message coming for you in approximately thirty minutes," Sanchez said, looking up at him from the opposite side of the desk.

Boxer checked his watch. The time was eighteen hundred.

"My guess is that you'll be leaving us soon," Sanchez commented.

"It can't be soon enough for me," Boxer responded.

"I can't say that I'm sorry to see you go either," Sanchez said. "You're not exactly an endearing person."

"I guess not," Boxer agreed. "But then again why should I be when I have little or no use for the people I'm with."

Sanchez fitted a cigarette into a gold-and-ivory holder, before he said, "Tracy is very angry at you."

"That's Tracy's problem."

"It might become yours. She knows there's a story in what Hayes told her and she wants it."

"She won't get it from me, and Hayes would be a fool to say anything more. He has already said too much."

"You know, the two of you do work for the same organization," Sanchez said, blowing smoke off to his left side.

"That's the Company's problem," Boxer answered.

"So Tracy has a problem and the Company has a problem, but you don't have any?"

"None," Boxer said.

"I think you're blind and I make it a practice to help blind people, whether they're physically blind and need to be guided across the street or psychologically blind and need to be guided toward some truth that they can't perceive, much less understand."

"Thanks. But no thanks," Boxer said. "I don't need your help."

"Nonetheless I'll give it. You do have a problem. Tracy is your problem and Hayes is your problem. Hayes has powerful friends."

"Like yourself?"

"Yes, like myself."

"And Tracy has a poison pen," Boxer said.

"That and considerable influence."

"Okay, Sanchez, you can rest easy for today. You've done your good deed. Now if you don't mind, I'll go to the radio room."

Sanchez nodded.

Boxer went to the door, stopped, turned, and said, "Thanks for the warning."

"My pleasure," Sanchez replied without a smile.

The message for Boxer came on schedule. Boxer was ordered to rendezvous with and take command of the *Shark* at approximately 0200 hours the following morning; then to proceed to twenty-seven degrees three minutes north latitude, twelve degrees sixteen minutes east longitude. The message came directly from Kinkade.

Boxer shredded the message and went down to the after deck. He beckoned to Sanchez, and when they were out of earshot of the other guests, he told him the news.

Sanchez's face remained expressionless. "The *Shark* and not the *Tecumseh*?" he asked.

"The *Shark*," Boxer repeated.

"How long do you think your transfer will take?"

"A matter of minutes," Boxer answered.

"I don't want my guests to be aware of what's happening," Sanchez said.

"But they'll notice I'm gone."

"And I can make it very mysterious. You'll rejoin us after the mission. I'd rather not have them aware of the *Shark*."

"How are you going to stop —"

"There are ways," Sanchez said.

"Drugs?"

"Yes."

"I don't like it," Boxer said gruffly.

"There isn't any other way."

"All right," Boxer said after a few moments of hesitation. "But not for the crew. It's too damn dangerous for them."

Sanchez nodded. "Not for the crew. You have my word on that."

Boxer gestured toward the guests. "A few of them are looking at us," he said.

"As soon as you came down here, all of them knew something had come up."

"See you at zero two hundred," Boxer said and walked away. He returned to his cabin and began to pack his things. Despite the danger he'd be facing, he was anxious to return to the *Shark*.

CHAPTER 17

Boxer made the transfer to the *Shark* in a matter of minutes and immediately took the CONN. He keyed the EO. "One five knots," he said.

"One five knots, Skipper," the EO answered.

"All hands now hear this," Boxer said over the MC. "Prepare to dive... Prepare to dive." He hit the klaxon twice and hurried off the outside bridge, looking back over his shoulder to make sure the sailor behind him dogged the hatch shut; then he went to the inside bridge, where the men and the equipment were bathed in the red glow of night lighting.

Bush was standing at the COMMCOMP. "Welcome aboard, Captain," he said extending his hand.

Boxer shook it. "Bush," he said, purposely avoiding the use of his rank, "everyone on the *Shark* calls me skipper. You will too. But we'll talk about various things later. Now I have to put this boat down." He let go of Bush's hand and keyed the DO. "Switching to AUTODIV."

"EPC set and DDRO set," the DO answered.

Boxer switched from night lighting to day. He set the AUTODIV for two hundred feet; then settled into the swivel chair in front of COMMCOMP and watched the instruments. "Making five zero feet," he called out over the MC. He glanced at Cowly, who grinned back at him.

"Skipper," the SO said, "do you want to have the *Mary-Ann* tracked?"

"Negative," Boxer answered. He glanced at the DDR. "Making one zero zero feet."

Bush leaned toward him. "Captain — I mean, Skipper — tracking any target is good practice."

"Absolutely right," Boxer answered, smiling at him. "But the sonar section aboard the *Shark* is so good that they don't have to track a known target."

Bush flushed.

"Making one five zero feet," Boxer announced. "Putting new course into AUTONAV and NAVCLOCK systems," he said and dialed in twenty-seven degrees three minutes North Latitude and twelve degrees sixteen minutes East Longitude into the two control systems.

"Skipper," the COMMO keyed.

"Go ahead," Boxer said.

"Message coming through for you in Cobra Code ... looks like a long one."

"Roger that... Set up the decoder," Boxer said. "I'll be there by and by."

"Sure ... glad to have you aboard," the COMMO said.

"Glad to be aboard," Boxer said.

"Roger that and out," the COMMO said.

"Making two zero zero feet," Boxer said, as he watched the EDG and the bubble on the level indicator come to center. "Dive completed ... lowering sail." He pressed a series of buttons that activated the sail's retraction mechanism. "Sail down," he said, as soon as the indication came on the COMMCOMP screen.

For the next few minutes Boxer got a quick rundown on the operational status of every section from each section officer, then a detailed picture of the *Shark*'s operation from Cowly.

"Everything is in fine shape," he said. "My compliments, Mister Bush."

Bush nodded.

"Where's Tom?" Boxer asked, realizing his friend had neither come to the bridge to welcome him, nor communicated with him by phone.

Cowly looked toward Bush.

"I've ordered Major Redfern to keep clear of the bridge unless he is summoned," Bush said.

"Oh," Boxer said, and opening the MC system, he said, "Major Redfern, report to the bridge immediately. Major Redfern, report to the bridge immediately."

"May I be excused," Bush asked.

"No," Boxer said. "You're on the bridge until I leave it."

Bush nodded.

Tom came running up to the bridge. "Skipper, am I glad to see you."

The two of them shook hands.

"How's Sue-Ann?" Boxer asked.

"Great. The senator sends his best," Redfern said.

"How are your men?"

"Ready for action," Redfern answered.

"Replacements for those we lost?"

"None yet," Redfern answered. "I didn't have enough time to screen the possibilities, but I will when we return."

"That leaves us eight men short," Boxer said.

Redfern nodded. "Will that present a problem?"

"I don't think so," Boxer said. "Tell your guys I'll pay them a visit later. Maybe even stay for a few beers."

Redfern punched Boxer in the shoulder. "It's great to have you here, Skipper."

Boxer nodded. "Listen, I have to go to communications," he said. "I can't hang around here and jaw with you."

Redfern tapped him on the shoulder again, turned, and left the bridge.

"Cowly, you have the CONN," Boxer said.

"Okay, Skipper," Cowly answered.

Boxer left the COMMCOMP and made his way to the COMMCENTER, stopping now and then to speak to some of the men.

"Message is complete and already in the decoder," the COMMO said.

Boxer sat down in front of the decoder. Anything coming coded in Cobra was for his eyes only. He switched on the printer and the decoder. The printed message began:

FROM: KINKADE ... DATE JUNE THE 16TH ... LANGLEY, VA.

TO: CAPT. JACK BOXER, *SHARK*.

RE: MISSION.

PROCEED TO 27 ± 3'N LAT, 12°16'E *LAT* ... *ENGAGE ENEMY AND DESTROY U. SEA STATION... TAKE GOLD BACK TO MARY-ANN*

RETURN WITH SAID VESSEL TO U.S.

OPERATION IS AS FOLLOWS ... TWO HOURS BEFORE YOU LAUNCH ATTACK SEND THREE RADIO SIG OF FOUR KHERTZ... THESE SIG WILL ACTIVATE EXPLOSIVE WW DEVICES ABOARD R TANKER THIRTY K NE OF YOUR POSITION... THAT WILL DRAW OFF SURFACE VESSELS... ATTACK TEN MINUTES LATER... SUGGEST NO PRISONERS BE TAKEN... CAPT BUSH IS TO ACT AS YOUR EXEC... YOUR CASUALTIES WILL BE PLACED ABOARD THE *TECUMSEH*... MAPS OF THE AREA WHERE THE ACTION WILL TAKE PLACE ARE IN BUSH'S POSSESSION...

GOOD LUCK, KINKADE

Boxer switched off the decoder and printer. The only thing of value in the entire message was the information about the radio signals. The rest of it was bullshit, especially the part about Bush. He wasn't about to let Bush act as his EXO. Bush was along for the ride and that was all he'd get. A ride.

Boxer took the printed message and ran it through the shredder. "Thanks," he said to the COMMO.

"Any time, Skipper," the COMMO answered.

Boxer left the SIGCENT. It was time to have a talk with Bush. He returned to the bridge and said, "Bush, let's go to my quarters."

"Yes, I think that would be a good idea," Bush answered.

Boxer led the way, and once inside his cabin, he dropped down on his bunk and gestured to Bush to sit in the chair opposite him.

"You may smoke, if you want to," Boxer said, taking a pipe off the shelf behind him and filling it with tobacco.

"I don't smoke," Bush said.

Boxer nodded and lit up. "You have some maps," he said. "Please place them in my chart case under the COMMCOMP."

"But they're top secret," Bush complained.

"Put them in my chart case," Boxer said. "No one on the *Shark* is a spy and if someone were, where would he go with them?"

"I'll require the usual written receipt," Bush said.

Boxer blew a cloud of smoke out of the pipe bowl but he said nothing about signing a receipt.

"Will there be anything else?" Bush asked.

"Yes," Boxer answered. "You're along to watchdog me and that's all you're going to do. Do I make myself clear?"

Bush flushed. "I was given to understand that I would act as your EXO."

"You were given to understand wrong," Boxer lied. "Mister Cowly is my EXO."

"I would like that confirmed."

"I'm doing that just now," Boxer said.

"I mean by radio."

Boxer leaned forward, took the pipe out of his mouth, and pointing the stem at Bush, said, "This is not the navy; this is a shadowy place between two government agencies. The rules and regs that govern either agency change like light that passes through a prism. The men aboard the *Shark* are the best of their kind, matched only by the men aboard the *Q-21*."

"I was briefed about your mission on Torpay," Bush answered.

"I'm sure you were," Boxer said, still pointing his pipe at him. "But you'd have had to have been there to fully understand and appreciate it. It was the men of the *Shark* who did it, not me or Harris, who was later killed, not any of the officers. It was the men."

"Captain — Skipper — without leadership these men, like other men, are just another sub crew."

Boxer put the pipe back in his mouth. "You'll learn," he said, "and then again maybe you won't. But while you're aboard, you will not take part in the operation of this boat. You're free to ask any man or officer any questions. But you will not be free to harass or discipline anyone."

"In other words, I'm an observer, nothing else," Bush said brittlely.

Boxer nodded. "Unless, of course, I ask, or order, you to do something."

Bush said nothing.

"That about covers what I wanted to say," Boxer said.

"I will, of course, file a complaint, when I return to base," Bush said.

"Everything we've been saying to one another is on tapes," Boxer said. "Those tapes go to our bosses. But if it makes you feel any better, go ahead and file your complaint."

"Are you finished, Skipper?" Bush asked.

"Yes."

Bush stood up and walked to the door. "Good night, or should I say good morning."

Boxer glanced at his watch. It was 0424. He had been aboard the *Shark* for two hours and twenty minutes. He looked at Bush, who was standing at the door and said, "Good morning, Mister Bush."

Borodine sat in his cabin and listened to a tape of the Brahms Double Concerto. He was in a melancholy mood. The tests he had run for the last few days to test the ASW capabilities of the surface were failures. The sonar operators had difficulty finding *Sea Savage* and even more difficulty, once they found the *Sea Savage*, to track it.

In disgust, Borodine had set the *Sea Savage* down on the bottom and had gone out to watch the actual salvage work.

The gold was there, but the bars were scattered over a very large area and the recovery was slow. Each bar had to be located with special metal detectors. This was done by careful sweeps over a predetermined area, which was placed under a grid that was carefully searched with a metal detector. As soon as the presence of metal was indicated, a two-man team was assigned to dig out the metal. More often than not, it was metal from the wreckage of the ship. The work was slow and laborious. In three days' work, a total of fifty bars of gold had been recovered. The experts in Moscow were sure that there were at least two hundred bars there.

The first side of the tape came to an end. Borodine reached over and reversed it. He was baby-sitting the operation and he didn't like it.

"I don't like anything about it," he said aloud, as the music came on again.

A beeping from his COMMCOMP made him lower the music and answer the call.

"Comrade Captain," the radio officer said, "the tanker *Kurskia* is entering our zone."

"Have you gotten a fix on her?"

"Just fifteen miles southwest of us," the officer answered.

"Signal Comrade Captain Danilov. Tell him to signal the tanker to keep away from the fishing grounds."

"Aye, aye, Comrade Captain."

Borodine returned to the music and his thoughts about Galena and Irena, his wife and the woman he was sure would become his mistress. He had never thought of himself as a man who could have a mistress, or as a man to whom women gravitated; yet, to his complete astonishment, this seemed to be true. He did not understand it. If he were a woman, he would not be in the slightest bit interested in a man like himself. And yet —

A knock on the door interrupted his thinking.

"Come," he said, sitting up.

Alexander entered the cabin. "Igor, I wanted your permission to call off the operation for today. My men are tired and so far today's pickings have been very lean."

"Of course," Borodine answered and going to the COMMCOMP, he keyed Viktor. "Stop the salvage operation for the remainder of the day... Have all divers return to the undersea station… Work will resume at 0700 hours tomorrow."

"Aye, aye," Viktor answered.

"Thank you," Alexander said. "The men are very tired. Though I know it cannot be done, I would like to shorten their work hours."

Borodine shook his head. "I'd like to shorten this whole damn operation and go home."

Alexander nodded. "Most of my men feel that way too," he said.

"Not that I mean to pry," Alexander said, "but are you well?"

"Yes. Why do you ask?"

Alexander shrugged. "You look as if something is bothering you."

Borodine hadn't realized that his various concerns were affecting his appearance. "I'm perfectly fine," he answered. "I just don't like sitting out in the open, so to speak." He said nothing about his marital problems.

"I can understand that," Alexander said. "In a way, it's scary not to see anything for miles and miles around, not even a hillock."

"I can't imagine what could have scoured this area so flat," Borodine commented.

Alexander shrugged. "Neither can I," he answered.

"Have you time for a game of chess?" Borodine asked.

"Yes."

Borodine smiled, took out his chess set, and set it up on a small table. "Black or white?"

"White," Alexander answered.

"You make the first move," Borodine said.

"It would be a pleasure." Alexander moved one of his knights.

"Skipper," the COMMO said, "we picked up traffic between the Russians... The trawler to the tanker *Kurskia*."

"Range?" Boxer asked.

"Thirty miles from us ... moving north."

Boxer put the information into the COMMCOMP. "Can you give me a speed?" he asked.

"Negative on that ... transmissions were too brief."

"Roger that," Boxer said. "Out."

He turned to Cowly, who was on the bridge with him. "We should be in the hot zone within a half hour," he said. "General quarters in fifteen minutes."

"Skipper?"

Boxer turned to look at Bush. "Yes, what is it?"

"I request permission to accompany Major Redfern and his men," Bush said.

Boxer's first impulse was to deny permission, without explanation. But then he said, "You'll accompany me."

"You intend to go?" Bush asked incredulously.

"Mister Cowly will take command of the *Shark*. The operation should not last more than a half hour. We'll spend more time in the decompression chamber than we will outside the *Shark*."

"But if something should happen to you —"

"You'll be in command," Boxer answered; then he added, "That's if nothing happens to you."

Intermittently, during the next few minutes Boxer looked up at the master clock on the COMMCOMP. Given their speed, the *Shark* would be just out of the Q-2Ts sonar range in fifteen minutes. He switched on the MC. "All hands ... all hands now hear this... All ships' operations switching to manual... All sections officers report switchover."

One by one the sections officers reported the change from autocontrol to manual operation.

Boxer keyed the EO. "Go to zero five knots," he said.

"Aye, aye, Skipper, zero five knots," the EO answered.

Boxer felt the pit of his stomach tighten.

Suddenly GQ sounded.

Boxer switched on the MC. "Now hear this ... now hear this... We are at General Quarters..." Then he keyed the COMMO. "Send the following three radio signals at three-minute intervals... Have your men stand by to monitor any transmissions... Stand by to send radio signals." Boxer gave him the signal frequencies. "Send signals," he said.

He watched the clock.

Two minutes passed.

The COMMO keyed him and said, "The tanker *Kurskia* is sending out a Mayday... She's burning... Her position is twenty-eight degrees, fifteen minutes north latitude by thirteen degrees twenty-two minutes east longitude."

"Keep monitoring her transmissions," Boxer answered; then he keyed Redfern. "Have your men ready to go in forty minutes."

"Aye, aye, Skipper," Redfern answered.

Boxer ran a last-minute check on all systems. All systems were go.

Borodine was on the bridge. "What the hell is happening up there?"

"Three separate explosions aboard the *Kurskia*," Viktor said. "She is burning."

Borodine began to sweat.

"She has sent out an international Mayday," Viktor said. "Danilov requests permission to go to her."

"Permission denied," Borodine said. "Those trawlers have to safeguard the undersea station. They can't leave. Patch me into the *Kurskia*."

"Comrade Captain," the COMMO said, "we can't get through to the *Kurskia*. She's still transmitting but not receiving."

Borodine switched to the MC. "All hands stand by to get underway," Borodine said. "Now hear this ... the tanker *Kurskia* is burning and needs help... She's just forty miles from here... We'll be with her in an hour's time... All deck details will report to Comrade Lieutenant Popov for further instructions."

Borodine keyed his EO, "Give me flank speed."

"Flank speed, Comrade Captain," the EO answered.

Boxer put the *Kurskia*'s last reported position into the AUTONAV system. Then he changed the depth from three hundred feet to one hundred and fifty feet.

"Comrade Captain," Lieutenant Popov said, "I have organized three rescue details: Two to remain on deck and one to go into the water to help the men who have been injured aboard."

Borodine nodded. "Have several sharpshooters on deck in case we have trouble with sharks."

"Aye, aye, Comrade Captain," Popov answered.

Borodine turned to Alexander, who stood quietly by. Each minute, he looked more grave. "Your men will be safe," Borodine said. "The trawlers are in place and the men are still decompressing."

"I think they should be told why the *Sea Savage* had to leave so suddenly," Alexander said.

Borodine keyed his COMMO. "Send a signal to the undersea station... Tell them why we had to leave the salvage area and that as soon as the rescue operation is complete we'll return... Use our code two for transmissions... I don't want them to misunderstand."

"Aye, aye, Captain," the COMMO answered.

"That satisfy you?" Borodine asked, looking at Alexander.

"Thanks," his friend answered. "I know the men will appreciate it too."

Borodine scanned his instruments. "There's been a shift in current and a change in water temperature," he commented.

"I imagine that happens now and then," Viktor answered.

"Current coming from the south now, and the temperature has dropped off zero two degrees," Borodine commented.

"Comrade Captain," the COMMO said, "the *Kurskia* reports her entire bow section is burning."

"Try to reach her again," Borodine said.

"I have been trying," the COMMO said. "But she isn't responding... I am beginning to send your message to the undersea station."

"Skipper," the COMMO said, "the *Q-21* has just sent a message to the men in the undersea station."

"What the hell are you talking about?" Boxer asked.

"The *Q-21* is answering the *Kurskia*'s Mayday... The message was sent in code three... We have broken that code."

"That means those damn trawlers are still on station," Boxer said, turning to Cowly. "That also means we have to get in fast and out faster."

"Twice as fast as we thought," Cowly said.

Boxer turned his attention to Bush. "Do you want to start earning your pay?" he asked.

"I want to be useful," Bush answered.

"Okay, you'll take the minisub and knock out those trawlers."

"Sink them?"

"Sink every one of them," Boxer answered. "I don't need to be depth-charged while I'm down there." Then to Cowly he said, "Send someone from the fire control section with Bush."

"Aye, aye, Skipper," Cowly said.

"Listen," Boxer said, "you go in at flank speed and hit them before they have a chance to fight back."

"I'll try," Bush said.

"Don't try," Boxer answered. "Do it, or you and the man with you are dead and maybe all of us are dead."

"What if the *Q-21* comes back —"

"She'll be back," Boxer said, "and we'll have a fight on our hands. Better go down to the launch bay and get yourself ready." Boxer extended his hand. "Good luck."

"Good luck to you too," Bush answered shaking Boxer's hand.

"I'll say this for him," Boxer commented after Bush was gone, "he got guts."

Cowly agreed.

Boxer turned his attention to the instruments. The current had increased from three knots to five but the temperature remained the same. He keyed the launch bay, "Prepare to launch minisub," he said.

"Launch detail ready," the section chief answered.

"Roger that," Boxer said; then he keyed his EO, "Stand by to reduce speed to zero five knots."

"Standing by," the EO answered.

"Target," the SO reported, "two hundred and seventy degrees ... range ten thousand yards ... speed zero."

"That's the first of the trawlers," Boxer said.

"Lieutenant Groody is with Bush," Cowly said.

"Boxer nodded and keyed the EO. "Reduce speed to zero five knots."

"Speed reduced to zero five knots," the EO answered.

Boxer watched the readout on the COMMCOMP. The speed was beginning to drop. He keyed the launch officer. "Have crew board craft," he said.

"Roger that," the launch officer answered.

"Target," the SO said. "Bearing two seven zero degrees … range nine thousand five hundred yards … speed zero."

"Is that the first or second target?" Boxer asked.

"First target," the SO answered.

Boxer watched the speed readout. The *Shark* was down to fifteen knots.

"Second target," the SO reported. "Bearing two seven five degrees … range eleven thousand yards … speed zero."

Boxer keyed the launch bay. "Commence flooding."

"Flooding started," the officer answered.

Boxer turned his attention to the speed readout. The *Shark* had slowed to eight knots. He keyed the EO. "Maintain zero five knots," he told him again.

"Will hold at zero five knots," the EO said.

Boxer turned on the TV camera to give him a picture of the launch area. The bay was flooding rapidly. "One minute to launch," he said, and counting. "Opening bay doors." He pushed the master control switch for the doors; they began to open just as the *Shark*'s speed reached five knots. "Bush, take her out."

"Roger that," Bush answered.

Boxer watched the minisub sink below the open doors and vanish.

"Out," Bush reported. "Out."

"Closing bay doors," Boxer said, reversing the position of the master switch. "Beginning pumping operation."

Within two minutes, the SO reported the four other trawlers. Boxer checked their position on the COMMCOMP; the six ships formed a ring with a diameter of three thousand yards. Obviously the undersea station was in the center of that circle.

"Skipper," COMMO said, "the *Kurskia* has suffered two large explosions and her bow section has broken off and is sinking fast."

"Roger that," Boxer said.

"Minisub closing fast," the SO reported.

Boxer glanced at the screen; Bush was doing forty knots. He glanced at the outside temperature. It had dropped ten degrees. He checked the speed and direction of the current. It was still coming from the south, but its speed was up to seven knots.

"Going in," Bush reported.

Thirty seconds later the deep roar of an explosion passed over the *Shark*.

"One out," Bush reported. "Going for the second one."

Forty-five seconds later a second explosion passed over the *Shark*.

"Skipper," the Commo said, "the Russians are calling for help and the *Sea Savage* answered... But the answer was in a different code which we can't decode."

"Okay," Boxer said to Cowly, "let's go down and get the gold."

"Let's go!" Cowly answered.

Boxer keyed the DO. "Make three zero zero feet," he said. Then he turned to the EO. "Flank speed for ten minutes; then drop to zero. I want to settle down nice and easy."

Two almost simultaneous explosions thundered through the water.

"They're after Bush," Cowly said.

"As long as he keeps them busy," Boxer said, "we have a chance of getting through."

"Passing through two zero zero feet," the DO said.

Boxer turned on the UWIS and focused on the surface. He could see the minisub weave in between the remaining trawlers. Then suddenly there was a huge flash on the screen and a second later the sound of an explosion swept over the *Shark*.

"Making two five zero feet," the DO announced.

Boxer watched the speed indicator. The *Shark* was slowing down.

"The target's dispersing," the SO reported.

Boxer moved his eyes back to the UWIS. Bush was on the tail of one of them.

"Skipper," the COMMO said, "there's a lot of message traffic between the *Q-21* and the undersea station."

"Roger that," Boxer answered; then to Cowly, he said, "Borodine must be going wild. He can't possibly get here in time."

"Speed at one five knots and dropping," the EO reported.

"Passing through two seven five feet," the DO said.

Boxer scanned the area. Directly off the starboard bow was the undersea station.

"Three zero zero feet," the DO announced.

"All engines stopped," the EO said.

The *Shark* gently bumped down on the bottom.

Boxer keyed Redfern. "Stand by to exit on the port side. Target is two zero zero yards off the starboard bow... I'll join you in zero three minutes... Stand by!" Then turning to Cowly, he said, "You have the CONN. Retrieve Bush as soon as he signals. Tell him he and Groody have done a good day's work." He left the COMMCOMP.

Cowly sat down and scanned the instruments. "Skipper, the current is coming from the south and running at eight knots. The temperature is five eight degrees." But Boxer had already left the bridge.

Borodine paced back and forth. As soon as he received word of the attack on the trawlers, he abandoned the rescue mission. But he was still too far away to do anything to stop the attack.

"Comrade Captain," the COMMO said, "the trawlers have broken off the engagement and dispersed."

"Losses?"

"Three sunk," the COMMO reported.

Borodine wiped the sweat from his brow with the back of his sleeve. "Now they'll go after the undersea station. He looked at Alexander. "Can you direct operations from here?"

"I don't have much choice do I?"

Borodine shook his head. "None."

He turned to his master control computer and looked at the ETA readout. They were still an hour away from the station. Then suddenly his eyes caught the outside temperature. It was five degrees and the speed of the current was one zero knots. It was still coming from the south. He ran a quick check on the speed and the temperature of the current over the last two hours and found that the speed had increased, while the temperature had dropped.

Borodine keyed the DO, "Go to periscope depth," he said.

"Going to periscope depth, Comrade Captain," the DO answered.

Borodine went to the periscope well and activated the instrument. "I think a storm is coming up," he said, answering Viktor's questioning look. "I want to have a look."

"Periscope depth," the DO answered.

Borodine placed his eyes against the binocular eyepiece and adjusted the instrument for daylight vision. "The surface is calm, but the sky is very gray," he said and retracted the instrument into its well. He returned to the master computer and put the readout of the current speed and temperature on an auxiliary video screen; then he keyed the DO. "Make two zero zero feet," he said.

"Aye, aye, Comrade Captain," the DO said.

As the *Sea Savage* pitched slightly forward, Borodine watched the video display. At one hundred feet the temperature dropped and the speed of the current increased. At two hundred feet the speed of the current had increased to eleven knots and the temperature had gone down a degree to fifty-seven.

"Comrade Captain," the COMMO reported, "the station reports the arrival of the *Shark*."

"Roger that," Borodine answered; then looking at Alexander, he said, "Take command of your men, Major." He handed him a throat microphone and a headset.

Redfern's men were in the exit chamber. Each man wore a wetsuit and an undersea communication pack, and each was armed with an air-driven gun capable of firing a six-inch dart with sufficient force to kill a man at forty yards. Each was issued a knife and four undersea grenades. Redfern checked every man to make sure he was properly equipped.

Then he moved to one side and said, "Listen up men. Our mission is to attack an undersea base. You all know what it looks like. You know what must be done. Lieutenant De Vargas will lead the assault team of twenty men. Sergeant Taylor will back him up. Sergeant Link will attack the installation. Link you know which one to hit?"

"The one marked with a red circle," Link answered.

Redfern nodded. "No prisoners men," he said. "We have to be in and out fast."

"Just how fast, Major?" one of the men asked.

Redfern looked at Boxer, who had just entered the chamber. "How fast, Skipper, do we have to be?"

"Very fast," Boxer answered. "The *Q-21* is on its way back. It should be here in about an hour. I want everyone back on board within three zero minutes."

"That's your answer, men," Redfern said. "Okay, let's get on with this. Sergeant Hellwig will oversee the transport of the gold from the station, or what will be left of it, to the *Shark*. The rest of the men will stay close to the *Shark* and be ready to move in as needed. If a man is wounded, he immediately returns to the *Shark*. Any man having difficulty breathing will immediately avail himself of the oxygen that will be dropped at various places along the way to the station. I suspect there will be some sharp fighting. The Russians are well armed and well trained. Be careful. Any questions?"

"Are we taking along bang sticks?" a man asked.

"Every fourth man will be carrying a bang stick," Redfern said. "There's bound to be all sorts of predators around once they get the scent of blood. Any other questions?"

There were none.

"Okay, Skipper," Redfern said, "we're ready to go … and good luck to all of you."

Boxer picked up the phone. "Flood the exit compartment," he told Cowly.

"Aye, aye, Skipper," Cowly answered.

Within moments water began to pour into the area.

Boxer donned his breathing mask and his communications pack; then he tested each one. "Ready to go," he said to Redfern.

"Ready," Redfern answered.

Boxer left the *Shark* and drifted to the bottom. The sea was cold and murky.

Redfern followed and the rest of the men came after him.

"De Vargas, move your men out!"

"Hit squad, let's get with it!" De Vargas exclaimed. Twenty men moved out after him.

"Let's see how well the rest of you guys know your jobs," Redfern said.

The men began to fan out: some of them went along the side of the *Shark* to the stern, while others followed De Vargas's team.

"Time for us to go," Redfern said, moving toward the bow.

In the murky light, the moving men looked like specters, figures that might be part of a dream.

Cowly keyed him. "Skipper, the temperature has dropped another two degrees ... it's down to fifty-six degrees."

"What about the current?"

"The same."

"Roger that... Any signal from Bush?"

"He's ten miles from here... Still trying to get another trawler."

"Call him in," Boxer said. "Make it an order."

"Roger that," Cowly answered. "Out."

"Ten four," Boxer said.

Suddenly through the gloom, Boxer saw the base.

"There it is!" Redfern exclaimed.

"I don't see any Russians yet," Boxer said.

"You will," Redfern answered. "I thought this damn water was supposed to be warm. It's damn cold."

Boxer was about to answer when suddenly the bottom blew up in front of them. The boom of the explosion crashed down on them.

"Mines!" Redfern shouted.

Another explosion followed, and another. The water turned grayer and three torn bodies floated off the bottom.

"No way to know where those mines are," Redfern said.

The men began to run toward the station. A half a dozen more mines exploded, filling the sea with debris and blood.

"Keep going men!" Redfern shouted.

Boxer ran alongside Redfern. He hadn't counted on mines and he was sure Redfern hadn't either.

"Major," De Vargas reported, "the Russians are moving toward us."

"Hit them hard," Redfern said.

De Vargas's men formed a front.

The Russians fired first. Using oxygen-fed rifles, they tore several holes in De Vargas's line.

"Christ," Redfern swore, "they have the range on us. Keep moving men. Keep moving!"

Boxer ran alongside of Redfern; they passed the bodies of a half-dozen men floating off the bottom. The fish were already at them.

De Vargas's men fired their darts.

Several of the Russian marines dropped to the bottom.

Boxer saw De Vargas launch a grenade. The explosion ripped through the Russian line.

"Our men are closing fast," Redfern said.

The entire area was suddenly illuminated by lights on the outside of the station.

"Major," Sergeant Link reported, "ready to blow the storage area."

"Blow it!" Redfern answered.

The next instant the boom of an explosion passed over them.

"Major," a man reported, "Link is dead, killed while trying to launch a grenade. Three men were also killed with him."

"Roger that. Try to blow that section."

"Roger that," the man said.

"Sharks," another man reported. "Sharks coming in ... sharks coming in."

Three bang sticks went off.

Boxer saw two sharks tear the bodies to pieces. He couldn't tell whether they'd been Redfern's men or Russians.

"We're taking heavy casualties," Redfern said.

"Keep pushing the men," Boxer ordered.

"Skipper," Cowly said, "Bush has the *Q-21* on his sonar."

"How far?"

"Twenty miles from here and moving fast," Cowly reported.

Suddenly the middle section of the station blew apart. The pressure wave staggered Boxer and Redfern.

"What the hell was that?" Cowly asked.

"We reached our objective," Boxer said.

"Tell Bush to get his ass back here. Go to one five zero feet and recover him; then come back here for us."

"Skipper the current is up to one zero knots," Cowly said. "But the temperature is holding."

"Roger that," Boxer said.

"Ten four," Cowly answered.

Boxer and Redfern moved quickly toward the blown station. There was still heavy fighting going on.

"Major," Sergeant Hellwig said, "we have the gold… We can move it as soon as the fighting gives way a bit."

"Roger that," Redfern said.

"Good work, Sergeant," Boxer said. He heard the *Shark* start up, turned and saw it slowly rise. He keyed Cowly. "Where's Bush?"

"Coming in, Skipper," Cowly answered. "We'll recover him right above you."

"Make it fast," Boxer said. "We don't have much time before the *Q-21* arrives."

"Roger that," Cowly answered. "Ten four."

"Let's go have a look-see at the gold," Redfern said.

"Get a casualty report," Boxer said, looking at the bodies strewn around the area.

When Redfern gave him the numbers, they were grim. Thirty-five dead; more than one third the entire force. And five incapacitated for various physical reasons.

"And all of the Russians?" Boxer asked.

"Sixty," Redfern answered.

"No wonder the sharks are here in droves," Boxer answered. Redfern nodded.

Cowly keyed Boxer. "Skipper, Bush is aboard."

"Roger that," Boxer answered. "How far is the *Q-21*?"

"Still out of range of our sonar," Cowly said; then he added, "We're heading back to you."

"Standing by," Boxer responded. "Out."

"Not much left of their station," Redfern said.

"Let's have a look at it," Boxer answered.

The two men moved slowly forward; there were bodies every few feet. Some had already been torn by the sharks and were now being eaten by smaller fish.

Boxer found himself wondering whether the value of the gold was worth the cost? It wasn't the kind of question he or any of the men with him should ask. But he knew it was the only question in all of their minds at the moment.

Redfern tapped him on the arm and pointed ahead and to the right, to where Hellwig was standing; then he said, "There's the gold."

"How many bars?" Boxer asked Hellwig.

"One hundred and fifty, Skipper."

"What's the price of gold?" Redfern asked.

"Eight hundred dollars an ounce," Boxer answered. "And each of those bars weighs over ten pounds each."

"That's a lot of loose change," Hellwig commented.

Cowly keyed Boxer. "Coming down, Skipper... I have the station on the UWIS."

Boxer turned around. The *Shark* was coming in some hundred yards from where he and the other men were now standing. "Tom, have your men ready to transfer the gold."

"Will do," Redfern answered.

With her power off, the *Shark* glided down, touched bottom and came to rest less than fifty yards from them.

"Skipper," Cowly said, "opening the number four cargo hatch on the port side."

"Roger that," Boxer answered and to Redfern, he said, "Let's move that gold."

"Will do, Skipper," Redfern answered.

Boxer moved out of the debris and made his way back to the *Shark*. He was becoming more and more worried about the *Q-21*. It should be coming up on the sonar at any moment.

"Skipper," Cowly said, "that temperature has dropped zero three more degrees. It has dropped to five four degrees and the speed of the current has increased by zero two knots to one three knots per."

"Roger that," Boxer answered. He was feeling the effects of both conditions. The cold was numbing and the speed of the current made moving against it difficult.

"Skipper," the SO said, "I'm getting irregular patterns from one eight zero degrees."

"Target?" Boxer asked, immediately beginning to sweat at the possibility that the *Q-21* was in range and he was still loading gold.

"I'm not sure," the SO answered.

"Cowly," Boxer said. "Check that sonar."

"Roger that," Cowly answered.

Boxer looked toward Redfern's men. They formed a human chain between the station and the *Shark*, each passing bar after bar of gold from man to man until they were stowed in the cargo hatch. One hundred and fifty bars didn't seem like much to transfer but the cold and the current made the job difficult.

"Skipper," Cowly said, "the DDC shows nothing... The SO says the pattern reminds him of a cold-water barrier... He's sure that's what it is."

"Have him watch it," Boxer answered.

"Roger that," Cowly answered.

Boxer breathed more easily.

"Skipper," Redfern said, "the last bar of gold is on its way to the *Shark*."

"Good," Boxer responded. "Get your men back on board. We're bound to have company soon."

"Okay, Skipper," Redfern answered.

Boxer started toward the *Shark*. The current was moving very fast and it seemed to be even colder than it had been just a short while ago. Suddenly, Boxer realized that there weren't any fish around the area. The sharks and the killer whales had gone. Even the small fish weren't around.

"Skipper," Cowly said, "the UWIS just went out."

"What?"

"The image left the screen and I can't get it back on," Cowly said.

Boxer was about to say that he was coming up on the bridge. But he couldn't do that. For the next three hours he and all of the men who had been on the mission would have to undergo decompression.

"Bush says it's because of the water temperature," Cowly said.

"Tell DDC to find out what's wrong and get that system back in operating order," Boxer said.

"They're already working on it," Cowly answered.

"Roger that," Boxer answered, looking at Redfern, who was waving him into the *Shark*. "I'll be there in a few moments," he said. "I want to make sure nothing is left for the Russians to use." He worked his way back to the destroyed station and, using his grenades, he blew up what was left of it; then he turned and started back to the *Shark*. The current was very strong, forcing him to bend into it in order to move against it.

"Skipper," Cowly reported, "the SO reports a target entering the outer limit of our sonar's range... Should have ID within moments."

"Roger that," Boxer said, reaching up to Redfern and De Vargas to lift him into the *Shark*.

"Positive ID... It's the *Q-21*."

"Let's get the hell out of here," Boxer said. "All men aboard ... hatch closed ... begin pump-out and decompression procedures."

"Pump-out starting," Cowly said.

"Flank speed," Boxer ordered.

"Flank speed," Cowly repeated.

The water in the chamber fell rapidly. In a matter of minutes, Boxer and all of the other men were able to remove their breathing gear.

Boxer immediately went to the phone. "Cowly, have COMMO patch me into all sections."

"Skipper, the SO just reported the sonar out," Cowly said.

"Just what the hell is happening?" Boxer shouted.

"According to Bush we're in a temperature screen," Cowly answered.

Suddenly, the *Shark* began to move sideways.

"EO," Boxer said. "Full power!"

"Full power," the EO answered.

"We're dead in the water!" Cowly exclaimed. "Skipper, we're pinned to the bottom!"

Borodine paced back and forth. No signals coming from the base meant it was totally destroyed. He stopped and looked at Alexander. "I knew those fishermen couldn't provide enough cover. I knew it!"

"Comrade Captain," the SO said, "I have two targets bearing one eight four degrees ... range four thousand yards ... contact lost ... contact lost."

"What the hell are you talking about?" Borodine said and going to the master control computer, he switched on the sonar display system. Nothing!

"Comrade Captain," the SO said, "the sonar shows no malfunction."

"Roger that," Borodine said. He had already run his own test from the console and knew that the equipment was functioning. Suddenly he remembered the falling temperature and the increasing speed of the current. He looked at the instruments. The temperature was down to forty-five degrees and the current was running at fifteen knots.

He keyed the EO. "Flank speed," he said.

"Going to flank speed," the EO answered.

"Switching all systems to manual control," Borodine said. "Helmsman steady on course one eight four degrees."

"Holding one eight four degrees," the helmsman answered.

Borodine turned to Viktor. "There's a thermal barrier between us and the *Shark*, and I'm going through it. My guess is that their sonar is out too. If we get through and pick them up before they spot us, we can kill them."

"It's a long shot," Viktor answered. "We might be the one to get killed."

Borodine looked at Alexander. "What do you say?"

"Do it," he said in a choked voice. "Do it for the men they killed."

Borodine nodded. "DO, make two zero zero feet," he said.

"Making two zero zero feet," the DO answered.

Borodine constantly monitored the outside conditions. The temperature was holding at four five degrees, but the current had increased to one eight knots.

Suddenly the needle on the depth gauge began to move.

"Comrade Captain," the DO signaled, "we're losing depth."

"I see it," Borodine answered. The *Sea Savage* had already lost fifty feet. "Trim her!" her ordered.

"Negative," the DO responded. "Can't trim."

257

"EO, full power reverse," Boxer ordered.

"Full power reverse," The EO answered.

"Still going down," the DO reported.

Borodine checked the speed of the current: it was moving at twenty-five knots. Suddenly he realized what was happening: they were caught in a huge river of cold water that was rushing out of the Antarctic Ocean.

"Going to two seven five feet," the DO announced.

"Stop all engines," Borodine ordered. He switched on the MC. "All hands, now hear this ... all hands, hear this... We're going to go to the bottom and stay there ... we're going to the bottom... Rig for crash... rig for crash."

The *Q-21* slammed hard on the bottom, rolling to port and then to starboard before she came completely to rest.

Now Borodine understood why the bottom was scoured clean.

The *Shark* was tossed over the ocean bottom. Regardless of the power Boxer ordered, it was no match for the force of the water pouring down on them and spreading along the ocean floor.

Boxer called his officers to the bridge. "All of you know we're in trouble," he said. "Sometime in the fifties the *Thresher* got caught like this off Cape Cod. She broke up before she hit the bottom. Well we're on the bottom. We can go much deeper than the *Thresher* ever could, but we can't just stay here and let the sea smash us to pieces, because that's what's going to happen. We've got to do something. Any ideas?"

No one answered.

"I'll listen to anything from anybody," Boxer said.

The EO raised his hand.

"Go ahead," Boxer said.

"Our power alone won't do it … but twice our power might," the EO said.

"Where will we get it?" Boxer asked.

"From the *Q-21*," he answered. "If they're close by, they have to be in the same fix that we're in."

"You're saying," Boxer said, "if I read you right, to join our power to the *Q-21* and save both boats?"

"That's the idea," the EO answered.

"You've got to be nuts," one of the signal officers said. "They wouldn't help us and we sure as hell wouldn't help them. We just killed sixty of them and now you expect the others to help us out of a jam?"

Everyone began to talk at once.

"Quiet!" Boxer ordered. "Quiet down. Just remember the *Q-21* is in the same fix we are and is probably being bounced around too. It's worth a try. COMMO get on the radio. Use their assigned frequencies."

"That's going to tell them we've broken one of their codes," COMMO said.

"Do it," Boxer said, as the *Shark* was suddenly lifted up and set down a few seconds later with a hard jolt. "One of those is going to open us up. Try to get the *Q-21* on the radio."

"Are you sure you want to do it that way?" Bush asked.

"Are you sure you don't want me to?" Boxer flung back at him.

Bush had nothing to say.

"We all want to live," Boxer said. "And so do the Russians. It's a chance for all of us to survive. Go ahead, try to make radio contact. I'll speak to Borodine. I know he speaks English."

"Aye, aye, Skipper," the COMMO answered.

Boxer dismissed his officers, telling them to have all their sections on standby. "I don't know what's coming," he said. "And I want to be ready for anything unexpected." Then he turned to Bush. "From now on, you'll be part of the bridge detail."

"Aye, aye, Skipper," Bush answered.

Boxer raised his eyebrows; then he nodded. Bush was turning out to be all right. Maybe even more than all right.

Borodine sat at his control console and waited to hear Captain Boxer's voice. Everyone on the bridge was absolutely silent. He had told them what was happening the moment his COMMO officer informed him that the Captain of the *Shark* wanted to speak to him.

"Captain Borodine, this is Captain Boxer speaking," Boxer said.

Borodine wet his lips and leaned forward. "You are coming through," Borodine said.

"I'll get right to the point," Boxer said. "We can get out of this together. Alone probably neither of us will."

Borodine wiped his brow.

"Captain, I have a radio fix on you," Boxer said. "You're less than a hundred feet off our starboard side. If this current —"

"The current is very strong," Borodine said.

"Too strong for either one of us to survive alone," Boxer said. "Your boat is being bounced around just as mine is. We must help one another."

"How?"

"Tie us together and use all our power to get to the surface," Boxer said.

Borodine was about to say impossible; instead, he asked, "How do we get the lines to each other?"

"Two men from the *Shark* and two men from the *Q-21*. It's our only chance."

Before Borodine could answer, the *Sea Savage* rolled to the port side. Borodine grabbed hold of the console. After a few frightening seconds, the *Sea Savage* righted herself.

"Captain," Boxer said, "it's our only chance!"

"I think so too," Borodine said slowly. "I will send four men out with lines."

"Four men with lines," Boxer answered. "The time is seventeen thirty. In one zero minutes my men will start toward your boat."

"The same," Borodine answered.

"Once the lines are in place," Boxer said, "we will slowly pull on them until the boats are lashed together."

"We will need more men to do that," Borodine said.

"We'll use as many as it takes."

"No arms," Borodine said.

"No arms," Boxer answered.

"You will stay in radio communication?"

"You will be speaking to me or Captain Bush."

The *Shark* was suddenly thrown into a different position.

"Skipper," the DCO reported, "seam has opened in the stern torpedo room."

"Roger that," Boxer answered.

"Repair underway," the DCO said.

Boxer returned to the conversation with Borodine. "You probably heard that," he said.

"Yes."

"The current is running at four zero knots and the water temperature is down to three nine degrees."

Borodine checked his instruments. "I have the same readings. They might get worse before they start to improve."

Boxer agreed.

"I am putting Captain Bush on the air, while I ready the men to go out."

"Captain Viktor Korzenko will stand by for me," Borodine said.

"Good luck," Boxer said.

"Good luck," Borodine answered.

"The following men will go out with me," Boxer said to the crew of the *Shark*. De Vargas, Taylor, and Hellwig. Redfern take command of the men working the lines ... I don't want any casualties. It's bad out there and could become worse, especially when the *Shark* moves. Be careful. There aren't any sharks or killer whales around, or at least there weren't when we came back. They had more sense than to stick around. Okay men get moving. We want to move fast."

"Are you sure you have to go?" Cowly asked.

Boxer nodded. "I can't ask Tom and his men to do something that I wouldn't do."

Cowly nodded.

"Bush will do fine," Boxer said. "Besides, he'll be following my orders."

"He's better than I thought he'd be," Cowly commented.

"Just a bit too rigid yet," Boxer said with a smile. "But if he stays with us much longer, he'll lose that too."

"Good luck, Skipper," Cowly said, jabbing Boxer in the shoulder.

Boxer nodded and hurried to the exit chamber.

Borodine quickly translated his conversation with Boxer for the officers who did not understand English. They were astounded by the proposal, but agreed it was worth trying. The only one who disagreed was Alexander. "It's a trick," he said. "We can't be sure what those men will do, once they're close to the *Sea Savage*. They can't be trusted."

Borodine understood his feelings and said, "We don't have anyone else who can help us. We must trust them and they must trust us. Our men will be as close to their sub as their men will be to ours."

Suddenly the *Sea Savage* was lifted up and slammed down on the bottom with such force that several of the readings on the instruments changed.

Borodine keyed his DCO. "Any damage?"

"AUTODIVSYS shows a malfunction," the DO said. "But the manual is operational."

"Roger that," Borodine answered. "Now you understand why we can't refuse Captain Boxer's offer. Alexander, pick your best men. Viktor, you take command. I'm going out."

Boxer was the first one out of the exit chamber. The water was numbing and the current almost swept him off his feet. "Tom," he said, "our first job is to secure three lines to the *Shark* on deck. Use spun steel cable. We're going to have to pull up on it."

"You've got it, Skipper," Redfern answered.

Boxer keyed Cowly. "Put on the deck lights," he said.

"Aye, aye, Skipper," Cowly answered.

Boxer moved away from the side of the *Shark* and swam up to the deck. Vargas had already secured one cable to the forward cleat and was working to secure a second cable amidship.

From the deck Boxer could make out the shadow of the *Sea Savage*. Suddenly her lights came on and illuminated every foot of her. She was almost as long as the *Shark* and unlike the

Shark she had a conventional sail. He was so busy looking at the boat that he didn't notice the men on her deck until Redfern came alongside of him and said, "Skipper, the Russians are securing their cables to their cleats too. That means we'll have a double set on each cleat."

"That might not be too bad an idea," Boxer answered, "just in case one snaps."

"Skipper," Cowly said, "the Russians are ready to bring their cables to us."

"Roger that," Boxer said. "Tell them to wait. I want to check if we're ready."

"Aye, aye, Skipper," Cowly answered.

"De Vargas are you ready?" Boxer asked.

"Third cable on," De Vargas answered. "Ready, Skipper."

"Cowly," Boxer said, "Tell them we're going to begin to move toward them."

"Roger that," Cowly said.

"Okay, Tom have your men get those cables across," Boxer said.

Within moments Vargas and his group moved the three cable ends toward the *Sea Savage*.

"There are the Russians," Redfern said, pointing to the three men coming toward the *Shark*.

"Skipper," Cowly said, "Captain Borodine requests direct communication with you."

"Patch him in," Boxer answered.

"Captain," Borodine said. "I have ordered my men to stop halfway between our two boats and exchange cables with your men."

"I'll do the same, Captain," Boxer answered.

Suddenly the *Shark* pitched violently up and came crashing down. Boxer was thrown to the deck.

"Holy Christ!" Boxer exclaimed, realizing Redfern had been pitched off the deck. "Tom, are you all right?"

"Shaken up," Redfern answered. "But all right."

"Skipper," Cowly said. "DC reports some damage to our air scrubbers... Estimates a two zero percent out."

"Roger that," Boxer said. Even as he spoke, he saw the *Sea Savage* rise up and slam down.

A few moments later, Borodine said, "two of my men have been killed... We must move faster."

"Will do," Boxer answered; then to Vargas he said, "Move faster Vargas. Give your cables to the Russians and take theirs back to the *Shark*. They have had two casualties."

"Roger that," Vargas said.

It took thirty more minutes to secure all the cables to the cleats on the two boats.

"Everyone on those cables," Boxer said. "Cowly patch me into the EO and put Mahony on the helm."

"Roger that," Cowly answered. "Mahony has been standing by."

Boxer waited until Redfern reported the men were at the cables. "Okay, EO give me enough power to hold steerageway."

"One thousand two zero zero rpms," the EO answered.

Though Boxer was certain Borodine was doing the same thing, he called him and said, "Using one thousand two zero zero rpms to keep steerageway."

"Yes," Borodine answered.

"Helmsman ease to the port," Boxer said.

"Easing to the port," Mahony answered.

"DO, vent all ballast," Boxer said.

The sound of rushing air filled the *Shark*. She rose slightly off the bottom.

"Pull on those cables men," Boxer said. "Pull!"

The *Shark* eased toward the *Sea Savage*. Over and over again the ballast tanks were flooded and blown. By a series of bounces the two boats drew closer and closer to one another, until after two hours of backbreaking work, they were securely tied to one another.

"All hands off the deck and inside the compartment," Boxer said.

"Roger that," Redfern answered.

Boxer stood alone on the deck of the *Shark*. Opposite him on the deck of the *Sea Savage* was Borodine.

"Good work, Captain," Borodine said.

"Good work, Captain," Boxer answered. "See you when we surface."

They waved to one another and leaving their decks, they entered their submarines.

As soon as Boxer was in the chamber, he ordered Cowly to start pumping water out and begin the decompression procedures. Then he keyed Bush. "Coordinate everything you do with the Russian Captain... Keep me informed."

"Roger that," Bush said.

Boxer sat down. He was bone weary. He looked at the other men. Some were already sleeping. He envied them.

"Blowing all ballast," Bush said.

"Roger that," Boxer answered.

"The Russians have blown their ballast too," Bush said.

Boxer didn't answer.

"Up six feet ... up one two feet ... up two five feet," Bush said. "Going to flank speed ... course two seven degrees."

"Good," Boxer said. "Very good." He could feel the vibration of the boats as they pushed through the sea.

Then suddenly the *Shark* was hurled down. He could feel the drop in his stomach.

"Going down ... one two feet ... one zero feet ... holding at ten feet," Bush said. "Holding at one zero feet... DO, one five degrees on diving planes."

"One five degrees on diving planes," the DO answered.

The two boats started to rise again.

"Making five zero feet," Bush said.

"Roger that," Boxer answered.

"Water temperature five five degrees," Bush announced.

"Skipper, it's gone up zero five degrees ... current still at four zero knots"

Boxer didn't answer. He imagined Borodine was receiving the same information and was reacting the same way.

"Making one zero zero feet," Bush announced. "Water temperature six zero degrees ... current moving at two five knots."

Boxer keyed Borodine. "Captain, I think we've made it."

"Yes," Borodine answered. "I think we've made it."

Fifteen minutes later, Bush announced over the MC, "Prepare to surface ... prepare to surface... Deck detail exit through hatches one and four... Standby ... standby... Bridge up, Mister Cowly."

"Bridge up," Cowly answered, pushing the control switch.

Bush hit the klaxon once. "Surface ... surface... Diving planes in neutral position... Surface."

"Done!" Boxer exclaimed. "Done!"

"It's a bright sunny day up here," Bush said a few moments later from the bridge.

"Good," Boxer answered. "I could do with a bit of sunshine. Have the men stand by. I don't want anyone to go aboard the *Q-21*."

"Roger that," Bush answered.

Boxer closed his eyes. He could rest for a while, even sleep until he finished decompressing. Then he'd meet Borodine. He looked forward to doing that very much. Despite the fact that they were enemies, they understood one another and in many ways were alike. They were professionals, doing what they were trained to do. In another time frame and another place, Boxer was certain they would have been friends.

A NOTE TO THE READER

Dear Reader,

If you have enjoyed the novel enough to leave a review on **Amazon** and **Goodreads**, then we would be truly grateful.

Sapere Books

Sapere Books is an exciting new publisher of brilliant fiction and popular history.

To find out more about our latest releases and our monthly bargain books visit our website:
saperebooks.com

Made in the USA
Middletown, DE
22 December 2024